# IDYLL THREATS

# IDYLL THREATS

## A Thomas Lynch Novel

# STEPHANIE GAYLE

**SEVENTH STREET BOOKS®**
AN IMPRINT OF PROMETHEUS BOOKS
59 JOHN GLENN DRIVE • AMHERST, NY 14228
www.seventhstreetbooks.com

Published 2015 by Seventh Street Books®, an imprint of Prometheus Books

Cover image © Bigstock
Cover design by Grace M. Conti-Zilsberger

This is a work of fiction. Characters, organizations, products, locales, and events portrayed in this novel either are products of the author's imagination or are used fictitiously.

Inquiries should be addressed to
Seventh Street Books
59 John Glenn Drive
Amherst, New York 14228
VOICE: 716–691–0133
FAX: 716–691–0137
WWW.SEVENTHSTREETBOOKS.COM

19 18 17 16 15    5 4 3 2 1

Library of Congress Cataloging-in-Publication Data

Gayle, Stephanie, 1975-
    Idyll threats : a Thomas Lynch novel / by Stephanie Gayle.
        pages ; cm
    ISBN 978-1-63388-078-8 (pbk.) — ISBN 978-1-63388-079-5 (e-book)
    I. Title.

PS3607.A98576I39  2015
813'.6—dc23
                                                                    2015011718

Printed in the United States of America

*For Cally Gayle, my mother*
*Every book I write is for you.*

# SATURDAY, AUGUST 9TH, 1997
## 2230 HOURS

I didn't make small talk, didn't ask about anyone's evening plans or even say good night. I snuck out the station's rear exit, the metal door squeaky with humidity, got into my cruiser, and drove to a secluded road. I parked and sat, watching the darkness grow, swallowing one tree at a time. I'd driven to the woods to think. Or not to think. To be alone. I did a lot of that.

An insect symphony played, all percussions. I didn't like so many bugs so near. I was city-bred, used to roaches and the occasional mosquito. Something pinged against my windshield. My hand went to my gun. Reflex. The action recalled last year's report on gun deaths that I'd read earlier today. In 1996, only fifty-five cops in the US died on the job from gun-related incidents. I bit my lower lip. In a year less likely to end in a police funeral, my partner, Rick, had beaten the odds. Been shot dead by a dealer. I could hear Rick in my head. "What can I say, buddy? I'm exceptional."

A bug adhered itself to the passenger window, its fat body vibrating against the glass. To hell with this. I turned the key in the ignition. Time to go home.

He sped past my cruiser, his convertible's top down. Doing 55 miles per hour, at least. I flipped on my lights and siren and cut a U-turn. The car fishtailed before the tires bit down. The frame shuddered as I lowered my foot. The driver slowed, then stopped his car. He stared ahead at the pocked road, hands on the wheel.

I approached slowly. You never know whether the guy you've

stopped is an upright father of four or an anxious kidnapper. If he was the former, I didn't want to scare him.

The crescent moon turned his gray hair silver. He turned toward me when I reached his door. Blue eyes. I've always been a sucker for blue eyes. "Sir?"

He started when I spoke. Not unusual. I'm a big guy with a deep voice.

"License and registration, please."

He handed over both. His watch was a TAG Heuer. A real one. I'd seen the fakes sold on Canal Street. His name was Leo Wilton. Age forty-nine. Address in Ashford, Connecticut. Thirty minutes east of here.

I considered running his plates. Screw it. Too much to hope he was a serial killer.

I returned his papers. "The speed limit on this road is 35 miles per hour."

"That right?"

"Lot of wildlife out here. Deer. They do nasty things to cars." Or so I'd heard. I'd been here seven months and not seen one. I suspected the locals invented things.

"Sure. Sorry 'bout that." He looked directly at me. Straight men don't stare into each other's eyes, unless they're about to fight. This guy wasn't angry. My body responded. My brain fought back. I was within town limits. I could be spotted. But it had been a long time since I'd scratched this itch. Six and a half months: a long winter, a stone-cold spring, and a summer with no skin in it. I craved contact.

"You see a lot of action out here?" He waved his hand at the trees, their needles pointy, ominous at night.

"Action?" He was hitting on me. I hadn't mistaken it. "Not exactly." In this town, with its picket-fenced homes, action was unknown. Everyone here was hetero or pretending to be. I gave him a small smile, just a quick pull of my lips. It was enough.

"You want to go somewhere?" he asked.

I chewed the smooth skin inside my cheek. I was off duty, but in uniform. A hell of a risk, but he looked nice in the moonlight, like a foil-wrapped gift.

"There's a place not far from here," he said.

Had I known what would result from this encounter—the secrets, the lies—I would've gone home and slept alone, again. But murder doesn't call ahead, warn you that it's coming. And if it had, I wouldn't have believed it. In this sleepy town named Idyll, murder seemed impossible. So I walked, lightheaded with lust, unaware that each step brought me closer to death and near destruction.

He led me to a disheveled shack I'd heard of but never seen. The cabin by Hought's Pond was condemned. In New York, to be condemned required one of three Cs: crack house, critters, or collapse. Here in Idyll, Connecticut, public disapproval was enough. The house, a shingled box, had a sunken porch, a rotted roof, and windows shot out by teens with BB guns. "Jack is a dooshbag" was spray-painted on the front door. Above the tag, a frayed No Trespassing sign dangled. This place was a blight in its postcard-perfect town. No wonder they'd condemned it.

He gripped my shirt and tugged me down so my face was level with his. I stiffened all over. He smelled of peppermint, his lips thin and slick. He reached under my shirt, his fingers tickling my abs. "Someone's been working out."

I grunted. We stomped up the creaking stairs in unsteady lockstep. My cock throbbed, halfway between pain and pleasure. Our bodies bumped. "Ah," I said. I nipped his neck. He held me closer. We crashed through the cabin door. My foot connected with a can. It rattled across the floor.

"Hey!"

We jerked apart. A couple lay on the floor, half-undressed. They reared back, as if struck. Near them, an oil lamp glowed. Too dim to warn this place was occupied. "You can't come barging in here," the girl said. She lifted her ass to wiggle into her jeans. Metal winked. Belly button ring. She was young. Twenty or so. Her hair a waterfall of brown. Her panties pink lace, a good girl's version of sexy. She smelled fresh-from-the-shower clean. But her tone and company told a different story. Even in the feeble light I saw her friend was daddy material. His hair thinning on top. He fumbled with his zipper and half rolled to his side.

"Let's go," I said, but Leo crossed his arms.

"Not so fast," he said.

"Faster." My lust had fled when I'd seen the couple. I touched his hand, but he yanked it back.

"You miss the No Trespassing sign?" Leo raised his voice to fill the space.

The girl thrust her face forward. A white oval with red lips. Just kissed. Pretty, and angry. "This your cabin?" she asked. Her tone left no doubt she knew the answer.

"Stop arguing," her friend said. He stabbed his arms into his jacket.

"He could arrest you," Leo said. He pointed to my badge.

The couple blinked. They hadn't noticed my uniform. But now they stared, eyes on my badge. I inhaled. It hurt. A lifetime of work, burnt to ash. And for what? A quickie in a rotting cabin? The man got up from the floor and hurried past, hand to his face. Like a pedophile on a perp walk.

The girl looked smaller now, her eyes on the door. "Guess you don't have any real criminals to chase, huh?" She shoved her feet in her sneakers, not bothering with the laces. As she stomped past, I smelled coconut. The door smacked shut and bounced, the wood warped by damp.

"Why the fuck did you do that?" I said to Leo.

"What?"

"Point out my badge. I'm not looking to advertise."

He spread his arms wide. "Now we have the place to ourselves." He smiled. I didn't.

"You don't bully people because you want a fuck. Got it?"

"Yes, sir." He saluted.

"I'll lead you to your car." I'd make sure the bastard left town, and fast.

He snorted. "I can find it. I've been here before. This place isn't a secret." He pointed at my badge again. "Except to you, I guess. Later, Chief." He stepped around a discarded condom. I let him go. He knew my rank. From the cruiser and my badge. He could report me. Ruin me. If he hadn't already.

Broken glass littered the floor. The space smelled of pond algae, like corpses in advanced stages of decay. Multiple people had come here for sex? Why? And how had I almost been among them? God, I was like Rick. My dead partner. Risking my career for a stupid fix. Moonlight shifted through the roof's holes. A pattern of spotlights played on the sprouting floor. A cracked window shivered. In it, I saw myself, a hulking dark shape. My badge glinted, the only bright thing in that lonely space. I bent down and blew out the oil-lamp flame.

**G**ravel crunched below as I rolled into the parking lot of Suds. I walked through the bar's entrance, though it wasn't open for business. Sunshine followed me inside, where the shades were drawn on all but one window. The door swung shut and the room succumbed to darkness. My shoes clomped on the worn flooring. To my left was the entrance to the Laundromat. Ahead was the bar, a twenty-foot expanse of Kentucky wood. Bought from some gone-bust establishment that had seen Prohibition come and go but hadn't survived the 1990s.

I sat on a stool and rested my hands on the cool wood. A small metal fan blew detergent and beer-scented air at me. Nate was absent. He'd inherited the Laundromat twelve years ago and bought out the bar two years later. Changed its name to that of the laundry, Suds. He'd said it worked for both.

Nate emerged through the swinging doors in back, where the kitchen was located. He carried two slim-necked bottles in each hand. His long hair was tied back with a red leather strip. An arrowhead rested in the hollow of his throat. He was the only Nipmuc in Idyll, or so folks claimed. He said he had cousins in town who were just as native, but they didn't look it.

"Hiya, Chief." He enjoyed the irony of addressing me by title. "Regular?" He walked behind the bar. Set the bottles down. Grabbed a mug and filled it from the sputtering coffeemaker.

"Thanks," I said. I got smirks at the station for drinking coffee here.

"You adding something?" Detective Wright had asked. "Maybe making it Irish?" He'd mimed tilting a bottle, in case I hadn't got the joke.

The liquor bottles behind the bar looked dull. I'd had too much to drink when I got home last night. It hadn't worked, hadn't kept my mind from returning to the cabin with its rotted timbers and sex-stained floor. My guilt wasn't drownable. But worse was how last night had returned Rick's death to me. I'd moved hundreds of miles to escape my dead partner. One stupid, impulsive action had brought him back.

I felt Nate's dark eyes on me. His gaze made me itch.

"Mind if I look at your paper?" I asked.

Nate pushed the *Idyll Register* to me. Sixteen pages of local news, town events, obituaries, and classified ads. Page 2 featured Mrs. Ida Lewisweather, who'd turned one hundred years old last Friday. Her tips for a long life? "A positive attitude and a nip of whiskey each night." The police blotter was on page 6. It included reports of smashed mail-boxes on Green Street and a burgled house on Whitman Road. They hadn't mentioned the rabid raccoon my men brought down. I was surprised. It had been quite the event.

I drank my coffee and tried to forget last night. Seven months on the job and I'd no idea that the abandoned cabin was a rendezvous spot. You could fit what I knew about this town into a shell casing.

"Refill?" Nate asked. He wiped the bar in slow, easy circles.

"Sure." I gazed up at the tin ceiling tiles. They reminded me of home, New York. The only thing in this town that did.

He topped my cup. "You've got a bag ready." He jerked his thumb toward the Laundromat. I owned a washer and dryer. Came with my house. But I was used to city habits: dropping off laundry to be washed and folded. It amused the locals, that I used the Laundromat this way. "I'll get it before I go," I said.

My right hand hurt. I flexed my fingers. The knuckles were skinned. I'd punched something last night. What? Not a person. I'd sped home after the cabin. Anxious to hide from others. To be alone with my thoughts. And to drink. I'd been full of bright ideas last night.

Nate filled the fridge with beers. He didn't talk much. I liked that.

He wore layered flannel shirts in winter instead of a coat. His age was impossible to guess. When things were very slow, he read slim books of poems. I'd overheard him say it was the Red Sox's year for the World Series. But everyone believes at least one crazy thing.

My radio crackled. I'd received complaints about dispatch responses. Last week, the mayor informed me that his roadside-assistance call had gone unanswered for twenty minutes. Instead of telling him to call triple fucking A, I said I'd look into it. And here I was, doing that. What a wonderful pet I made.

"10-78 for Nipmuc Golf Course." Why did they need a detective?

Nate set a bottle down. "The golf course?" he said. "Something happened out there?"

Another crackle. "10-38 at the Nipmuc Golf Course." Murder? No way. These yokels didn't know their codes. Time to school them.

Outside, the glare made me wince. I made a visor by lifting my hand to my brow. I swore under my breath. The idiot who'd botched the dispatch and robbed me of my second cup of coffee would pay.

Two patrol cars were parked on the street near the golf course. I pulled behind the second and hauled myself out of my seat, the movement unwelcome. I kept still and waited out the nausea surge. The air was cool, but it would turn inside out by noon, become sticky like taffy. August in Idyll required two shirts: one for work and one for post-work.

"Excuse me, sir. Stop!" A flush-faced cop hurried toward me. Yankowitz. My first day on the job, he'd parked across two spots, including mine. I wrote him a ticket. Ever since, he's real nervous around me. "Oh, Chief Lynch. Sorry. I didn't see your car." The one I was standing beside? Jesus, how had he passed his exams?

"They found a body," he said.

"Who did?" The ten code was correct? No fucking way.

"The groundskeeper found her. It's a dead woman." He hop-stepped side to side, like he had to pee.

"Who's here?"

He pointed toward the golf course. "Hopkins and Thompson. I was nearby. It's street-sweeping day."

"You got here first?" I popped the trunk and grabbed my case, the movements more habit than thought. Did I have extra gloves? Yes, by the spare tire. Good.

He gulped and nodded. "Dispatch called. They didn't say it was a dead body." They had. He hadn't known the code.

I slipped surgical booties over my shoes. "Stay here. Let no one through." I walked through the woods surrounding the golf course. The air smelled of sap and the pines blocked most of the sunlight. I was grateful; the sunshine hurt my eyes. Birds chattered, their songs needles to my brain. The trees thinned, and a lush circle of grass expanded before me. The ninth hole. Its flag was missing. Nearby, an officer squatted, his back to me.

I walked toward him, careful where I set my feet. The sun haloed his bright hair. Officer William Thompson. Only ten months on the job. Nicknames included "Slim," "Rookie," and "Hoops." (He'd played basketball and was, by all accounts, terrible.) But I called him Billy, as in the Kid. He couldn't grow more than blond fuzz on his face.

"Billy." He spun, his thin body quick in the pivot. The dead woman lay belly down on the grass. I stepped closer. She was white, thin, and young. Her face, turned toward me, was covered by long brown hair. Her T-shirt punctured by bullet holes. Multiple. The last gunshot victim I'd seen was Rick. I swallowed, my mouth cottony. This was different. Just the job.

Impressions surrounded her. Too many. "How did you get here?" I said. The air smelled of blood. Its metallic taste coated my mouth. I swallowed, and the dark flavor slid down my throat.

"Drove over from the station." He stood and wiped his cheeks. His eyes were red. Shit. He'd been crying.

I counted to five. "How did you get to the body?"

"Walked, like you did, through the trees." He pointed. "Jim led me to her."

"Yankowitz?" He nodded. "So whose shoe prints are these?"

He rubbed his nose. "Mine, probably. He didn't get near her."

"We'll need your shoes for exclusion. His too. Please tell me Hopkins wasn't here." He said nothing. "Fuck!" He flinched. "You know anything about securing a crime scene?" I pointed to my covered shoes.

"I've never worked a murder." Of course not. He was a rookie cop in a small town.

"Know her?" I asked.

"Yes." He inhaled deeply through his nose. Mucus rattled. "Cecilia North. She hung out with my sister, Jenny."

That explained the crying. "She live nearby?"

"Spring Street." He pointed. "Couple of streets that way. She just finished college. Been living with her parents since then." Pretty college grad. Whole life ahead of her. The headlines wrote themselves.

"You okay?" Maybe I should swap Yankowitz in. Then I thought about his parking job. I couldn't let him near the corpse. He'd probably move it.

He sniffled. "Sorry. I just didn't expect to find her like this." He set his shoulders back. "What can I do?" His voice was hoarse, but he was trying.

"I need the ME, a crime team, and one of our detectives. Radio for those." I'd let him stay, for now.

I noted the time, date, and location. Then I examined the corpse. She wore jeans and a black T-shirt. It had holes made by bullets. How many? One in the middle of her back, one up and to the right, and a third below that one by ten inches. Wait. There, above her left kidney, was shot number four. Behind her, a short path of flattened grass and a snail's trail of dark blood. She'd fallen, probably after the first shot, and crawled. Not far. Her hands, flung in front of her, were empty. She wore a silver ring on her left pinkie. Pink sparkles on her right hand. Glitter? A part in her hair allowed me a glimpse of her right eye. It was brown-green. There was something about her. What? I checked her tan arms for track marks. None I could see.

Billy stopped talking into his radio. "Better call the staties, huh? This isn't the sort of thing we get in Idyll." No kidding. When I'd interviewed, I'd assumed their stats were fudged. Two rapes in six years and no homicides in five? But it had all been true.

Sirens sounded, far away, the sound as familiar as my father's voice.

"What was she like?" I asked. Not every day I got a cop as a character witness.

He looked at her, and then away. "She was funny. Loved animals. Sassy, but not mean. You know how girls can be mean?" I didn't. I'd never had much time for girls.

The sirens got louder, shriller.

"Don't suppose you know who did this?" I asked.

"She was nice. No one . . ." He trailed off because someone obviously hadn't liked her.

The sirens stopped. "If that's the crime guys, let 'em in. But no more of our men come near unless it's a detective. Where's Hopkins?" Where had my other scene-mucker gone? What damage was he wreaking? Best check on him.

"At the clubhouse. Want me to call the staties?"

"I want the ME." Until he came, I'd visit with Hopkins. I kept to the edge of the course, my eyes to the ground. The grass was brilliant, as if each blade had been hand-painted emerald.

A brisk four-minute walk brought me to the clubhouse parking lot. A pickup truck and police cruiser were the only vehicles there. Officer Hopkins stood with his thumbs tucked into his utility belt. The belt needed another hole punched in it. Hopkins was a twenty-year veteran of the force, and he looked it. He stood opposite a man with skin as leathered as a baseball glove and iron-gray hair. The man raked his hand through his hair, over and over.

Hopkins introduced me to Cal Jackson, the groundskeeper.

"I'm Police Chief Lynch," I said. "You found the body?" I kept my voice low and gentle.

"This morning. I couldn't believe it." His Adam's apple bobbed, prominent in his thin neck.

"Did you touch her?" I asked.

He lowered his eyes. "I wanted to be sure, so I poked her arm with my finger." He shook his head as if he could dislodge the memory from his skull.

Hopkins said, "He found her around seven thirty a.m. Says she couldn't have been here before ten p.m. last night." Near his foot was a latex glove.

"Why not?"

Mr. Jackson tapped his watch. "Charlie sweeps through at ten p.m. He's our watchman."

"Would he have checked the whole course?" Not hard to picture a tired man shining his flashlight over the grounds and going back inside.

"Charlie's reliable," he said.

"Charlie's last name?" I asked.

"Fisher."

"Anything strike you as out of place this morning?"

He rubbed his chin stubble. Pointed downhill. "Just her."

"Thank you, Mr. Jackson. If you think of anything else, please, give me a call." I gave him my card. "Hopkins, where are our detectives?"

He glanced over his shoulder, as if one stood behind him. "I don't know."

"Here's a question you might be able to answer. Whose glove is by your foot?"

He glanced down. Hitched his belt up. "Mine."

"And you dropped it at a crime scene because . . . ?"

He widened his stance. "It fell out of my pocket."

I stared at him until his flabby face got pink. "There's no corpse here," he said, as if that was a valid defense.

"Don't tell me what the scene is! And don't drop stuff that the techs are going to have to bag and test. Do you have any idea how to do your job?"

He put his hands on his hips. "Yes."

"Pick up your shit," I said through clenched teeth.

"Um, Chief Lynch?" Mr. Jackson said.

"What?" I kept my eyes on Hopkins. Watched as he picked up his litter.

"Someone's down there." Mr. Jackson pointed. At the ninth hole, someone stood by the body. Someone not in uniform.

Fuck. Maybe I should deputize Mr. Jackson. So far, he was the only one giving me intel and showing common sense. I hustled back to the ninth hole, arriving corpse-side short of breath. "Who are you?" I said to the man bent over the corpse.

He turned and rose, nearly matching me for height. A scar bisected his cheek. Faded white. Old injury. He had bright-blue eyes. "I'm Damien Saunders, the medical examiner." His voice was quiet. I'd expected someone older or rumpled. Would've preferred it. I didn't need handsome now.

"Chief Lynch." We shook hands. He had calluses. Odd for an ME.

"She's dead, in case there was any doubt. Rigor indicates she's been that way several hours, but don't quote me." He walked around her and stared from a different angle.

A foot away, Billy watched, chewing on a fingernail.

"Billy, how's the crime team coming?" I asked.

He dropped his hand from his mouth. "They're on the way."

"Good. Send a detective to interview the night guard, Charlie Fisher."

"Which one?" he asked. Like we had a bullpen to choose from.

"Either. Hopkins can give you the address." He followed the path I dictated. Good. Soon the ME would insert a rectal thermometer into the victim. Billy didn't need to see his childhood friend violated.

"What's this?" Dr. Saunders said. He peered at her shimmering hand.

"Glitter? Or drugs?"

"Unusual." He pressed a gloved finger to her hand and lifted some of the crystals.

"Shouldn't we wait for the techs?" I said.

He lifted his finger to his mouth and licked the crystals. *Pop! Pop!* The noises came from his half-open mouth.

"What the—"

"Pop Rocks," he said. "The candy. Didn't know they still sold it."

"She had candy on her hand?"

He glanced at the victim and said, "Maybe she robbed the wrong baby." Most MEs I'd encountered had an odd sense of humor. This guy was no exception.

"Thorough killer." He gestured toward a starburst hole in her back's center. "Close range."

"Or panicked," I said.

Crime scenes have moods. Angry. Cold. Confused. This was jumbled. It felt hurried and planned. Four bullets was no accident, but it didn't feel like an execution. What the hell had happened here? I regretted last night's drinks. What I needed was a clear head. What I had was a skull filled with wasps.

A whistle drew my attention toward the clubhouse. The crime-scene guys came, tools in hand. One said, "Great, when we finish, we can get in a game."

Another said, "Sorry, Gary. Golf is a thinking man's sport."

The head of the team nodded hello. He was a burly man who looked as though he chopped trees for exercise. Sequoias. "This is going to take time," he said. He looked at and around the corpse.

"Problems?" I asked.

"Lots of impressions." He stared at the ground. "Only the ones we need help. The rest just add noise. It looks like you and your men have been square-dancing here."

"They're new to murder," I said.

He glanced at my gloved hands. "You're not. Aren't you the big-city copper they hired?"

"I am."

"Police chief, yeah?"

"Chief Lynch."

"So who's the detective in charge?"

"I am."

He said, "Shouldn't you have a detective here?"

I crossed my arms. "I was a detective for fifteen years in New York. Did homicide for twelve."

He looked at my feet. "Least you're dressed for it." He barked orders at his team.

"She's been dead a few hours?" I asked Dr. Saunders.

He checked his thermometer. "Seven or so."

The techs took pictures. A sketcher drew the scene. The victim shimmered. Was it the light? I blinked. Just around her hand. The one with the Pop Rocks on it. I squinted so hard I felt wrinkles form. She couldn't have moved. Just a trick of the light. Or last night's drinks.

Billy returned from his errand. "You okay, Chief?"

I stopped squinting. Did I look hungover? Worried? I unclenched my jaw. "Fine. Where are my detectives?"

"Finnegan's hunting down the watchman," he said. "And Wright's at the clubhouse, interviewing the owner."

"Good. I'm going to notify her parents. Get Wright to send patrols to canvas every house within two miles. See if anyone heard the shots." They should've. Not much competing noise out here.

"You want to talk to her family?" he said.

"I'd prefer it if someone experienced informed her parents. And I don't see anyone qualified here."

He nodded and looked at his boots. I hadn't intended that parting shot just for him, but I wasn't going to waste time explaining that.

## 1015 HOURS

The Norths' house was a white two-story with a navy-blue front door. Pink roses bloomed in front. The wide driveway held three cars. A woman unloaded groceries from the rearmost one. "Mrs. North?" I said. She tightened her grip on the bags. "Ma'am, I'm Police Chief Lynch. Is your husband home?" Better to break the news to both.

"Jeffrey? He's just back from the hospital. His mother had hip surgery. I'm going to make her a pie." No, she wouldn't. But she didn't know that yet.

"I need to talk to you. May I come inside?"

"Why, certainly, but what's this about?" Her voice fought to stay steady, but pitched upward.

"Your daughter." I took the groceries from her. "Cecilia." They had two. Billy had told me. Renee was older.

She opened the side door without keys. "Cecilia? She's inside, sleeping."

I almost missed the next step. Could Billy have made a wrong ID?

In the kitchen, Mr. North sat at a round table, sorting papers. A pair of half specs rested on his sharp nose. "Hullo," he said. "Anything the matter?" His T-shirt read "World's Greatest Dad." What a thing to be wearing today. I introduced myself. He rose and shook my hand, then invited me to sit. There were four chairs. One too many for their family now.

"He wants to talk to Cecilia," Mrs. North said.

Before I could correct her, he said, "She hasn't come downstairs."

"Really?" She glanced at the clock. It had a different bird at each hour. The little hand approached the robin. "Cecilia!" she called. No answer. "I'll just go get her."

We listened to her footsteps grow faint. She yelled, "Cecilia!" again. Then silence. Mr. North cocked his head to the side. The clock ticked, the only sound besides our breathing.

Mrs. North returned. "She's not there. Her bed's made."

"I didn't see her leave." Mr. North was alert to danger now. Too late.

"Mr. and Mrs. North, I have some bad news."

I'd had the techs take an instant photo, of her face only. She didn't look bad. Could've passed for sleeping. The photo was what convinced them. Not my words and not knowing that Billy Thompson, whom they called "Will," had identified her. Mrs. North clutched the photo. She checked it every few minutes as if it might change. We sat at the table. The liquid inside Mr. North's mug had stopped steaming.

"I thought she was sleeping," he said, again. As if the repetition could protect him from the terrible fact that his child had been killed.

"When did you last see her?" I asked.

Each time I asked them a question, it was like starting a wind-up toy. They'd spring to life, then slow down, stop, and stare blankly. "Around nine p.m. We were watching TV. She came down to say good night. She hadn't felt well since she'd come home from the pool. That's why we thought she was sleeping in," he said.

"Is her car here?"

Mrs. North wiped her cheeks. They were dry now, but she didn't notice. "Yes, it's parked in front of mine. The Toyota." She reached past a mug and grabbed a jar of raspberry jam. Then she rose and stuffed it inside a cluttered cabinet.

Mr. North said, "It's Cecilia's jam. I put it out for her breakfast."

"Do you have any idea why she left? Why she was at the golf course?" I waited for them to process the question. They were operating under shock, but were still functional and polite. Some witnesses were like this. They answered questions because they'd been raised to respect the police. What they didn't realize, or perhaps they did, was that once I stopped asking questions, it would get worse. They'd be alone with their thoughts.

"Maybe she went for a walk," she said. Her hands rested on the table. I pictured her dead daughter's hands, small and empty.

"No," her husband said. His knee banged the table. Mugs shook; a pen skittered and rolled into a saltshaker. "If she'd wanted to go for a walk, she'd have said so." He reached to steady the mug, but his hand made it shake worse.

"What was she wearing, when you last saw her?"

"Sweatpants and a T-shirt." So she'd swapped the sweats for jeans before she left.

"And neither of you heard anything after you'd gone to bed? A door or a phone?" The silence grew elastic. It stretched so far, I thought they'd lost track of the question.

"No," she said, at last.

"Who would *kill* her?" Mr. North asked.

A whistle chirp split the air. I spun in my seat, looking for the source.

"The clock," Mrs. North said. So that's what a robin sounded like. High-pitched, cheery, and inappropriate. "Cecilia gave it to Jeffrey for his birthday last year."

He rubbed his eyes. "I hate the damn thing. But I couldn't get rid of it, because she . . ." He sobbed.

I cleared my throat. "Had she mentioned anyone bothering her lately, any strange encounters?"

He shuddered. "No. Nothing like that."

"Does she have a boyfriend?"

Mrs. North said, "She did, until just before graduation. Matthew Dillard. Nice boy. But he got a job in New York, and he and Cecilia agreed that a long-distance relationship would be too much." Last I checked, Manhattan was three hours away. Long-distance was a relative concept.

"You have a picture of Matthew?"

"You don't think—" She stopped because she saw I did. I wondered if the nice ex-boyfriend had shot her daughter and left her on the golf course like a discarded ball.

"She has one tucked into her mirror." She made no move to get it.

"I could fetch it." I watched their faces for resistance. They remained blank. "It might help me get a sense of her, to see her room."

"Oh, I see. Well, yes, I suppose she—" Mr. North stopped and winced. He'd forgotten. That his daughter couldn't care whether I saw her bedroom.

Mrs. North led me upstairs, down a carpeted hall. Its plushness dampened footsteps. She stopped in front of the first room on the left. "I just want to look around," I said. Her hand went to her throat and she backed away.

The victim's bed was covered with a handmade quilt. Atop it was a book, *Extraordinary Animals*. I moved the book and discovered one neat hole in the quilt. Cigarette burn. Secret smoker. A poster of Brad

Pitt hung beside a World Wildlife Fund map of endangered-species regions. Pictures were tucked into the seam of the dresser's mirror. I examined them. Cecilia North with three girls in field-hockey uniforms, the pale skin beneath their eyes streaked black. A Halloween picture in which she was Scarecrow and another girl Dorothy. A boy kissing her cheek. I bagged that one. A fortune-cookie slip atop the dresser advised: "Expect the unexpected."

Desk drawers contained notepaper, pens, pencils, a bird guide, and a well-thumbed paperback dictionary. Two packets of tissues, stamps, some bookmarks. Movie-ticket stubs and a copy of her graduation program. A small silver flask. I uncapped it and sniffed. Rum. Nothing taped under the drawers. I swept between her mattress and box spring and found a tiny pink vibrator. Put it back. Her closet contained shoes, bags, clothes, and stuffed animals. The oddest was a three-toed sloth. A box of mementos held an old corsage, more photos, a graduation tassel, her learner's permit, and a volunteer award from the Idyll Animal Rescue League.

Her denim-jacket pocket held a condom. A half-smoked joint was hidden in a winter coat. So she'd lived a little. Her bookshelf had textbooks and childhood favorites. None of it told me anything about her death. Only of her life. No diary. She had a small pink bottle of perfume. It smelled like a department store. Beside it was a spray bottle. Coconut. *Oh hell.*

Coconut. I sniffed again. The scent from the cabin. I reexamined the photos. Brown hair, yes. And hazel eyes. The tilt of her chin. A little aggressive. What was it Billy had said? She was sassy. She had been, I recalled. The way she'd snapped at me in the cabin. Challenging me. But I hadn't thought it was *her* this morning. How had she come to die only a few hours after I'd met her?

Downstairs, the Norths sat at the kitchen table in silence. "Did you find anything?" Mrs. North asked.

"No. I'll send someone by, to talk to Renee later." Their older daughter. They'd have to fetch her home. "I'm sorry for your loss." Mrs. North still held the photo of Cecilia. I extended my hand. She pulled it to her chest. Her husband put his arm around her and said, "We don't need it." Her shoulders rounded and she handed it to me.

Inside my car, I worked a time line. I'd seen the victim around 11:00 p.m. The ME said she'd been dead seven hours. So about an hour after she left the cabin, she was shot. I glanced at her ex-boyfriend's photo. He was young, blond, with a pointy face this side of weasel. Not the guy at the cabin.

The boyfriend would be the prime suspect. Unless I told the detectives that there'd been a man with our victim last night near Hought's Pond. But to tell them would require an explanation of my cabin tryst. If you give a cop a choice between a gay man and a leper for a partner, he'll take the leper every time. Trust me. I've been a cop twenty-two years.

I didn't have to tell the truth. I chewed my cheek until I tasted blood. No, any lie would collapse if the cabin man were found. He'd recognize me. And he'd talk.

"Shit." I slammed my hands against the steering wheel. The car felt stuffy. My chest hurt. This tiny fucking town was closing in on me.

## 1200 HOURS

The desk sergeant covered his phone's mouthpiece and asked, "Any word on the homicide?" I walked past without comment. He called, "Are the staties coming soon?" I grunted and slammed my door, rattling the brass nameplate. It said Chief Stoughton. Seven months and they hadn't changed it. At my old station, I would've offered more on the murder. But this wasn't my old station. The carpet underfoot was unstained. The file cabinets opened and closed, no kicking required. And my door had someone else's name on it.

The phone rang, a button lit green. Active call. I snatched it up.

"Chief Stoughton?" The voice was soft, female.

"Chief Lynch."

"Oh, I'm sorry. The directory said—"

"It needs updating."

"Shirley Winston from the *New Haven Register*. I heard you had a murder. Can you confirm that—"

"No comment."

"Why, Chief, you haven't let me finish my question."

"Would you prefer that I let you finish and then say 'no comment'? It's too early. When I know something, you'll know something." I hung up. Time to see if my detectives had done any detecting.

The *rap-rap-rap* on my door torpedoed that idea. "Come in, Mrs. Dunsmore." She came, her orthopedics quiet on the carpet. She surveyed my office, looking for faults and finding plenty. Mrs. Dunsmore was a secretary, presumably mine, but I'd sooner lay claim to a rabid dog.

She dropped a manila folder on my desk. "Time to review the applications for patrol supervisor."

"I'll do that once I get this murder squared away." I pushed the folder aside. The bright pain inside my forehead exploded into a supernova.

"We need a patrol supervisor." She pushed the folder toward me.

"Did you know Cecilia North?" I asked. Distraction. It worked on wild animals, occasionally.

"She was in my grandniece's Girl Scout troop. Nice girl." She clasped her hands at her waist and asked, "When will the state officers be coming?"

I set my mitts atop the folder. Stopping our tug-of-war. Afraid she'd win.

"Why does everyone think we need the staties?"

She shuffled to my window and examined the plant on the sill. She'd given it to me on my first day. I'd poured coffee and soda on it. Plucky thing wouldn't die. It had a cop's constitution. "We don't solve murders," she said.

"That's going to change. Excuse me."

I exited my office and scanned the station. Heard the desk sergeant answer the phone, "Idyll Police." It still sounded like a joke. Idle police.

The space was half full of uniforms. Most patrols were back from the golf course. I clapped my hands until only the desk sergeant was speaking. "Quick announcement," I said. The men formed a wobbly circle around me. "If a reporter calls you, stops you on the street, or climbs into your shower, the answer to any question she has is 'no comment.'"

"What if it's a he?" someone called. Wiseass.

"By all means, offer him some soap. And then tell him 'no comment.'" They laughed. A bunch of straight guys never tempted by another man. Or were they? One cop, Klein, laughed harder, his eyes checking his colleagues. Bingo.

Our detectives, Wright and Finnegan, sat farthest from the coffeepot but closest to our only interview room. Visually, they made quite a pair: Wright, tall, thin, and black, and Finnegan, short, schlubby, and ashen white. My first month here, I thought of them as Wright and White. Finnegan's desk was covered with chewed pens, takeout containers, and files that belonged in cabinets. It was dominated by a plaque that read "A clean desk is the sign of a full dumpster." Wright's desk was tidy. Near his phone sat a photo of his wife and kids. It needed dusting.

I cleared my throat. They looked up. "Any news?" I asked.

"Some, sir." Finnegan, from Boston, had an accent that could strip paint. "I drove to Charlie Fisher's house in Coventry. He was drinking coffee with his wife." I imagined the scene. Old Mr. and Mrs. Fisher drinking from mugs that said "Decaf is the Devil's Blend." "Charlie said he'd made his rounds at nine thirty p.m., a half hour earlier than usual. He needed to drive his wife home from a church function."

"He see anything?"

"Said the course was fine. Walked the whole thing. Always does. They've told him he can use a cart, but he prefers to walk. Says it's more effective even if it's not efficient." Good old Charlie, walking the course. Not likely he'd miss a body. "Poor bastard." Finnegan scratched his chest. "He asked if he'd come at his usual time, if it would've made a difference."

"So you don't think he did it?" I said.

"He's sixty-plus years old. She could've outrun him easy."

"She couldn't outrun a bullet."

"He owns a shotgun. Used for hunting. I checked it out. Smelled dusty."

"Okay. The timing matches what her parents said. Sometime after nine p.m. she leaves the house and ends up dead around midnight. Let's find out how. I want Billy to help."

"You want Hoops?" He didn't say more. Billy was young and raw. And he'd trampled the crime scene.

"He's an Idyll native. He knew the victim." I held up my hand. "I know. You think that's a problem. If it is, we'll cut him. But for now, keep him in the loop." Billy's youth was an asset. He'd do as I said and keep me informed. No questions asked.

Wright said the techs had retrieved three bullets from the scene. "Handgun." He scanned his notepad. "Three people in the area heard loud noises. Two said around midnight and the third said sometime after eleven thirty p.m."

"Did they call it in?" I asked.

He held up a finger. "One did. A Mrs. Riley. Dix checked it out. He made a loop around the block. Nothing. Since he'd only got the one report and he saw nothing, he thought—"

"It was a car backfiring?" I'd seen tourists in New York make the opposite mistake. Hit the deck when an old taxi drove by. Always good for a laugh.

"Yup." Wright put his notepad in his inner pocket. Unlike Finnegan, his clothes fit. Because, unlike Finnegan, he still had a wife. "I'm going to look in on our boy, Anthony Fergus." He leaned forward on his chair. Ready for action.

"The wife beater?" I asked. Anthony was heroin skinny, in need of a dentist and anger-management classes. Wright had hauled him in two months ago. His wife had dropped all charges two hours after his arrest. Showed up with tears in her black-and-blue eyes and apologies on her lips. It had steamed Wright but good. He'd broken the coffeepot. Dunsmore had complained, but I'd told her to let him alone. I knew what it was like to watch a perp walk. I'd broken more than coffeepots.

"Why are you looking at him? We've got a murder," I said.

"Plenty of wife beaters graduate to murder." He wiggled his brows.

I leaned against his desk. "They usually kill their wives."

He scooted his chair back. "He owns a gun." He made a pistol with his thumb and forefinger.

"He's not the only person in town who does."

"He worked at the golf course. Maintenance. Was let go for missing work too often." He fired his finger gun.

I looked at Finnegan. He studied his fingernails. "And you think that makes him a suspect?" I asked.

Wright said, "I think it's worth checking where he was last night."

"Make it quick. We've got work here that *needs* doing," I said.

His ass was out of his chair before I'd finished.

"You think Anthony Fergus shot our victim?" I asked Finnegan.

He no longer feigned interest in the state of his hands. "I think we don't have any likelier suspects," he said. An attempt to back his colleague. So he was loyal. There were prices for loyalty. I almost warned him.

I asked, "What did the techs give us?"

"Besides a lecture on not destroying the crime scene?" He tapped his desk with a well-chewed pen. "Another lecture on the rewards of patience."

"Start getting us background on the victim. And get an interview with her employer. What did she do?" Her parents had been vague.

"Insurance, human resources. Working with new employees. Those gunshots prevented a slow death by boredom." Real cops regard desk jobs as hell on earth. It's funny, given how much paperwork we do.

"We'll need a tip line," I said.

"We'll have to hire extra help." Money woes were a regular gripe. The station leaked. On rainy days, wastebaskets were deployed. Not Washington Heights, but not Beverly Hills.

"You okay being full-time 'til this wraps?" I asked.

"Sure thing." He was my half detective, a casualty of budget cuts. I needed the selectmen's blessing before I changed his status. Ah, well. As Rick used to say, "It is better to ask forgiveness than beg permission." That nicely summed up my dead partner's philosophy.

Back in my office, the phone rang and rang. Mrs. Dunsmore answered it when the feeling moved her. "Chief Lynch."

"Chief, hello. Lieutenant Doug Martin, from the Eastern District Major Crime Squad." Ah, the staties. "Heard you got a homicide. Young white woman?" He didn't wait for my response. "I'm assigning Detective Carl Revere to liaison with you." My headache migrated to my eyes. I thought about that old proverb. The one about keeping your enemies closer. Plus, if I let him in, everyone would stop asking about the state police.

"I look forward to meeting him." My tone said otherwise.

"I'll send him to tonight's press conference."

"There won't be one."

"Girl found dead on a golf course? You'll need one."

"I'd like to get the autopsy results first."

He said, "Ah, I see. ME giving you a hard time? He's an odd duck."

The doctor had tasted the victim's Pop Rocks. Unorthodox, yes. But again, most MEs were. *You think he's handsome*, my inner voice said. *Shut up*, I told it. *Blue eyes*, it said. *What is it about blue eyes with you?*

"If you'll excuse me, I've got a murder to clear," I said.

"Sure thing."

As pissing contests went, I'd been in bigger and wetter. I didn't like being told I'd host an outside detective. He'd probably expected gratitude. Color us both surprised. I scanned the Filofax I'd inherited. Under "Medical Examiner," the typed "Franklin Connor" had a red line through it. Below was handwritten "Damien Saunders." I dialed his number.

"Chief Lynch." His voice, deep and slow, suited his purpose. No hurry needed around the dead. "I've scheduled your autopsy for Tuesday at eight a.m. And before you ask, I'm sorry, but I have bodies in queue. I can't do it sooner."

I fought my reflex to argue. The cause of death wasn't much of a mystery. "Eight a.m. Tuesday is fine. See you then." I hung up, wondering how he got his scar.

Billy fetched me lunch. I didn't want to leave the station. The last murder in Idyll was in '90. Domestic. Wife confessed on scene. This one looked tougher. I ate three pizza slices and made lists of things to check. It felt like the old days, the good ones. Except I knew something about our murder case that I couldn't share. Who was I kidding? The good old days had been full of secrets.

Back in the pen, Finnegan had Cecilia North's college transcript. An average student. Involved with animal rights. Otherwise unremarkable. Wright, returned from chasing Anthony Fergus, worked at his typewriter, pecking with one forefinger at a time.

I said, "Victim's autopsy's scheduled for Tuesday morning. I'm going." Finnegan wrinkled his nose. Not a fan of the morgue.

"How's the tip line coming?"

"Once they get us a number, we're in business." Finnegan lit a cigarette. "They claim it's in use for the Morris case." He exhaled a stream of smoke, keeping the butt balanced on his lip. Trick of a longtime smoker.

"Wasn't that put to bed before I got here?" I took a shallow breath. Smoking bothers me. It's inconvenient in my line of work. But so is being gay.

"Yup."

"Tell the genius in charge of getting us a number that if I don't have one in an hour, I'm going to visit his house and cut *his* phone line. Then I'm going to cut every cable around his house. Maybe I'll puncture his car tires."

"Will do," Finnegan said. He sketched a two-finger salute.

Wright stopped typing. He looked up and said, "Anthony Fergus claims he was home watching TV last night. *Walker, Texas Ranger* reruns. I'll check *TV Guide*."

"Do that after you've pulled and reviewed the victim's phone records." Jesus, it was lucky Idyll had few murders. Chasing local apes wasn't how you solved them. "Eastern District wants to send us a helper. Carl Revere. Know him?"

Wright said he'd seen him at a few police functions. "He looks like he came from 1954." He made a buzzing gesture and moved his hand over his head. "He supervising this?"

"No, he's not." I pointed to their desks. "I want this one resolved quickly. All overtime will be covered." Wright whistled. "Don't tell the troops, or I'll be double-checking time sheets for a month."

"A month?" They laughed. "You think we're rookies?"

"See you tomorrow."

"Good night, Chief."

I was out of sight when Finnegan said, "You ever known a chief to attend an autopsy?"

Wright said, "Or notify the victim's family? What's he on?"

## 1900 HOURS

I drove past the Sutter place on my way home. Framed by thunderclouds, it looked more desolate than usual. The large farmhouse flaked white paint chips onto its weedy lawn. The abandoned red barn had a hole in the roof the size of a man. Its large pasture contained no cows or horses. The only animal on site was a goose with a bad attitude. At the end of the farm road was a tee intersection. Turn right and get dinner? Or turn left and revisit the golf course? I turned right. I'd revisit the course later. They were going to have a job, making the grass green again where she fell.

I parked at Suds, where I ate most of my dinners. The bar was nearly empty. Nate had told me Sunday nights were his worst. "Puritans," he'd said, shaking his ponytail. "Don't like to drink on Sundays. Not in public, anyway."

Donna Daniels was behind the bar, her pale arm reaching into the ice chest. She leaned so that I got a good look at why the regulars called her "DD." It wasn't because of her initials. She straightened. "Chief!" Too late. No choice but to approach and hope she wouldn't fuss. Why hadn't I asked Nate if she'd be working tonight? Because she might hear of it and interpret it as interest on my part. Donna interprets respiration as interest on my part.

"How are you?" She tilted her head, ready to listen to my worries. "Tough day, huh?" Of course she knew about the murder. Bet the whole town knew.

"I'm fine, thanks. Hungry."

"What can I do you for?" She sounded like a TV waitress.

"Steak and cheese."

"Peppers, onions?" She knew my order. "Anything else?" She tucked a strand of hair behind her ear, pierced twice. I said no thanks and she twirled and wiggled to the kitchen, ignoring the waves of a thirsty patron. Two minutes later, she passed him again. He waved his empty glass at her. No joy. She came right for me, pink lipstick now on her lips.

"I heard the news," she said. "Murder on the golf course. That girl? Cecilia North? Real nice. A couple years younger than me." That seemed generous. I'd lay a fiver that they weren't born in the same decade.

"You gonna catch who did it?" the man nearest me asked. He wore an ancient leather jacket and a Red Sox cap. He leaned in as if I was about to confide.

Donna rolled her eyes. "Don't hassle the man, Larry. He's here to eat."

"I'll take it to go," I said.

"Haven't had a real murder since 1987," Larry said. "Man got run down outside the train museum."

"That was a hit-and-run," the man beside Larry said. He played with a matchbook.

Larry turned to him. "Man died, didn't he?"

"Not the same as murder. It's vehicular homicide or some such, right, Chief?"

"Would you guys knock it off?" Donna said. "He didn't come here to explain the law to you monkeys." Both men scowled but quit yapping. Too wise to piss off their booze source.

Donna fluffed her hair and said, "This fall will be your first Idyll Days."

"Yes, it will." Why the sudden shift in topic?

She rested her muscled forearms on the bar. Giving me an even clearer view of her assets. "I work the kissing booth. It's for charity."

"That so?" I made a show of checking my watch.

She patted my hand with her damp fingers. "Let me go check on your order."

Larry watched her walk, his eyes on her ass. He leaned on the bar and said, "I think she fancies you." His breath was 90 percent vodka. I almost told him I didn't fancy her. But he wouldn't believe me. What straight man would?

Someone tapped my shoulder. I turned. Male. Brown hair. Weak chin. "Hi, Chief. I'm Sam Franklin. I live over on Grove Street, near the Norths. You don't think I need a new alarm system installed, do you? Because of the murder on the golf course? I've got two girls. Both in middle school."

"Do you have an alarm system now?"

He nodded. "Motion-sensor lights too."

"Fancy," Larry said.

I shot him a "shut up" look and said, "Don't upgrade your alarm." I wondered if he would, anyway. People like to create and maintain the illusion of safety. I couldn't blame him, not with two kids.

Donna returned with my dinner in a large brown bag, stapled shut. "I put some extra pickles in." She winked.

I fought the urge to tell her that pickles were my favorite. Rick wasn't beside me to appreciate it. He'd loved the jokes that sailed over people's heads because they had no idea what or who I was. When we'd get out of hearing range, he'd elbow my ribs and say, "Oh, honey, you are too bad!" And his effete impression would send me into fits. The way he'd wave his hands and roll his eyes.

"Thanks." I set the money down before she could argue. I could eat my way through this town and never pay a bill. Seems like Chief Stoughton did. First few places I paid, the owners looked bewildered. Some cops dig that shit. Not me.

It was a four-minute drive home. The realtor who'd sold it to me described it as a perfect "starter house." It was a brick rectangle with a lawn and mailbox. I used the side door. The front was for people selling things and formal occasions. The side was for family and friends. Day by day, I was learning the rules of small-town life.

Inside, I wrestled my jacket off. Hung it on the wall rack, its crooked trio of pegs set into a splintered pine board. A shop-class project made by the former owner's kid decades ago. I dropped my takeout on the scarred kitchen table and grabbed a beer from the avocado-colored fridge. Below, the diamond-patterned linoleum peeled. Could I glue it down? I recalled the Norths' kitchen, with its bright-yellow walls and sugar and flour canisters. Even their unmatched mugs looked good. My place hadn't been updated since the late seventies. Furnished with its dead owner's belongings.

I brought my dinner to the beige-and-brown living room. Maybe there was a game on. A gust swept through, rustling papers. I walked through the living room and down the hall, peering into the old "sewing room," now a graveyard for my unpacked boxes. Past the bathroom with its black and pink tile. The spare bedroom had wallpaper patterned with sailing ships and a window painted shut. At the hall's end was my bedroom. The window near my unmade bed was open, the gusting air fragrant. I slammed it shut. The only furniture was a full bed, a bureau missing two drawer pulls, and a lamp covered with brown-and-white shells on its base. The curves of the shells looked swollen, as if the lamp was infected, breaking out in bulbous hives.

Cecilia North's bedroom had more personality than my whole house. I'd had twenty-two more years to accumulate a life. So where was it? My mind ran backward. Her spray bottle, her teddy bear, her map of endangered species. She'd bought her father a clock, and he kept it though he hated it. She'd inspired love. The gunshot wounds had made a rectangle on her back. She'd inspired hatred.

I returned to the living room and sat in my brown, corduroy recliner. Ugly as sin, my sister-in-law, Marie, said of it. She'd begged to buy me a new one. My brother, John, had laughed. "You'd sooner convince Father McMann to eat a burger on Friday," he'd said.

I grabbed a notebook from my side table, a glass circle above a curved piece of metal. The only piece of furniture in my house I liked. I made notes. The ones I couldn't share. John Doe at the cabin. Shorter than me, with thinning, fair hair. Clothes? Khakis, maybe. A collared shirt. Shoes? Damn it. He hadn't made an impression, had worked hard not to. And I'd been so worried about being caught, exposed, that I'd let him walk by with his hand raised to his face. On his hand, a ring. He'd worn a wedding ring.

The phone rang. I walked to the kitchen and picked up the large-numbered push-button phone. An instrument for the vision-impaired. "Hello?"

"Lynch. It's Lee." Lee was from my old precinct. We hadn't spoken since my going-away party. What a sad affair. Even before the heavy drinking began. "How are ya?" Ah, that accent. If you could distill New York into a sound, it would be Lee's nasal voice. It made me positively nostalgic.

"Good. You?" I said.

"Same old, same old. Oh, 'cept they finally got us a new sergeant. Flynn, from the 151st. He's not fucking awful." I'd had my eye on that job, once upon a time. "Anyways, I wanted to let you know we're having a memorial for Rick on Tuesday, the nineteenth. St. Anthony's. Can you make it?"

My nostalgia dried up like the Gobi after a hard rain. "Aw hell. Sorry, Lee, but we caught a murder." *Thank you, Cecilia North.* "I'm gonna have to make sure the locals don't Barney Fife it."

"That's too bad. Maybe you're unlucky." He swallowed. "I didn't mean—"

"Forget it." I looked out the window above the sink. Saw in the twilight that the grass needed mowing. Christ. How did people do this stuff? "I'll send flowers."

"Sure. Good luck with the murder, Lynch."

"Thanks. Take care, Lee."

On August 19th of last year, my partner had died, gunned down. Apollo St. James had fired twice at Rick and hit him once. Rick had fired between the first and second shots. And I had shot twice, when it was too late, when Rick was down. Five shots, and I was unhurt. That's why Lee apologized about the unlucky comment. Because there'd been talk. Why hadn't I gotten hit? Hadn't I tried to save Rick? That talk had broken what remained of my heart. And the rest of it, what no one else knew, had driven me here.

A bird called out. Not a robin. It didn't sound like the Norths' clock. I wondered if they'd toss it, or keep it, because of Cecilia. It was just a clock. But they'd never see it that way. I understood.

# MONDAY, AUGUST 11TH
## 0900 HOURS

I found the mayor waiting in my office. Behind my desk, in my chair. "Chief Lynch!" He smiled. Many of his teeth were fake. He'd once enjoyed success in hockey.

"Mayor. To what do I owe the pleasure?"

His face crumpled. "I heard the sad news. That poor young woman. And her family." He rose and gestured to my seat.

I remained standing. "The Norths."

"We must do everything we can." He walked to the window. "Perhaps set up a scholarship in her honor. We could host a pancake breakfast." He rubbed his gut.

"We ought to find and arrest her killer, first."

He nodded. "Yes."

"You'll want this resolved as quickly as possible."

"Absolutely." He crossed his meaty arms over his chest.

"I'm going to need more manpower."

"Mmmm hmmmm."

"Money."

He harrumphed. Had I been impolite? Perhaps. But I didn't want any nonsense when it came time to sign checks. "Finnegan needs to come on full-time. Overtime for patrol. Plus, we'll need people on the tip line. Which you can mention at the press conference, if you like."

He grinned. He'd had eggs for breakfast. "When?"

"Your office can set it up. We have to wait for the autopsy results."

"Good thing we hired you. All that detective experience. I told

39

the selectmen." He came closer. We were matched for height, but the mayor liked food more than I did and it showed. People called him handsome. I suppose he was, if you liked the chinos-and-boat-shoes look with Kennedy hair. Too L. L. Bean for my taste.

"Solve it quick. Don't want any shadows on our upcoming festivities," he said.

Ah, Idyll Days, the brainchild of a prior mayor who guessed that people would pay to visit a tiny New England town and pretend that things were quaint. It worked. Idyll Days brought four thousand tourists to eat, drink, and buy local goods.

"The Eastern District crime squad is lending us a detective," I said.

"Wonderful." He cracked his knuckles. "But if we have him, why does Finnegan need to be full-time?" Ah, so he had been paying attention.

"A case like this needs police with more experience than writing parking tickets and shooting rabid animals." Or chasing wife beaters.

He tutted me and walked toward the door. "Now, now, they're good men, up to the task. I'll get my office working on that press conference." He paused on the threshold. "But you'll be careful about the money, won't you? I'd hate to go back on my word." He let me puzzle over that. "About your car." Before I could respond, he said good-bye and walked away.

When I'd arrived in January, the selectman had fussed over my exclusive-use patrol car. In New York, I'd never owned a car. Never needed one. But here? Without a car, I'd starve. I'd protested. The mayor had gone to bat for me. He'd said it wasn't very neighborly to lure me from the city and then strand me without transport. His backing came at a price. Damn politicians.

In the detectives' pen, I asked if they'd seen our statie visitor. "Detective Revere?" Finnegan's tone, all innocence, made me suspect its opposite. "He called earlier, for directions. Should be here any minute."

"When did he call?"

Chins propped on fists. They thought, hard. "Twenty minutes ago?" Wright said. "Dunno. We've been busy." He waved his arm over piles of paper like a game-show hostess.

"Don't tell me." They'd fucked with him.

"Maybe he stopped off on the road," Finnegan said.

I raised my brow.

"For a date."

Wright laughed. "I hear the rest area by Exit 14 serves all kinds."

Finnegan nodded, face solemn. "I too have heard such rumors."

They didn't have to say more. I got it.

Gay jokes were a staple of police stations. At my old precinct, they were tossed about, fast and furious. But so too were racial epithets and ethnic slurs. Everything and everyone was fair game. And in the melting pot of New York, there was plenty of diversity. Here, diversity was Wright, our only black cop, and Yankowitz, an overweight Pole whose people had probably arrived three boats after the *Mayflower*. Here, gay jokes weren't casual. They were knives flung with malicious intent.

"You two go there a lot?" I asked, my voice cool.

Wright pointed at Finnegan. "I think he's earned some kind of frequent-visitor stamp. Right, Finny?" Finnegan tossed a pencil, missing Wright's eye by inches. Close, but no cigar. Too bad. I left them to their fun.

In my office were several folders marked Urgent. Mrs. Dunsmore's handiwork. I knew what they contained. Requests for vacation time, work roster sheets, equipment inventory forms, résumés for patrol supervisor, budgets. Mind-numbing paperwork. Sure was a good thing I had all that detecting experience.

A knock at the door. "Who is it?"

"Billy, sir."

"Come in."

The heat had curled the hair about his ears. "I've returned from talking to Cecilia's friends. Should I share my notes with you or give them to Detective Wright?"

"Sum it up for me first."

"I spoke to Susan Hill and Deidre Lipschitz. Can you imagine a more terrible name?" He pursed his lips. "Susan was Cecilia's college roommate. Deidre was a friend. Neither girl could think of anyone who had a grudge against her. Last year, Cecilia signed a PETA petition protesting the fur industry, but so did a hundred other students. Not a likely lead, is it?" He looked up from his notes.

"No. Anything else?"

"I made a list of ex-boyfriends, and I looked 'em up."

I hadn't told him to do the second part. "How far back did you go?" I asked.

"Third grade, John Ward. Only two have records. Josh Kelly had a DUI two years back. Michael Schwartz was a surprise. Arrested for public indecency."

"When?"

"Six months ago. But it seemed like he just got really drunk and started flashing people." I didn't see how Michael Schwartz's willy-waving was related to our murder. "I have a copy of the report." He handed it to me.

"Did Susan or Deidre mention a man in Cecilia's life? A new boyfriend?"

"No."

Damn. Cecilia must have kept it mum. Billy was good-looking. Ladies responded. They'd have told him, if they'd known.

"Let Wright know what you got. Tell him I told you to check the ex-boyfriends." Wright wouldn't like Billy checking records. "Next time, ask before you run reports."

"Yes, sir." I returned his file to him. He paused at the door. "Chief? I appreciate you letting me help. I know you don't have to." He gripped the doorframe, as if for support. Had I ever been that young or vulnerable? "Thanks." He closed the door.

Before I got through the vacation requests, there came another knock. The person who entered had military-short hair and a well-tailored suit. FBI? No. Not wary enough. "Chief Lynch," he said. He straightened a millimeter. And then I got it. Like someone out of the 1950s, Wright had said. "I'm Detective Revere. Eastern District Crime Squad."

"Welcome to Idyll."

"Thank you. I hoped we might meet for a few minutes to discuss the case. Then I can meet the team, get caught up."

"I'll take you to them." His posture was impeccable, but my genes triumphed. I was taller by three inches, and stood close so he knew it.

He said nothing as I walked him through the station, even when confronted by the three-foot-tall softball-league trophy, crowned with a jockstrap no one would claim and thus no one would remove.

Finnegan sat at his desk. He tugged the world's ugliest brown tie and grunted into the phone. "Nah. Nah. Huh? Ugh. Okay." He hung up.

"Finnegan, meet Detective Revere. Where's Wright?"

"Talking to the golf-course owner. Something about a surveillance camera."

Detective Revere thrust his hand out. Finnegan stood and shook it. We all looked at the board. Crime-scene pics and a recent photo of the victim were attached to it. Revere picked up a paperclip. "Has anyone ruled out accident?" he asked.

Finnegan said, "We don't get a lot of drive-by shootings on the golf course."

Revere coughed and bent the paperclip's end. "I'm not suggesting the shooting was accidental. Just that she wasn't the target."

"What leads you to suspect mistaken identity?" I asked.

He unbent the clip, straightening the metal into a line. "Just a hypothesis. She was out in the dark. The course isn't lit at night. I checked. It's possible she was at the wrong place at the wrong time."

"I'd say she was definitely at the wrong place at the wrong time." Finnegan said.

"Time of death?" Revere asked.

I said, "We're waiting on the autopsy. Most likely near midnight."

He said, "Where do I sit?" I pointed to a desk we used as a dumping ground for catalogs, broken equipment, and half a dozen phones whose origins no one could explain. His face looked like he'd sucked a lemon.

"Who's handling where she worked?" I asked.

"I've got an appointment tomorrow morning," Finnegan said.

"Make it early afternoon. I'll ride with you," I said.

He arched a brow. "I'd love the company." Sure he would.

Revere said, "You're working the case?"

"Problem?" I said. Maybe he wouldn't need a desk.

"I've never known a police chief to work a murder."

"Small-town economics."

He set the unbent paperclip on Finnegan's desk. "Perhaps you'd point me towards the bathroom? I've been on the road a long time."

I pointed. He walked. Finnegan swept the paperclip into his trash. Wright approached, a giant soda in hand. "Get anything from the golf-course security camera?" I asked.

"Nada. It hadn't been turned on in months." Wright set his drink down and loosened his tie.

Revere returned from the toilet. He and Wright met. Updates were given.

"She was shot on the golf course, but that might not have been her destination," I said. Time to lead them to the cabin. "She doesn't live far from the course. She might've been headed home."

"From where?" Wright asked.

"You tell me. Are there places in Idyll where young people go at night?"

"If they want fun?" he asked. "Out of town."

"And if they're making their own?" *Come on, guys. Say the cabin.*

Finnegan said, "We've busted kids near the train museum. They love to pretend to drive the trains after they've had a few rum-and-cokes."

"What about the Sutter place?" I asked. Perhaps if they thought of abandoned places they'd get to the cabin.

Wright said, "Have you ever been to that place? It has an attack goose." He made his hand into a beak. Opened and closed it as he said, "Honk, honk, fuckers. Better security than an electric fence."

None of them suggested the cabin. Maybe they knew as little as I had. Revere cleaned junk from his desk while Wright checked the victim's phone records. Finnegan added notes to the time line. I stared at the board. Nothing but her body for evidence.

Maybe the autopsy would reveal something. Maybe she'd been sexually assaulted. Or done a shit ton of drugs. It's not terrible to hope for such things. It's practical. If our girl had gotten plugged by complete, random chance, it was a crime without origin. And we'd have more chance of locating the Holy Grail than solving it. I returned to my office and mulled over how to lead the detectives to the cabin. By the end of the day, I still had no answer.

# TUESDAY, AUGUST 12TH
## 0800 HOURS

I hated everything about the morgue. The formaldehyde smell, the damp, chill air, the red biohazard bins. What I hated most was the drain in the floor. Picturing what sluiced down that hole made my molars ache. On an aluminum table, Cecilia North lay nude. I could have drawn her bikini based on the contrast between her pale and dark flesh. Her torso was grotesque. A golf ball would have fit inside one of her exit wounds.

Dr. Saunders was scrubbed and gloved, his eyes bright behind a plastic face shield. "Got an early start. Already did the clothes and charted the wounds. And I've got good news," he said. "She's still got a bullet in her. Lodged in a rib." He pushed a metal block under her back. I kept my eyes on her left heel. It had a pale, half-moon scar.

He slit her chest and glanced up. "Not nauseous, are you?" I said no, but his grin showed he saw through it.

"No defense wounds. Nothing to indicate a struggle." He cut through her ribs and folded her skin back as if it were a blouse. I looked away. I was fine at autopsies, always had been, even that time a bit of kidney hit my hand. I hadn't gotten sick. So today was harder than usual. Seeing her, dissected like a lab frog, was harder. Because her corpse reproached me. For keeping silent about the cabin. *You're fucking up my case*, I imagined her saying. *Why?*

"Now, for that bullet," he said. I turned back to watch. The slippery sucking of her flesh made me grimace. Then came a high ping. The bullet hitting a metal bowl. The sound punched my gut as I thought of Rick's wound. The one that killed him.

"Got it," he said. "Nothing like a bullet to make your day, huh?"

"I wouldn't mind a suspect." I tried to smile. It felt wrong, so I stopped.

"You okay, Chief? You seem a little foggy." He said it like a man used to hearing excuses. I wasn't making any.

He cut into her abdomen. "She ate before she died. At least four hours. Looks like meatloaf and salad." The smell of gastric acid made me breathe short and hard through my mouth. Mrs. North said they ate at 7:30. So at least 11:30 p.m. for time of death. So far, so good.

He said, "You ever think about what your last meal would be?"

"What?" I pulled my hand back. It had been stroking her foot's scar, as if I could comfort her. Goddamn. *Pull it together, Lynch.*

"You know how death-row inmates request a final meal? Ever think what yours would be?"

I had. We'd played this game, Rick and I. We'd given it lots of thought. "A good steak, medium-rare, mashed potatoes with cream cheese and chives, a toasted roll with real butter, and a slice of blueberry pie with vanilla ice cream."

He reached for paper towels and knocked them to the floor. "I'll get 'em," I said. I bent and picked them up. When I stood, my shoulder knocked into the metal table's edge. "Ow!"

"You okay?" He touched my shoulder. His fingers felt hot, even through my layered clothing. "I'm sorry." He gestured. There was blood on my jacket. He pulled his gloves off, tossed them in the biohazard bin. Snapped on a fresh pair.

"It's okay." I held out the paper towels. Feigned indifference, though his touch had shaken me like a damn martini.

He grabbed two sheets, lifted his plastic shield, and wiped his shiny face. "Guess you've given your last meal some thought." His blue-eyed stare was too much. I returned to the end of the table. Kept my eyes on her scar.

"Stakeouts get boring," I said.

He weighed the remains of her liver. The scale's arrow marker ticked back and forth.

"No doubt it was the bullets that killed her," I said.

"There's more to do, but that's the current theory."

He weighed her organs, as if it meant something. It did, to him. To me it looked like a grocery horror show. "I'll have the report sent over," he said. He walked to the sink, his gory hands held out and away from his aproned body.

I left. The doors thwapped behind me. The gray hall was empty of people, living or dead. I hurried up the stairwell and outside, where the bright sunlight stung my eyes. I held on to the railing, its pocked, metal surface rough against my palm. I checked my jacket. Her dark blood on it. So much for leaving her behind.

An hour later, I was at the station. It smelled of blueberries. The desk sergeant talked into the phone about a car accident. He said he'd send someone immediately. He set the phone down. "Berries?" He pulled a green pint from under his desk. Held it out.

"No, thank you."

"My sister-in-law has a farm. Down the road, near Pond Street."

"Wonderful."

"Any time you want berries or apples, let me know." He put a call through, at last, to request an officer check out the accident. I had a clue as to why our response times were slow.

When I found him, Finnegan looked like something the cat threw up. And he smelled like half a pack of cigarettes. "Rough night?"

"You have any ex-wives?" he asked.

"No."

He scratched his stubble. "I've got a collection. Number three wants more money. She gets loquacious when she's angry." He had a habit of breaking out twenty-five-cent words rarely enough to surprise me every time he did it. "How'd the autopsy go?"

"Blood and guts," I said. "The ME found a bullet inside her."

"That's good," he said.

I nodded. It was.

He belched and rubbed his chest. "'Scuse me. We've got an appointment with Helen O'Donnell at noon. She runs Human Resources at Liberty Insurance."

"I'll see you later, then," I said.

My desk was piled with more folders. Patrol-supervisor résumés were on top. I could review them and select the best. Or I could ignore them and watch Mrs. Dunsmore seethe. The second option appealed, but I opened the folder. Some candidates were underqualified. Two were overqualified. That worried me more. Why would a cop leave his station for a demotion? I set aside four and wrote, "Follow up." Then I went through the vacation requests. Either the men thought I was born yesterday or they couldn't count. I marked them and moved on to citizen complaints. Besides crazy Elmore Fenworth, we had Caroline Ross, who took exception to every ticket issued her. There were a lot. Lady couldn't drive or park.

A trio of door raps raised my head from Ms. Ross's complaint of misogyny disguised as a ticket for blocking a fire hydrant. "Come in, Mrs. Dunsmore."

She wore her church bingo outfit, a black dress brightened by a lacquered parrot pin. "Good morning, Chief." She saw the open folder in my hand. She couldn't have looked more surprised if she'd caught me masturbating. "Is that—?"

"The citizens' complaints. Nothing unusual or unexpected."

"You've reviewed the résumés?"

I held the folder out. "I have."

She took it. "Very good."

"You can take the vacation requests too."

She frowned. This wasn't expected behavior. I smiled. "That's a lovely dress."

She smoothed the fabric. "Thank you." She hurried out.

Finnegan didn't look better when I next saw him, but he stood and said, "You want me to drive?"

"Sure." I regretted my decision when I saw his car. It resembled his desk. The backseat showed his devotion to Dunkin' Donuts and McDonald's.

He drove with one hand on the steering wheel. "Wright located the ex-boyfriend," he said. Matthew Dillard had been traveling since the murder. "Doesn't look like our guy." I didn't tell him that wasn't a surprise.

At Liberty Insurance, I stepped onto a parking lot the size of four football fields. "How you want to play it?" Finnegan pointed at the tall, glass building.

"Friendly, curious. But if we meet any resistance, you keep nice."

He said, "So you want to be bad cop?"

"Who said anything about 'want'?"

He laughed. That prompted a coughing fit. He hacked, hands on his knees.

"Goddamn, Finnegan. Keep your lungs inside your body."

"Ah, fuck off." He waved a hand at me. Then he straightened and checked me for a reaction.

I smiled. No one had dared tell me to fuck off since I got here. It felt good to be back in the club.

The head of Human Resources, Helen O'Donnell, sat in a corner office. She wore a navy suit that struggled to keep up with her. "Everyone was shocked to hear about Miss North," she said. *Everyone*? *Miss North*? Interesting choice of words.

"What was her job?" Finnegan asked.

"She welcomed new employees. Got them set up in the system."

"I see. How was she at it?"

She clucked her tongue. "It was too soon to tell. But she spent a lot of time with people." She implied this wasn't desirable. "She'd explain the finer points to new hires."

"Was that usual?" He hadn't missed her tone.

"Protocol is to greet the new hires, give them their materials, and once they've read it, if they have questions, they may schedule an appointment. It's more efficient." This lady really took the human out of resources.

"Were there any problems with other staff? Disagreements?"

She shook her head before he'd finished his question. "No."

"Had she made any friends while here?"

"She got on well with Jenna Dash." Jenna got first-name treatment, unlike our victim. Why?

"We'd like to talk to Jenna," he said.

"She's meeting with members of our risk-management team."

"When will she be done?"

"Oh, not for hours. The survey involves a lengthy questionnaire and then she has to conduct interviews."

"We don't have time to spare. We're investigating a murder. I'm sure you appreciate that," I said.

"Of course, but this survey has taken months to develop. Thousands of dollars—"

"Cecilia North was twenty-two years in development. Which is more important, would you say?"

She made a noise in the back of her throat. Then stood and pulled her jacket down. It resisted. She walked to the door and barked an order at an underling. We waited in silence until the underling appeared, followed by a woman. Jenna Dash. Her face was pale, her blond hair pulled tightly off her face. Her body resembled a butternut squash. I saw why Ms. O'Donnell favored Jenna. Cecilia had been thin.

"You wanted to see me?"

"Jenna, these policemen are investigating Miss North's death. They want to speak to you."

"Oh," she said, looking at us. "Oh."

"Is your office nearby?" I asked.

"It's just down the hall."

"You can talk here," Ms. O'Donnell said. "I'll fetch another chair."

"No, thank you. We'll join Miss Dash in her office."

Jenna led us down a hall, past employees who stopped talking as we walked by. She stopped before a door and fumbled her keys. "Sorry," she said. She unlocked the door. Small tchotchkes lined her shelves. In a tank near her phone, a fish swam laps.

"You worked here before Cecilia?" Finnegan asked. He sat. I followed suit.

"Yes." Her face had regained color. "I was hired last September. Cecilia started June first. I was assigned to show her the ropes. She was super nice."

"Did she like her job?" he asked.

"I think so. She is—was—really outgoing. She didn't have trouble meeting people. She always remembered names." She flushed. Guess she didn't have it so easy.

He hummed agreement. "And Ms. O'Donnell? She was Cecilia's boss?"

"Supervisor. We don't use the 'b' word here." Too bad. Ms. O'Donnell was perfect for the "b" word.

"How did Cecilia get on with her supervisor?"

Jenna rotated a candy jar filled with mini chocolate bars. "Ms. O'Donnell can be tough. She thought Cecilia spent too much time with new hires, but," she lowered her voice, "they came back fewer times with questions after they'd been processed by Cecilia. I did an informal study." She typed on the keyboard, her fingers fast. "See?" She swiveled her monitor so it faced us. We stared at a graph with four colored lines plotted in various arcs. "Cecilia is blue. Her line is way below every other person in HR for follow-up questions related to new hires."

I admired her handiwork. She blushed until her ears turned red. "I like graphing. That's why they have me conducting surveys. I did some ethnographic studies in school, and now they've decided I'm the Margaret Mead of insurance." She turned the monitor. "Cecilia's average would have been even lower if she didn't have Gary Clark."

Finnegan looked like a dog that's heard the word "walk." He took a chocolate from the candy bowl. "May I?"

"Of course." She proffered the bowl to me.

"No, thanks." I patted my flat stomach. "Watching my weight." Too late, I spotted a calorie counter taped below a picture of a thinner Jenna. Damn. I might not know much about women, but I know plenty about self-loathing. Jenna's face glowed red.

"Who's Gary Clark?" Finnegan asked.

She fumbled the candy bowl back onto her desk. "He works in the Life section. He started in mid-June. He's a boomerang."

"A boomerang?"

"Yeah. He turns up with a new question before you've answered the last one."

"So he took up a lot of Cecilia's time?"

"She used to say that Gary was the nine-to-four in her nine-to-five."

"Did she mention what it was specifically that he needed help with?" Finnegan had his notepad out. Its wire top was unspiraling.

"Little stuff like how to get reimbursed for expenses or how to set up voicemail."

Stuff he should've figured out himself. Finnegan looked my way. I nodded.

"You obviously liked Cecilia," I said. "Was there anyone here who didn't?"

"Not really, no." She looked down at her desk.

Finnegan said, "We won't repeat it." I wasn't the only one telling lies today.

She twisted a ring around her middle finger. "Patricia Jamison and Cecilia had the same job, but Patricia's been here two years. She wants to be seen as this nurturing sort. You know, 'My office is open anytime.' But she's not good at it."

"And Cecilia was?" I asked.

"Cecilia liked people. I think Patricia thought Cecilia usurped her role."

"Is Patricia in today?"

Jenna's brows descended. "Ever since we learned about Cecilia, she's been offering to help us if we're grieving. As if I'd go to her." Her eyes welled. "Sorry." She honked into a tissue. "Why would anyone shoot Cecilia?"

I gave her my card. "It's our job to figure that out. Where does Patricia sit?"

A small smile appeared. "I'll take you to her." With her smile, she was quite pretty. I almost said so, but I knew she wouldn't believe me. Not with that calorie counter taped above her candy bowl.

While we stood outside Patricia's office, Finnegan nudged me. "You don't think Cecilia was shot because she became the nicest one in the office do you?"

"No. But it'll be helpful to talk to someone who didn't like her."

"What about O'Donnell?"

So he'd noticed. "I'm hoping this one is chattier."

"Right then," he said as the door opened. Patricia Jameson wore a flower-print dress and granny glasses and had the reddest hair I'd ever seen. And I'm fourth-generation-from-the-boats Irish. She gave me a dead-fish handshake. Then she suggested we come inside. Her office contained nothing personal. Even I had an unwanted plant.

"You're here about Cecilia North." She sat. All her office items were aligned at right angles. "It's such a tragedy." *Tragedy* is a word out-siders use to describe terrible events.

"You were close?" Ah, Finnegan. He was winning me over today.

"She often came to me for advice." She rubbed her hands together. If she were playing poker, I'd call that movement a tell.

"I thought Jenna Dash was assigned to help Cecilia?"

Scorn pulled her lips back. "Jenna is in charge of surveys and studies. She hardly communicates with others outside of her data collection."

"How was Cecilia, once she got settled?" I asked.

She set her hands flat on the desk. Her veins were ropy and very blue. "She tried hard. But she wasn't always punctual, and time is money. She took two sick days when she only had one. And she spent too much time answering basic questions."

"Was she reprimanded?"

"Ms. O'Donnell spoke to her, but nothing was added to her record." How would she know? She saw me look at Finnegan and said, "Cecilia told me." She'd left the lie too late.

"Did she seem troubled lately? Worried?" I asked. She shrugged. "You've said you were close. I'd hoped you might know if something was bothering her."

"Things have been busy with the new crop of hires. We didn't have a lot of time to be chatting." I said nothing. She bit her lower lip and added, "Lately, she seemed distracted. I asked what was wrong, but she said she hadn't gotten enough sleep."

"Is there anyone you can think of who might have wanted to harm her?"

She adjusted her stapler. "No, but you might ask Gary Clark. He spent enough time in her office." There he was again. Gary Clark.

"Is there anything else you can think of about her last days?" Finnegan asked.

"She borrowed three dollars from me Friday to get a sandwich. She was going to pay me back, but—" She read our faces and said, "Of course, I don't care about the money. It's just so hard to believe she won't be here again." The crocodile tears came. I would've left her to sniffle, but Finnegan handed her a tissue. I gave her my card. Then I threw three singles on her desk. "I'm sure Cecilia would have wanted you to have them," I said. She looked as though I'd slapped her. Good.

Ms. O'Donnell gave us Cecilia's office key after she warned us not to review any files in there, which were confidential. She said she couldn't believe we'd find anything to help us. "She lacks imagination," Finnegan said, as we examined Cecilia's desktop.

"And a heart," I said.

There was an aloe plant on the file cabinet. Pictures of friends and family on her desk. A greeting card urged her to "Practice random acts of kindness and senseless beauty." Finnegan tossed her daily calendar into a bag. I looked through her folders.

"Are those the confidential, do-not-touch folders?" he asked.

"Are they?" I held one up. "Gary Clark." There was a picture. He was handsome in a preppy way. Blond hair, brown eyes, conservative shirt and tie. Mid to late thirties. Was this the man from the cabin? Maybe. It had been dark.

"Is that the face of a killer?" Finnegan asked. "God, I hope so. I swear, the more clean-cut killers you get, the better guys like me look."

"Let's see if we can find the real article." Maybe in person I'd know if it was him. And maybe he'd recognize me. I bit my cheek. Ouch. I still had a sore. "I need to go to the gents. Find him, will you? Ask some basic questions, get a feel for him."

"You okay?" he asked.

"It's nothing. Sometimes after I have coffee I—"

"Say no more," he said. "I'll meet you back here."

I used the toilet. Washed my hands. Imagined what Finnegan was doing. I should've gone with him. If Clark was the guy, I'd know. But then he'd see me. He'd ask questions. I crumpled my paper towel into a tight ball. "Fuck!" I tossed it at the garbage can. Missed. Instead of doing my job, I was hiding in the men's room. And how long could I hide? I slapped my hands against the sink. The exposed pipes juddered.

A man entered the bathroom. I pushed off from the sink and left to pace the hall.

Two minutes later, Finnegan returned and said Gary Clark was at an insurance seminar until Thursday. "But, get this, his colleague asked if he'd had another car accident." We walked to the elevators. "Why would police show up about a car accident?"

"Look into it. You learn anything else? Is he married? What's he drive?"

"Didn't ask, and a Honda Accord. Why?"

"Curious. Any pictures on his desk?"

"Didn't see." He was giving me side-eye, so I stopped with the questions.

We talked about small things on the return trip: graffiti tags near the middle school, and the burglaries that had occurred in the mayor's neighborhood. I'd heard a lot about those, mostly from the mayor. But my mind was back at the insurance company. I'd have to send Finnegan again, or ask Clark to come to the station. Where he would see me. No, Finnegan would have to go back. My cheek throbbed.


## 1530 HOURS

At the station there was a spike in the chatter. Wright found us. His face was calm, but his eyes weren't. "You need to see this," he said.

"See what?" We followed him. I noticed his shoes were worn at the heels. He walked heavy for a slim guy.

"Revere found it." He sounded annoyed.

Wedged onto a rolling cart was a bulky television attached to an ancient VCR. Revere held a remote control. When we'd gathered around, he hit play. A bodega appeared on screen, the frame focused on the cash-register counter. The store was empty. Someone walked into sight. She looked up, right at the camera. Cecilia North. "When was this taken?" I asked. She looked down, at the cashier. Only the back of his baseball cap was visible.

"August ninth," Revere said. She smiled and handed the cashier a soda can. He hit a register key. "At Cumberland Farms."

She looked at something in the rows below her waist. Grabbed a packet and gave it to the cashier. She spoke, and then laughed.

"Who's the cashier?" Finnegan asked.

"Donny Browning. Lives in Willington."

She smiled, waved, and left. Another person entered, an older white male. He headed for the back, out of frame in seconds.

"That's it?" I asked.

Revere hit the remote's stop button. "That's it."

"What's the time?"

"Nine forty-two p.m. She told Donny she was going to see a friend." The man in the cabin, no doubt.

"Who?"

"Didn't say."

She'd walked out of the store and gone to the cabin, where we met. Less than two hours later, she was dead. "No one's said boo about meeting her that night," Finnegan said.

"Did the cashier come forward with this?" I asked.

"No," Revere said. He tugged at his dress-shirt cuffs.

"How'd you find it?"

He said, "Good old-fashioned police work." I clenched my jaw. "I went door-to-door, covering all buildings within a two-mile radius." We should've done that. We had done that, or so I'd thought. But we'd missed this. What else had we missed?

"Good work. I want to see this Donny Browning."

"I can type up my notes in fifteen minutes," he said.

"I'd like to talk to him myself."

"He worked the rest of the night. The tape shows him there until five thirty a.m." Revere sounded like an exasperated parent, explaining a simple concept to a whining child.

But I wasn't his child. "Tapes can be faked."

"And destroyed, which he didn't do. Honestly, this kid's not bright enough to edit a videotape." He looked annoyed. The others enjoyed this. Finnegan and Wright might think I was too hands-on, but they didn't like Revere. And they sure as fuck didn't like being upstaged by him.

"Pick him up," I said to Wright. "Bring him in."

"Yes, sir." He saluted me. His smile got wider as he walked past Revere.

Forty minutes later, I met the cashier. Donny Browning had close-set eyes, a weak chin, and a baseball cap he had to be told to remove. His nicotine-yellowed fingertips would've outed him as a smoker if his stink hadn't first.

"So, Donny. You saw Cecilia the night she died."

His eyes jackrabbited about the room. "I want my lawyer."

"You have an attorney you'd like to contact?" What gas-station employee had a lawyer on call?

"Yeah. Douglas Browning. My father."

I let him place the call. Twenty minutes later, his father came to the station loaded for bear. I must've looked furry, because he went straight for me. "Why are you interrogating Donny?" He wore his money: leather briefcase and a fancy, silk-blend suit.

We talked in my office. I wanted home-court advantage. "Donny saw Cecilia North the night she was murdered. We want to ask some questions about his interaction with her."

"He's already answered questions."

"We have a few more. Donny might remember something that helps us catch her killer." That deflated him. He couldn't fault our cause.

"I'll join you." He brushed my office lint from his suit. "I've seen the news. Abner Louima. Seems you New York cops like to play rough with suspects."

Abner Louima. The papers and TV were full of him. The Haitian resident of Brooklyn who'd been arrested, then sodomized with a broom handle by two New York police officers while in custody. No doubt people would be taking to the streets in protest soon.

"We're not in New York," I said.

Mr. Browning harrumphed and followed me out of my office.

When his father entered the interview room, Donny looked scared. Mr. Browning sat at the same side of the battered table as his son. But he was careful not to touch him.

Mr. Browning said, "Did they ask you anything after you called me?"

"No," Donny said. He squirmed in his chair.

"May we continue?" I asked. No one objected. "Donny, what time did Cecilia come into the store?"

"Ten o'clock or so." He was off by almost twenty minutes, but that wasn't a crime.

"Had you met her before?" He shrugged, his hands limp in his lap.

"Answer," his father said.

"We went to middle school together. And I saw her at the store sometimes. Mostly to fill her car with gas."

"How did she seem that night?"

Mr. Browning put his hand in front of his son, as if protecting him from sudden braking. "You want my son to speculate as to Miss North's mental state?"

Stop grandstanding, Perry Mason. There's no judge here.

"It would be helpful to know if she was agitated," Revere said. I hadn't wanted him here, but he'd caught the tape. So he got to sit at the big boys' table. He lounged in his seat, not a care in the world. Not his usual attitude. An act for the Brownings.

"She seemed fine. She bought Pop Rocks and a Coke. They used to say that if you ate them at the same time, you'd explode. She said she was going to take a big risk."

"You're sure she was joking about the candy?" Revere asked.

"Sure. What else would she be talking about?" He pushed his lower lip out. The resemblance to a chimp was uncanny.

"Did she say anything about this friend she was meeting?" I asked. "A name? Maybe she said 'he' or 'she'?"

"I don't think so. I asked if she was headed out for the night or if she was going home, and she said she was meeting a friend. I told her to have a good night."

I leaned forward. "Donny, why didn't you mention this? We've been asking everyone to come forward with any information they have."

His eyes started up like a pinball again. "I don't pay much attention to the news. I didn't know she was dead until this morning."

"But you didn't call us when you realized."

Mr. Browning said, "Donny sold her a soda. I don't think he thought that was going to help you find a killer." He glanced at the walls, then down at his wrist. Checking the time. I'd had the men remove the large school clock from the wall my first week here. I liked to keep the men deposited in here guessing about the time, about how much they had left as free men.

"Your son is the last person we know who saw Cecilia North alive. You think that's irrelevant?"

"I think you should be looking for this woman's friend, the one she was meeting."

"The one we wouldn't have known about if we hadn't talked to Donny." Not exactly true. But he didn't know that. None of them did.

"I think he's told you everything he knows." Mr. Browning looked at his briefcase. His small supply of patience was nearly spent.

"Do you know any kids who hang out on the golf course?" I asked. Donny looked at his father, then away. "Do you?"

"No," he said, fast. Too fast?

I left some breathing room for him to elaborate. He didn't, so I asked, "Do you know anyone who owns a gun?"

His eyes got skittish and he tapped the table. "Do you?" I repeated.

"Dad," Donny said. His voice crept toward a whine.

Revere said, "Do you know who killed Cecilia North?"

That took everyone aback. Donny recovered first. "No." He bit a fingernail.

"We're through here," Mr. Browning said. "My son answered your questions. I'm going to take him to his place now." His place. So they didn't live together.

Donny took his cap from the table and followed his father from the room, eyes glued to the carpet. "Interesting," Revere said.

"Wasn't it?"

We exited the room to find Mrs. Dunsmore waiting, arms crossed. You could lose a dime in her frown lines. "I just saw Douglas Browning," she said. It sounded like an accusation.

"His son, Donny, saw Cecilia North the night she died," I said.

"Watch out for Mr. Browning. He's a big-time lawyer. Sued the town years ago. Claimed building permits were being blocked unfairly. Got a quarter of a million dollars. Bankrupted the town and moved his family away."

"So he's not popular?"

"Not here. But it's best to stay on his good side. Assuming he's got one."

"Hmm. Any word on when the carpenter is coming?"

"Carpenter? What carpenter?" she asked.

"The one who's supposed to swap the nameplate on my door." When I'd arrived in mid-January, I was informed that changing the nameplate required the town carpenter. Forms to be filed, work orders to be placed. Mrs. Dunsmore filled out the forms and orders. I wondered if she'd even obtained the forms.

"He's working at Town Hall this week." She didn't miss a beat.

Unlike the rest of us. God, if Revere hadn't pounded the pavement, we'd still be wondering where Cecilia went between the time she left her parents' house and wound up dead. And they still didn't know about the cabin. I bit my cheek. Ouch.

In my office, tilted back in my chair, I contemplated options. How to get them to the cabin. Call in a tip? Or cut out the middleman?

Leave a pink slip on Wright's desk, saying Cecilia had been seen at the cabin. He wouldn't check who took the tip call until he'd swept the cabin. My gut rumbled. Manufacturing evidence. Did I want to start down that path?

"Needs must," my gran used to say when I'd complain about chores.

I used the phrase on rookies, years later, when they'd moan about having to interview a drunk whose pants stank of his own filth. "Needs must," I'd say, and the men would laugh and say, "Ah, lay a little more of that Irish wisdom on us."

I missed that camaraderie, the quick laughter at jokes heard a hundred times. Idyll wasn't friendly despite the locals' insistence to the contrary. Newcomers were subject to suspicion. And I had secrets to guard. I didn't trust my men here to keep them. Not yet. Maybe not ever.

I could put the pink slip on a desk before any of them arrived tomorrow.

Needs must.

# WEDNESDAY, AUGUST 13TH
## 0630 HOURS

I breathed hard and sharp through my nose as I crunched up, turned to the right, punched fast. Back down to the floor, inhaling through my mouth. Crunch up and to the left. Two more punches in sync to a sharp exhale. Sometimes, when my brain got stuck in a revolving door, I'd work it loose with exercise. My gut was feeling it. My brain remained mired, like those animals that got trapped in tar pits and turned to fossils. I crunched down and up. I wasn't a fossil yet. I sat up and shook my head. A drop of sweat spun off my hair to the carpet. Time for push-ups.

Rick had challenged me to a push-up contest two weeks into our partnership. I laughed, sure he wasn't serious. "What you afraid of, Sasquatch? Losing?" he'd asked. I'd checked the room to see if there was some joke I didn't get. Nearby, Detective Lee shrugged. So, after more taunts from Rick, I'd agreed to set my hands on the less-than-clean linoleum and complete a set of push-ups until one of us gave out. The son of a bitch had surprised me. His arms were wiry and he fought for it, but eventually he'd collapsed, cheek to the floor, and had said, "Christ, were you a Marine?" And I'd kept doing reps, just to show what a good sport I was. When I'd stopped, he'd given me his hand and helped pull me up. "Guess that makes you the muscle," he'd said, his smile revealing a chipped tooth. "That makes me the brains." And he'd insisted on buying me a soda, which was the traditional prize awarded in the station. The prize for closing a stone-cold case or for winning the March Madness pool. Always a goddam can of soda from the wheezy, tilted vending machine.

I stopped, my elbows bent, stomach quaking. A soda can. I'd seen soda cans inside the cabin the night I'd tried to hook up with Leo Wilton, where I'd met Cecilia North. She'd bought a soda that night. One of the cans could be hers. Could have prints. Could put her at the scene. I pushed myself up and toward the shower. If I hurried, I could make it into the station before the others. And fake a note pointing them to the cabin.

A half hour later, I sat behind my desk. My office plant stood at attention as I tried my hand at forgery, again. This was my eighth attempt at replicating the floral script of our tips line coordinator, Joanne. I botched the victim's name, making the C's spike too hard. No good. Checked my watch. Fuck. Wright would be at his desk in twenty minutes. A knock at my door. Damn it. I fanned my folders over my handiwork and said, "Come in." Billy entered, looking all of sixteen years old.

"Hi, Chief. I heard about the videotape."

I expected half the town knew by now.

"And?" I pinched the skin between my thumb and finger, trying to stave off the headache I felt at the base of my skull, its tendrils squeezing my nerves.

"Is there anything I can do?" he asked. "To help?"

No, unless . . . "You know where Cumberland Farms is. Where might Cecilia go from there? If she was meeting someone and wanted to keep it private?"

His face crinkled in thought. God, if I'd looked like him twenty years ago, I'd have brought the West Village to its knees.

He said, "There's the railroad museum. And the woods by the golf course."

"Anywhere else?" *Come on*, I thought. He had to know.

"The cabin by Hought's Pond."

"Hought's Pond?" Did my voice sound anxious?

"Yeah. It's between Cumberland's and the golf course, but the woods are closer."

"I thought they were going to tear the cabin down?"

Billy relaxed against the door. "They've been saying that for years.

It belongs to the Sutters. Well, the son now that his parents passed. But he lives in California. The town's been all over him to fix the cabin or demolish it, but he says he has fond memories of it. Doesn't want to spend the money, more like. And he's got the town over a barrel because they want him to leave the farm as is."

"Really? Why?" Its lonely pastures and sinking barn gave me the creeps.

"They think it looks old-timey. And they don't want shiny, new condos on the land. It would ruin the whole Idyll Days image."

"I see. Why don't you check the railroad museum? We know she bought a Coke and some Pop Rocks. See if you find any trace of 'em near the museum. You know how to bag evidence?" He got red, remembering his crime-scene massacre. He nodded. "I'll take a look at the cabin."

"Should I radio you if I find something?" he asked.

"No. Just bring it in." It was a fool's errand. He'd find nothing of value, but he felt included, valuable. We both got something we wanted.

☀

The cabin looked worse in daylight. It leaned toward the pond, as if drunk. Ivy crept through its sunken steps and twined around a front window that looked like a jagged tooth, only its bottom third of glass intact. I used my foot to open the door. A leaf skittered across the floor. Bottles, wrappers, condoms, and matchbooks littered the place. A charred section of wall showed where someone had played firebug. I looked for evidence of my last visit. There were faint smudges in the dust that could be partial footprints. I could sweep, erase any traces of myself, tamper with the crime scene, as Rick had done once. My mind seesawed.

"Where's the baggie?" I'd asked Rick. We'd gone through the crack house where Marshall Clements had died. Now it was time to submit our evidence. I couldn't find the baggie with white powder. Rick had grabbed it, though it was on my side of the scene.

"What?" He stretched like a cat in a puddle of sunlight.

"The baggie. You had it last."

His eyes were blank, like a shark's. "Tommy, boy, I don't know what you're talking about." He picked up his bags. Whistling as he walked away. The sunlight glinted off his copper hair. A golden boy.

I hadn't thought he'd tamper with evidence. His grandfather was awarded a Medal of Valor. He was a third-generation cop. It was his birthright. And now he was corrupting, from the inside out. And still my partner.

I massaged my eyes. Brought myself back from the past. Set my case down. I'd have to move around the cabin, but I wouldn't brush the floor. I couldn't. Rick had fallen prey to addiction, had briefly loved other things more than being a cop. I didn't.

There were two Coke cans. One under a window, the second by the door. I bagged both. I looked between squeaky, rotted floorboards and in filthy corners for the Pop Rocks or anything else that might indicate she'd been here. She hadn't carved her initials inside a heart on the wall. Unlike "JL + BG." But under those initials I found a button. Small. White. She'd been wearing a T-shirt, so it wasn't hers. But her date had worn a dress shirt. Could he have lost a button?

I walked outside and breathed deeply. The air was wet. It felt like you could wring it out. Nearby, something splashed in the pond. I checked its edges again but found nothing but a fishing bobber riding shallow ripples. The sickly smell of the water, the cabin, knowing what I'd almost done there—I couldn't get away fast enough.

Back at the station, Billy presented me with five bags. One contained a Coke can so sun-bleached it had to be at least two years old.

I said, "I found some too. They look a bit fresher."

He rubbed his forehead. "I didn't think it looked likely, but I figured that's not for me to decide." He hesitated. I waited him out. "Her family's been asking me questions. About the case. I don't know what to tell them." His face got hangdog.

I put my hand on his shoulder. "Look, I know it's not easy. Most police go their whole careers without having to work an investigation so close to them. I'm happy to pull you off." I stepped back. Gave him time to consider it.

He didn't think long. "No. It's okay. I'll explain to the Norths that I can't talk to them." He looked at his shoes and said, "The funeral is set for the eighteenth. They're waiting because Cecilia's grandmother is still recovering from surgery."

The eighteenth. Five days from now.

"You, uh, got something." He pointed to my shirt. I started to explain that it was a bloodstain from the autopsy, but then I recalled I'd dropped the jacket at Suds.

"What?" I looked at my shirt.

"You've got, um, hairs. Long ones." He pointed. Hairs clung to my shirt. Too light and long to be mine. "Maybe you got them at the cabin." The thought didn't cheer me. Nor did I buy it. I'd been careful at the cabin. Touching as little as possible.

"Or maybe it's your girlfriend's?" He smiled. Eager to hear all about her. He assumed I was straight. Small-town boy. Probably thought everyone he met was.

"Nope," I said. I pulled the hairs from my shirt and dropped them above my waste bin. They floated slowly, as if reluctant to mingle with the trash. Long, blond hair. Maybe they came from Donna, courtesy of her dye bottle. She got awful close, when opportunity allowed.

Billy left. I shoved aside a folder of parking citations to make way for a report form and found the autopsy folder. My finger stabbed the intercom button. Mrs. Dunsmore was in for it. Hiding vital reports under busywork? Shit. It wasn't her fault. My finger released the button. This morning, I'd pushed the folders around when Billy had come in. Trying to hide my false tip. I'd buried the report. I kicked my desk. Welcomed the pain in my toes.

I opened the report. Cecilia Elizabeth North. Age: twenty-two. Height: five feet, six inches. Weight: one hundred and eighteen pounds. Cause of death: exsanguination. She'd bled out. How long had she been conscious? A minute? More? Had she known her life was seeping away as she lay on the damp grass, panting her last breaths?

No sign of sexual assault or activity. Disappointing. Sex yielded DNA. We had nothing more. I flipped the sheet. Dr. Saunders had attached a note to the last page. *"Looks like your bullet came from a Smith & Wesson .45."*

In the detectives' pen, Wright and Revere sat, backs to each other, each sifting papers. "Good news," I said. They looked up. Revere's shoulder cracked. He winced. "The bullet taken from our vic came from a Smith & Wesson .45 handgun." Revere stood and wrote this on the board. "And earlier, I spoke to Billy about rendezvous spots and he suggested the train museum—"

"We told you," Wright said. He did his finger-pistol thing, and then blew imaginary smoke from his finger's end.

"And the cabin by Hought's Pond."

"Oh, right. That dump."

"I checked out 'that dump' and found two Coke cans. Maybe she was there Saturday night."

"Where's the cabin?" Revere asked. Wright showed him on the map. "You think she walked?"

"Might've got a ride," I said. "He could've had a car, her friend."

"We're assuming the friend is male," Revere said. "What if she's female?"

"She snuck out. Smart money has it her friend was male," Wright said.

"What if she was romantically involved with a woman?" Revere asked.

"What? A lesbo?" Wright shook his head. "You seen our girl? Too pretty. Besides, she had a boyfriend, remember?"

Revere said, "Maybe college broadened her horizons."

Wright laughed. "Right. Well, if you find the girlfriend, bring me to the interview. I want to hear *all* about it." Of course he did. Straight men find the idea of two women erotic. But present him with two men? He'd be revolted. To be fair, I'd always found the idea of a man and woman together puzzling. I get it, intellectually. Survival of the species and all that. But otherwise? Nah.

# THURSDAY, AUGUST 14TH
## 0835 HOURS

I was due to stand before a swarm of press, concerned citizens, and selectmen in a couple of hours. So my two-day shadow had to go. I scraped a razor along my cheek. Stubble collected along the blade like metal filings to a magnet. Day five and nothing to show but the videotape, autopsy report, and ballistics findings. No suspects and no witnesses. The phone rang. My hand was specked with shaving foam. It rang again. I cursed and wiped my hand on a towel. The answering machine picked up.

The machine announced it had a message. It insisted on telling me the date and time. Then a beep, click, and my mother's voice. "Hi, Tom. I called Benson's. They'll send a wreath to St. Anthony's for Rick's service. Give us a call. Or stop by for dinner soon. Dad sends his love. Bye." I'd called and asked my mother where to order flowers for Rick's memorial. She'd taken this as a charge to do it herself. I'd call later to explain I couldn't make it home. I wouldn't mention what had happened the last time I showed up for a last-minute dinner invitation.

The table setting should've tipped me off. My family didn't use the china except for holidays and dinners with deans. My brother, John, and his wife, Marie, exchanged furtive looks over their glasses. Were they having another child? Bit late, for both of them. And should Marie be drinking wine? The doorbell rang.

"I'll get it!" my mother said. A minute later, she brought in a man wearing a velvet jacket with a paisley pocket square. Slender and smiling. Chris Danforth. My mother knew him through her charity work with the New York Foundation for the Arts.

"Chris was in a revival of *The King and I* on Broadway." My mother squeezed my forearm. My muscles contracted under the pressure.

He was seated across from me at dinner, half visible through the spring bouquet set there for his benefit. We weren't flower people. He asked about my work while he sawed at his chop. I was polite but brief. Homicides don't make nice dinner conversation. Not the sort I'd seen recently: a wife bludgeoned with a hot iron, a man hog-tied and carved up.

"Your mother tells me you like boats," he said to me.

"Did she?" I had, as a child. John smiled brightly at me. I kicked his leg under the table.

"Ow!" he shouted.

Marie sussed the situation and asked Chris if he was preparing for future roles. He ducked his head, as if embarrassed by the attention. Bullshit. No actor I'd met hated attention. "I'm auditioning next week for the chorus of *Rent*."

"How exciting!" my mother said. This from the woman who fell asleep when she attended a Broadway show. She claimed all that singing and dancing tired her out.

"You know it's a musical?" John asked Mom. I didn't respond to his wink. He was on my shit list. He'd known what they'd planned and hadn't warned me. Some brother.

Chris asked about my parents' work. Mom talked about her Brontë research. "I've always preferred Anne to her sisters. More common sense and a better writer."

Chris said he'd loved *Wuthering Heights* in high school. She wrinkled her nose.

"Emily wrote that," I said.

Dad talked about his study of philosophy, and his latest subject, Albertus Magnus.

"And what do you study?" Chris asked my brother.

John stopped petting his wife's hand and launched into a lecture about how climate change is real and we're going to be the means of the planet's destruction. Cheerful stuff.

"What a remarkable family." Chris showed off his veneers. "You weren't tempted by academia?" he asked me.

"No." All that reading? Just a one-way ticket to Sleepy Town.

"Tom always wanted to be a cop," John said. "And unlike most boys, he didn't outgrow it."

"I always wanted to perform," Chris said to me, as if we shared a secret. Then he grabbed a flower from the bouquet, tucked it in his napkin and waved it above the table. He opened the napkin and nothing fell. Everyone applauded except me. I knew where the flower was.

At my mother's insistence, I escorted our guest to the door after dinner. Chris adjusted his pocket square. I wondered if it meant something. There'd been a whole gay subculture of kerchiefs. Colors and styles indicated preferences and persuasions. I'd never learned them. He patted my arm. "If you ever need help—"

"Help?"

"Navigating your way out of the closet—"

Had he prepped that exit line, just in case I didn't respond to his smiles?

I pointed behind me. "They know I'm gay."

"But not at work, right?"

What did he know about being gay on the force? Did he know about Jackson's memo to our lieutenant? The one that complained of his partner's "multiple unwarranted and unnatural physical advances?" The one pinned to our memo board. The one we'd laughed at for weeks. Typical cop humor. Did he know how the only "out" detective in our precinct had transferred after only two months? Did he think being gay at work made you a hero? It made you a target. Unless you worked in a field like acting.

I opened the door and waited. He left. I slammed the door. Nothing angered me more than other homos telling me how to be gay. This asshole was upset because I didn't represent "gay" with a big grin while standing on a rainbow-colored parade float? Fuck him.

"Is Chris gone?" My mother entered the foyer prepared to back out, hopeful of interrupting something.

"Don't ever do that again," I said.

She got close. Combat position. "I thought you two might hit it off." The lines about her mouth deepened. "I see I was wrong." She gave me a disappointed look. I knew that look well.

In the living room, John and Marie laughed, their hilarity escalating into hiccups. "Oh, you didn't!" Marie said.

My mother got on her tiptoes and smoothed my hair. "I just want to see you happy." Angry as I was, I knew she'd meant well. They all did.

Now, back at my house, I pushed a button and erased my mother's message. I'd call later to decline the dinner invite. Who knew where her good intentions would lead this time? Better not to find out.

Something crashed on a hard surface. Tiles. The bathroom. I hurried to find my toothbrush cup smashed into shards. The toothbrush's bristles rested on the dirty tiles. I'd need to buy another. I picked up glass pieces.

The glass. What was it? I looked at the uneven shards, opaque in my shadow. There'd been glass in the gutter, when Rick died. Some homeboy's broken forty a foot away from Rick's body. My eyes had stared at those shards after the EMTs shooed me away and bent over him, working his chest like a bellows.

My hands clenched. I felt a sharp pain. "Shit!" A piece of glass was stuck in my index finger. I pulled it from my finger pad and dropped the glass in the trash. Ran water over the wound. Pink water swirled down the drain. I looked for a bandage and found one behind an expired bottle of aspirin. My hands botched the job: the bandage puckered. But I hadn't time to do it over. I was running late and still had to finish my shave.

When I reached Town Hall, cars filled every parking spot. I cruised past, once more. Nope. Not one free, except for a handicapped spot in front of the arched brick doorway. I thought for a second. No, I couldn't. I bumped my car over the curb and parked on the grass between the lot and Main Street.

The press conference was in the Porter Room, named after the town's founder, Isaiah Porter. His portrait hung outside the room. A cheerless man in a weathered hat, holding a Bible. The room's heavy wooden door opened to reveal seven rows of occupied folding chairs. News crews were present. At the podium, Mayor Mike repeated the tip-line number. He spotted me and waved his arms as if landing a plane. "And here, ladies and gentlemen, *as promised*, is Chief of Police Thomas Lynch."

When I reached the podium he said, "Where have you been?" The mic picked up his question. There were titters from the audience.

"I'll take your questions now," I said.

A black woman wearing a pretty scarf said, "Shirley Winston, *New Haven Register*. Chief Lynch, do you have any suspects?"

*Yes, but I'm not sure who he is.* "We're pursuing several leads." She pursed her lips and gave me a look that said she'd heard that line before.

John Dixon, from the *Idyll Register*, asked if the murder could be the work of a serial rapist/killer. He was underfed and wore a suit two sizes too big.

"No. It's an isolated incident. There were no signs of sexual assault."

He scratched his nose with the pink eraser of his pencil. "Perhaps this is the killer's first victim? A trial? Maybe he'll advance as he goes?" He sounded hopeful.

My breath emerged as a huff into the microphone. "I'm not sure what sort of TV shows you've been watching, but this isn't a serial killing. And it's not entertainment."

John Dixon sat down and shut up.

I fielded questions about motive (I wouldn't speculate) and one about a town curfew (unnecessary). There wasn't much else to say. The reporters would have to pad their pieces with thoughts on what a shock murder was in this sleepy community. The mayor took me aside when the news crews shut off their lights and wound their cables. "I assume you've an excellent excuse for being late." The stains under his armpits were two shades darker than his shirt.

"New information came in. I'm sorry. It took precedence." The lie came easy.

"We couldn't reach you at the station."

"I was talking to the techs, from home."

The mayor walked with me out of the building. "Next time, call ahead to say you'll be late." He squinted and said, "Is that your car?" He didn't need to ask. Its side read "Police Chief."

*You mean the one you threatened to take away?* "There weren't any spaces."

"Not even the handicapped one?"

"I didn't think it would be right to park there."

"You need to treat your vehicle like you would a lady, Chief." He withdrew a pair of aviator sunglasses and put them on. "With respect."

## 1130 HOURS

I poured flat soda on my plant and looked down at the parking lot. My car glinted in its reserved spot, safe for now. The mayor had bought my lie, but he'd been unhappy. Maybe he and the selectman had hedged their bets, not changing the nameplate on my door.

The phone rang. "Chief Lynch," I said.

"Hello Chief, this is Mr. McKinley, owner of the Nipmuc Golf Course. I'm just following up about last night."

"Last night." What was he talking about?

"The trouble?" He waited for a response. I said nothing. "Charlie saw some teens by the ninth hole last night."

"Oh." First I'd heard of it. "I could send an officer to keep an eye out after Charlie's left." I didn't need ghoul-hunting teens on the crime scene.

He said, "The murder . . . well, I don't want people to associate the course with it."

Good luck with that. "I'll assign someone for a week." It would be a dozer. Maybe I'd send Yankowitz, or Hopkins. He was still acting pissy for my scolding him at the clubhouse. "Did Charlie give a description of the kids?"

"Yes, when he called the station last night." So that's why he thought I knew. Because Charlie had called it in. The desk sergeant and I were due for a chat.

"I'll send someone tonight, after Charlie finishes his rounds. How's that?"

"Fine. Thanks, Chief."

I hung up the phone. A tentative knock lifted my gaze. I had a visitor. "Come in." Yankowitz opened my door, his face the definition of confused.

"Help you?" I asked, my tone less than pleased. He usually stayed away from my office. Had never been inside as far as I knew.

"There's a man here. He says he knows you."

"And?" His posture implied there was more to this story. He looked over his shoulder. Then back at me.

"I pulled him over on Sparrow Street. He was doing 45 miles per hour. It's a school district. No school now, but there are day programs for kids."

*Stop the presses*, I opened my mouth to say.

"His name's Leo Wilton." My open mouth snapped shut. The man I'd picked up. The man at the cabin.

"He insisted on seeing you. Says you'll straighten it all out."

"He's here?" I tried to look around Yankowitz.

"Yeah."

"Send him in."

"Okay."

Twenty seconds later, Leo Wilton stood in my office. "Close the door," I told Yankowitz. He did, his face no less confused as he left.

"Hello, Chief." Leo looked older under the fluorescent lights. His grey hair looked slightly green. "Had a feeling we'd meet again. Had no idea it would be so soon."

"You seem to have a lead foot," I said.

"Your officer there is very by-the-book." He sat and crossed his leg. "Tried to give me a fifty-dollar ticket."

"He takes speeding seriously."

Leo pulled a paper from his pocket and held it out. The ticket.

"And you came here because?" I asked.

He sniffed. "Come on. Don't play dumb. Make this," he wiggled the paper, "go away."

I waited, saying nothing.

"Get rid of this and I won't have to tell your ticket buddy how well we know each other."

Blackmail. He wouldn't tell on me if I waived his ticket. I almost called his bluff. He wore a wedding ring. I'd bet he had adult children. Jesus. I couldn't believe I'd almost fucked this guy.

I beckoned him near. He leaned forward. I grabbed the ticket from his hand. Tore it in half, and half again. "Happy?" I asked.

"As a clam." He looked me up and down. "If you ever want a rain check . . ."

I'd rather sleep with Mrs. Dunsmore.

"Bye," I said. "Send my eager beaver in, will you?"

He winked on his way out. I fantasized about blacking that eye.

Yankowitz came. I told him to close the door and have a seat. He did both at the pace of an injured snail.

"Tear up that ticket." I nodded at his booklet, held tightly in his hands.

His mouth formed a perfect ring. "But why?" He looked down at his booklet like it was his infant child.

"It's a freebie," I said.

"Freebie?"

He couldn't be this naïve. There are all sorts of currency in policing. Internal, like choice car assignments, overtime, sick days when the station knows you're healthy, lies told by your partner to your wife about your whereabouts. External freebies like not seeing a taillight out or getting information and knocking down a felony to a misdemeanor. Police stations are like prisons. Every interaction is worth something. Even a meter maid like Yankowitz ought to know this.

"He did me a favor, so I'm doing him one," I said.

"But . . ." he said. He let his thought die, unspoken.

"I'm sorry," I said. "I won't ask for this kind of thing often."

His face was no longer confused. It was disappointed. I nearly threw my stapler at him. How dare he look at me like that? Over a goddamn speeding ticket?

"Is there anything else?" I asked.

"No, sir." His words soft, sad.

"Okay then. Thank you, Yankowitz."

He left my office without further comment.

I hoped to God Leo Wilton started taking another route, one that skipped Idyll. Or he learned to let up on the gas pedal. I couldn't keep intervening. I didn't want to. Once this case was put to bed, I wouldn't.

I gathered all my ducklings by the crime board. Billy stood, having no chair. "Your finger's bleeding," he said, pointing. Sure enough. Blood dripped down my finger. "First Aid kit is by the coffee. I'll get it." He loped away.

"Watch Hoops go," Wright said. "Go, Hoops, go."

"Your kids learning to read?" Revere asked Wright. Wright had two young kids, one boy, one girl. Their skin was two shades lighter than his, courtesy of his white wife. Milky coffee, that's what they'd called it back at my old station. Biracial light.

"How'd you know?" Wright asked Revere, his tone pure suspicion.

"You sound like a *Dick and Jane* book," Revere said. He pointed at Wright's family photo. "They don't have different books for your kids?"

"My kids?" Wright's voice got lower. "You think they should have some Ebonics version? Learn to read *Hustle, Shawanda, Hustle* instead?"

Revere said, "I just meant *Dick and Jane* is what the Chief read as a kid. I thought maybe your kids had more modern books."

"Don't knock *Dick and Jane*," I said. I watched Wright. He looked ready to blow. I didn't think Revere was racist, but I wasn't sure Wright would believe that.

Billy returned, kit in hand. "Cut yourself?" he asked. The interruption distracted everyone.

"Thanks. Why don't we start?" I unwrapped the bloody bandage. "Has anyone heard from the golf-course security guard recently?"

Billy said, "He called last night. Saw teenagers near the ninth hole."

I gave him the bad-dog look. "When were you planning on sharing this information?"

My cut was inflamed, the skin swollen. Great.

Billy flushed redder than a baboon's ass. "Today. Later today."

"In the future, when news related to the murder scene, or hey, let's make it the murder, comes up, find me. Now, what have we got?" I daubed antiseptic on my finger and bandaged it again.

"That hardly seems relevant," Revere said. "Thrill-seeking kids." He stared at me. Boy, he'd picked the wrong man on the wrong day.

I said, "Kids at the crime scene? They might hang out there often. They might have seen our victim the night she died. Who knows? Maybe one of them owns a gun. Let's gather information before we exclude it."

Revere said, "So we should inform you of all developments, what, every ten minutes?" He leaned against his desk. His posture was casual, but his face was stony. Wright smiled at Revere.

"I'll swing by the course tonight after Charlie's gone," I said. Claiming it marked it as important. And it avoided Revere's question. I didn't want the men to think I loomed. But I didn't want them excluding me, either.

"It's gonna be a snooze," Finnegan said. "Or were you planning to practice your game?" He swung an imaginary gold club. Good old Finnegan. Quick to keep the peace.

"The ex-boyfriend is out," Wright said, plowing ahead. "We've got confirmation from a hotel clerk and three folks at the investment firm he visited. He was in London."

"No chance he had it done?" Finnegan said.

Billy said, "He's a nice guy. I don't think—"

I interrupted. "Anybody know nice guys who had people killed?"

All the men raised their hands. Wright said, "I knew a nice guy who had his wife killed while he was at church with their kids."

"I knew a nice guy who had his boss whacked over a measly two hundred bucks," Finnegan said.

"Better to say that he doesn't fit the profile," Revere told Billy. "'Nice' doesn't cut it."

"Listen to the good detective. 'He doesn't fit the profile.' That's good stuff there. The kind that gets you into the State Police," I said.

"Well that and some gooooood ass-kissing," Wright said. If it was time to kick Revere, Wright was first in line.

"My ass-kissing can't compare to the Chief's," Revere said. "I mean, what does it take to get appointed Police Chief? It probably surpasses kissing ass."

I could punch him, or let it go. I counted silently to twenty. "Kissing doesn't begin to cover what I did for this job." Finnegan laughed. "Now that we've covered the sexual perversions of promotion, does anyone have any other news?"

Revere said, "I've gone through the past twenty years of handgun murders. Four looked similar, but all but one was resolved and the killers are still inside."

"Holy Mary, Mother of God," Finnegan said, sketching a sign of the cross.

"And the other?" I asked.

He tapped a folder. "John Murray, age twenty-seven, shot three times in the torso four years ago in Meriden, outside a used-car lot. He made a little book, but nothing major. No solid leads. The case is still open. So far, no connections to our girl."

Finnegan tapped Gary Clark's picture that he'd pinned to the board. "I spoke with Mr. Clark this morning. He works at Liberty Insurance, where he spent a lot of time with our victim. But to hear him tell it, he saw her twice a week, for ten minutes tops. And he kept switching his tune. One minute it was 'I don't need help; I've been in insurance for years' and the next it was, 'Who can understand HR policies? They're so confusing.'"

Wright leaned back in his chair and said, "So he was defensive. Man gets nervous when the office girl he's chatted up is murdered." So far, Wright was the resident skeptic. Questioning every theory but his own: that wife beater Anthony Fergus had plugged our girl.

I'd checked on Gary Clark. He had no priors. A couple moving violations. Nothing spectacular. Nothing dodgy. Just a married insurance jockey.

Finnegan said, "He's a liar. When I first visited Liberty, his colleague asked if he'd had another car accident. I mentioned it to Clark and he brushed it off. Says it was just a fender bender; the other driver was insured. No biggie."

"And?" Revere said.

"There was no accident. He never filed a report. I talked to the Waterbury cops. They've no record of an accident that day until six p.m. Clark said it happened before work, which is why he didn't show."

"So he lies about a car accident. Why?" Revere asked.

"To get out of work. Guess who called in sick that day?" Finnegan opened a bag of chips. The crinkle activated my salivary glands. I'd missed breakfast and hadn't eaten lunch yet.

"Our girl?" Wright said.

He pointed at Wright. "Give the man a Kewpie doll."

"What's a Kewpie doll?" Billy asked. Revere groaned but didn't answer.

I said, "Could be coincidence, but why don't you check? See if her parents remember her being home sick. Ask if she stayed in *all* day." I stuck my hand into Finnegan's bag of chips.

"Ta," I said. He harrumphed. The chips' saltiness just made me hungrier.

"There's also her mobile-phone records," Revere said, so soft we all leaned in.

"Come again?" Wright said. He'd reviewed the phone records.

"She called one number several times. Here." Revere pointed to a repeating number he'd highlighted in pink.

Finnegan took the paper. "Isn't that the Liberty Insurance number? She called work?" He pulled a mangled calendar forward and paged through its sheets. "Twice on a Saturday? And three times when she was at work? Why not use her office phone?"

"You think she called Gary Clark," I said to Revere.

"Maybe. The main line gets you the company directory. She dials using her mobile phone and her number shows as an outside call. If she uses her office phone, her name appears on the phone display. If she was seeing him, she might prefer to call on her mobile."

Wright scowled. This was the second time Revere had shown him up. I also had egg on my face. I'd let Clark off my radar. Shit.

"And now for the bad news," Finnegan said. "He has an alibi. Poker game with his buddies. It's a regular thing."

I said, "Right. Check it. Twice. Any matches on the gun? No?"

"Hey, about that," Wright said. "The techs were annoyed."

"Annoyed?" What had we done to piss them off now?

"You got the ballistics report from them?" Wright asked.

"Yes, but the initial ID came from the ME. Why?" My stomach wanted lunch, and I didn't need the crime-scene techs' bitching to keep me from it.

He shrugged. "They were peeved we knew before they did."

"Yeah? They should work faster then," I said. That burger place I kept hearing the guys talk about. Where was it?

Billy said, "Dr. Saunders? How does he know bullets?"

"He took a course or makes them on the weekends," I said. "Does it matter?"

"I heard he's a fairy," Billy said. He waved his hands close to his chest. He looked like a dim-witted T. rex.

"Saunders?" Wright said. His brows popped up like bread from a toaster.

"Yeah," Revere said. He moved some papers, to unfurl a map. "It's not a secret. He's openly out." He looked up at the others, a crease bisecting his forehead.

Finnegan said, "I'd heard rumors."

"I wouldn't want him handling my body," Billy said, making a show of shivering.

"You'd be dead," I pointed out.

"Afraid he'd want to play doctor with you?" Finnegan asked. Wright laughed.

"Damn straight," Billy said. Finnegan and Wright slapped their knees.

"Damn *straight*," Wright said. "Classic."

Billy grinned, delighted to be one of the guys. "Hey, what do you get when you cross an Eskimo with a gay dude?"

"What?" Wright asked.

"A snow blower," Billy said.

My hunger was gone. The gnawing in my stomach something different now.

Wright said, "Snow blower. Ha." He smacked his knee again. "Ha."

Finnegan laughed until he coughed a phlegm ball into his food-stained handkerchief.

My finger throbbed. "Back to work," I said. I left them to their stupid jokes.

So Dr. Saunders was gay. And out. Good for him. But then he worked with the dead, and they tend to be more forgiving.

## 2235 HOURS

Pine trees surrounded me at the golf course's edge. I watched the silent greens, now a monochromatic gray. Bugs hummed and chittered. Every few minutes, I lifted my feet and ran my fingers over my ankles and calves. Checking for bumps. The locals had gleefully shared tales of Lyme disease, and I'd developed a fear. I rubbed my arms, cold. My jacket was still at Suds, being purged of Cecilia North's blood.

"I heard he's a fairy." Billy's voice returned. A fairy. Right. All gay men were weak, effeminate. In a fight, I'd whip Billy's skinny ass from here to Timbuktu.

But I'd learned to control my temper. My parents, embarrassed by their brute son, sat me down for repeated talks on why we don't hit and how physical violence solves nothing. "Not true," I'd said. "Kevin Hurley hasn't taken lunch money from any of the young kids since I held his head in the toilet and flushed it." My father wrapped bandages around my knuckles and asked when I'd learn not to be baited. "Tommy, you've got to get a thicker skin. This one's going to be peeled from you if you keep on this way." But I kept scrapping, until I made it into the police academy. I loved policing and didn't dare lose it. Fighting could cost me my new career. So I quit, cold turkey.

An owl hooted behind me. My feet crunched dried pine needles. Would the kids come after being chased by Charlie last night? Probably not. This was absurd. But I'd said I'd do it. Had said it in front of my men. I'd stay until midnight or half past and then radio someone to take the last few hours.

Stars sparkled in the dark sky. Underneath the same sky, years ago, Rick and I had sat eating soggy pizza on a tar-paper roof, watching a suspect's windows. Rick's back was against the roof's entry door, his binoculars by his knees. He'd said, "Would you look at that, Tommy?" I'd arched my back and tilted my head to follow the line of his pointing finger. Above us was a dark-violet sky. Clouds scuttled past. No moon in sight.

"What am I looking at?" I'd asked.

"Pollution. Certainly not stars." And then he'd laughed, to show he was kidding, that he didn't care if he couldn't see constellations.

He always protested what he meant most. And when he got low, it was my job to jolly him along. "Stars? What're those?" I'd said.

"Ah, dummy. How'd you end up with parents like yours?" He'd scooped up his binoculars. He knew my parents were professors. It amused him no end.

"Stork got the wrong address," I'd said.

"Probably got tired of carrying you."

I wasn't heavy, but I had forty pounds on Rick, who stood 5'8" in boots. We'd nicknamed each other within hours of being partnered. I called him Leprechaun. He called me Sasquatch.

"Just think. Somewhere there's some poor Sasquatch family wondering where their dear baby is." He made his arms into a scoop and rocked them side to side.

"Imagine my parents, wondering where their assistant professor of sociology is."

He'd laughed and let his arms fall to his sides. His body loose, the tension gone. Mission accomplished.

Rick got it. I complained about my family not understanding why I became a cop and he said, "Shit, Tommy! What the hell else you gonna be, a shoe salesman? Jesus! You're natural-born murder police. You got the jazz."

The jazz was instinct and luck, the kind only cops have. Those with jazz lasted. Those who didn't have it usually went down the hall to Vice and put in for their pensions like clockwork.

Hearing him say I was born to work murder? I never wanted more. Rick understood. Like no one else.

I slugged him in the arm and said, "Keep up with the sweet talk and I might turn straight for you."

He barked a laugh. "Hands to yourself, you perv."

Someone whispered. I scanned the area. Nothing. A burst of light streaked through the sky. A falling star. Holy shit. I'd never seen one before. What should I wish for? To solve this murder. What else?

1. Get laid.
2. Get the nameplate on my door replaced.
3. Get the mayor off my back about my car.
4. Stop thinking about Rick.

A voice called from across the green. "Come on!"

Four forms approached, two of them all limbs. Teenagers. "Where's the candle?" one asked. They stood near the ninth hole. A flicker of light. "Stupid lighter." The flick came again, followed by the firefly glow of a candle, then two. In their weak glow, I made out three boys and one girl.

"What now?" a boy asked.

"Look for the stuff," another said.

"What stuff?" the girl asked. The candle cast shadows on her face. "I thought we were here to make contact."

"Casings," the boy wearing a hoodie said. "Evidence from the crime. It will put us in touch."

These idiots were trying to find evidence so they could commune with the murder victim? Jesus.

The shortest boy suggested that they say the St. Anthony prayer.

"What's that, Kevin?" the girl asked.

"Please, St. Anthony, look around. Something's lost and must be found." I hadn't heard that prayer in years. Rick once invoked it at a hopeless crime scene. The team had laughed. Praying for evidence. The last resort of an Irish Catholic cop.

The boy holding the candle urged them to hurry up.

"There aren't going to be any casings," Kevin, the small one, said. "The cops have already been here."

Candle boy laughed. "You think our cops got this figured out? They couldn't find their own ass if you handed it to them."

My cue. I burst through the trees. "Freeze! On the ground now!" The kids spun. Kevin put his hands up. "Down!"

Kevin and hoodie boy hit the ground.

The girl, still upright, said "What?"

"Police!" I said.

The fourth kid, the joker, ran. I pursued. Couldn't find my own ass, huh? I wasn't going to lose his. He huffed and puffed, out of reach. My side cramped with each jagged breath. Boy, he was quick. I sprinted, reached forward, and grabbed his T-shirt. My hand clutched the thin fabric. I tugged it toward me, hard.

"Ack!" He jerked backward and stumbled. His hands went to his throat. I pulled him to his feet. "Come with me." He stood, muttering about police brutality. He smelled of pot and sweat.

"You don't stop running your mouth and I'll show you brutality. Let's go join your friends."

I'd expected they'd taken off, but all three remained where I'd left them.

"You're all coming to the station." I radioed for a patrol car. "Better prepare how you'll explain this to your parents."

After I'd requested assistance, I made them face me, an impromptu lineup. "Why are you on the golf course?" They shuffled their feet and stayed silent. "This isn't a multiple-choice question. Why?"

"We were trying to make contact," Kevin said.

"With the murder victim, Kevin?"

He stepped back, surprised I knew his name. He nodded.

"So you were here last night too?" They started in with quick denials. "Don't insult my intelligence. You were here last night."

"Yes," the girl said. "But the guard came through."

"Did you see anyone else during your visits?"

"Besides the guard?" she asked.

"Besides him," I said.

"No."

"Nothing out of the usual?"

Hoodie boy said, "You mean related to the crime? Like the killer?"

"I mean anything," I said.

"I saw a flashlight," he said.

"When, Chris?" the girl asked. "You never said."

"Last night. But then the guard came and we all had to run, so—"

"Where was the light?" I asked.

Chris pointed toward the eighth hole. "That way, but closer to the edge, skirting the woods, you know? It would come and go, like it was being flicked on and then off."

"You never said," she repeated.

So someone else may have been on the course last night. Someone Charlie Fisher hadn't seen. I'd send Revere to check the woods around the eighth and ninth holes tomorrow. Show him that following an "unimportant" tip might earn us forensics.

Fifteen minutes later, the patrol car came. The officers looked around. "These guys?" they said, pointing to the kids who stood, fidgeting.

"They were trespassing. I want them booked."

Hopkins said, "We'll have to call their parents." He made it sound like a deal breaker. If he were any lazier, he'd be dead.

"I look forward to it. Especially that one's." I pointed to the teen who'd run. "What's your name?"

"Michael Jackson," he said.

"Shut up," hoodie boy said. "We're in enough trouble."

At the station, I learned my young offenders' full names. Hoodie boy was Christopher Warren. His punk friend was Luke Johnson. The girl was Tiffany Haines. And last and shortest was Kevin Wilkes. They sat on a bench, near each other but not touching. Luke stared, glassy-eyed, at the Most Wanted posters. Probably looking at his future. He was the one the desk sergeant, Mahoney, had recognized. "Tagging more bridges, Luke?" he'd asked when the kids had filed into the station.

"Nah," Luke had said. "Trespassing."

I'd hung back and asked Mahoney, "He got charged?"

"Juvie court. Got public service. Picking up trash. Not surprised to see him again. No dad at home. And his mother, well, she's a piece of work."

During the next hour, three sets of horrified parents came through the door. Mr. and Mrs. Wilkes were first. When I'd explained why Kevin was at the station, Mrs. Wilkes had said to her son, "You were supposed to be watching a movie with Chris!"

"I was, at first," Kevin said.

"And we told you not to hang out with the Johnson kid," his father said. He massaged his temples. "We're going to have a serious conversation. Starting with how many weeks you're grounded."

Mr. and Mrs. Warren came next. "Chris? Sweetheart, are you okay?" Mrs. Warren hugged him, her diamond earrings throwing sparkles all over the room. Chris nodded, hands clutched at his sides. His ginger hair was a shade lighter than Rick's. In my office, he hung his head while I recounted the night's adventures. "I'm sorry," he said, before his parents spoke. "I'm so sorry."

"Now, now," said Mrs. Warren. She patted his shoulder.

"Are you pressing charges?" Mr. Warren asked. He smelled like a stiff drink but looked white-collar. I bet he got a big holiday bonus, doing whatever he did.

"No. Chris appreciates what he did was wrong. But I think a punishment is in order." Chris stood. He was nearly eye level to me. He stuck his hand out. "Sir, I'm sorry. I'll never do anything like that again."

I shook his hand. "Glad to hear it."

He gave me a crooked smile and his resemblance to Rick grew stronger. I'd called that smile Rick's "rueful charmer." Seeing it again made my chest loosen.

Tiffany's mom and dad were nice but absentminded. I got the impression that Tiffany was smarter than either parent and all of them were aware of this imbalance. When I asked why she ran with a bad crowd, she said, "Only Luke is bad. Or tries to be."

Tiffany suggested her own punishment: more hours spent at the Animal Rescue League.

"Didn't Cecilia North work there?" I asked.

"Yes." She looked down. "But she was older, so I didn't know her."

After midnight, only Luke remained. The desk sergeant hadn't lied about his mother. We'd thought she was on her way after our first phone call, but she thought picking up her son from the station was "optional."

When she finally showed, she said, "What's he supposed to have done, now?" She took out a cigarette. I pointed to the No Smoking sign taped behind my desk. She rolled her eyes.

"He was caught trespassing on the Nipmuc Golf Course."

"Oh?" She'd expected worse.

"And he tried to run from me." Luke shrugged at her. She fingered the cigarette. "But what really bothers me, Mrs. Johnson, is what your son was up to. He was looking to remove evidence. That's interfering with a crime scene."

"I'm sure he's sorry, aren't you?" She elbowed him.

Luke crossed his arms. He stared at my desk.

"Don't you have a curfew?" I asked.

Luke and his mother went slack-jawed at this idea. "Well, you've got one now. Until school starts, I want you home every night at nine p.m."

"What?" His shout ricocheted off the file cabinets. "You can't do that."

"I'm the chief of police, son. I'll conduct random checks. If I stop by your house after nine p.m. and you're not home, I'm sending you to juvie court. And I'll recommend that your mother attend parenting classes."

"What?" She bested his shriek by twenty decibels. "You can't do that!"

She didn't know that, not for sure. "I hate to repeat myself, but I'm the chief of police. Mrs. Johnson, take Luke home. And make sure he obeys his curfew." She tugged on his shirt and complained about police abuse.

My wall clock read 2:21 a.m. I rubbed my gritty eyes. My keys jingled as I picked them up. My mind flashed to Rick again. He used to spin his key ring and whistle the theme to *The Andy Griffith Show* before going home. Every night. A whirl of the key ring and that damn whistling.

I stole his key ring. After he died, I took it from his desk. Put his keys on another ring. No one noticed. It wasn't distinct, just a double circle of metal, bought at any bodega for fifty cents. It wouldn't mean anything to anyone. It's inside my gun safe. Sometimes I see its dull metal glint as I retrieve or put away my gun. And I think, "There you are." But of course he isn't. He's dead.

# FRIDAY, AUGUST 15TH
## 1030 HOURS

The morning crew was deep in the business of small-town policing when I arrived at the station, still tired. Chasing teenagers and acting like the paternal police chief had exhausted me. I trudged toward my office. Scarlet fingernails, snapping in the air, stopped me.

Joanne Devon, ear to the phone, jerked her head. She stopped snapping and pointed to a pink memo in front of her. "Yeah?" she asked. "What night was that?"

I picked up the thin memo. Mrs. Ashworth. 115 Lakeside Drive. Saw two men on the golf course the night of the murder.

I looked at Joanne. She put her hand over the phone and said, "Sounds credible. I tried raising Wright, but he didn't respond. Finnegan's in later."

"I'll take it," I said. "Thanks."

She rapped her knuckles against the desk and said, "Sure, ma'am. I'll pass on your concern." She hung up and said, "Half the town uses this number for complaints. That one was about garbage pickup. Fourth one so far. We should make Public Works answer these calls."

"You know her?" I waved the pink paper.

She scrunched her petite nose. "Just to talk to at the market. She's British. Moved here years ago. Loves dogs."

The phone rang. Joanne squared her shoulders and said, "If this is another garbage complaint . . ." She picked up the handset and was all sunny professionalism. "Idyll Police Station. Homicide tip line."

I headed back outside. Time to discover what Mrs. Ashworth knew.

I got two feet inside Mrs. Ashworth's cottage before her yapping Pomeranians tried to take me down. Each attacked a shin. I grunted and kicked them free. They barked and rutted against my legs. I'd need to call the sexual-assault team if they didn't let go.

Mrs. Ashworth, who smelled strongly of peppermint, said, "Down boys!" Her voice was devoid of authority. Her face was broad and cheerful. She'd make a great Mrs. Claus. I took advantage of the dogs' distraction and scuttled past them. Following her petite back, I passed photos of the Queen, Buckingham Palace, and an English tower I felt I ought to recognize. Inside the kitchen, a man-sized map of London hung over a side table filled with tchotchkes: souvenir spoons, thimbles, and commemorative coins. Everything was covered in a film of dog's hair. My skin itched. I fought a sneeze. Lost the battle. It tore through my sinuses.

"Bless you," Mrs. Ashworth said. She held up a kettle. Fur clung to its greasy bottom.

"No, thank you." I rubbed dog hairs from my pants legs. They clung like burrs to the polyester.

"Just take a minute." She turned the knob on the aged, white stove. A tick, a puff, and then a whoosh as fire rushed to the surface of the gas ring. The stench of methane reached my nostrils.

Seated at the two-person kitchen table, I said, "You said you saw people on the golf course the night of the ninth?"

She raised her eyeglasses from the chain she wore around her crepey neck. Peered through them at the kettle. "Hmm?"

I repeated my question. Behind me I heard the clack of the dogs' nails on the bare floor. Shit. Incoming.

"Yes, that's right."

The dogs appeared, pink tongues protruding. Their eyes locked on my legs. I moved them aside and under the table. The dogs panted and yipped. Playtime.

The kettle shrieked. Mrs. Ashworth grabbed it from the stovetop, humming under her breath. I tried to avoid the dogs. Easier said than done. They kept feinting toward me, their eyes wild with delight.

I watched as the gas ring of flames blazed, forgotten. She'd burn the place down before I got a damn answer.

"How many people?" I asked. "On the golf course?"

"Ah!" She held up a flowered, blue tin. "Orange pekoe. Do you like orange pekoe?" Her gold wedding band was loose on her hand. Her husband "had passed" a decade ago. Just after they'd moved to the States. I wondered if all Brits were as batty as she was.

"Two people? Three?" I asked.

She scooped a bunch of dried stuff from the tin. It looked and smelled like potpourri. God, was it? She put it in a mesh container. Then she swirled the teakettle and poured hot water from it into the sink.

"This is how you make a proper cuppa." She lowered her voice, sharing a great secret. By pouring the hot water down the sink?

She put the mesh container into the teapot and poured the remaining hot water over it. "There," she said. "Where were we?"

Losing my damn mind. "How many people were on the golf course?" The smaller dog began humping my shoe. It felt like a mini-jackhammer had attached itself to my toes. I jerked my foot back and forth. The dog clung, unshakeable.

"Two men." She set the teapot on the table. It sported not one, but three, doilies.

"Now the cups." She went to the cupboard.

"Your range is still on," I said.

She glanced down at the blue flames. "Oh! Sometimes I think I'd forget my head if it weren't attached."

I pushed my foot so that the dog was stuck between it and the table leg. It yowled. I pulled back and it hurried away to its friend.

"Shasta! What are you up to, poppet?" she asked the dog.

As eyewitnesses went, she ranked between Blind Bill and Wazoo. Blind Bill was an alcoholic who gave out information when he needed another bottle, and Wazoo was a junkie who often needed to trade a story for a get-out-of-jail-free card. Both were unreliable at best and absolute liars at worst.

She turned off the gas, set two cups down, and said, "They weren't playing golf."

"Who?" I asked.

"The two men on the course." She looked at me as if I were the one in the room half short of a loaf.

The other dog lunged at my calf. He got in two thrusts before I picked him up and dropped him near her. He barked.

"Hush, Samson," she said. "Mummy's talking."

"Two men," I said, sitting again.

"I suspect they'd had too much to drink." She poured the tea into the cups. The smell strengthened my suspicion she was serving potpourri.

"Why do you say that?"

"Well." Her plump cheeks got rosy. "One of them was relieving himself."

"He was peeing on the golf course?" I wrote this down.

She bit her lip. "Yes. On the grass by the eighth hole."

"You saw him urinating?"

She shook her gray hair. "Not exactly. I saw his pants were down at his ankles." She sipped her liquid potpourri.

"And the other man?" I asked. "What was he doing?"

"Just standing there. He seemed anxious. Maybe because of his friend."

"How were they standing?"

"Upright. By the eighth hole." She was giving me that "my, you're dim" look she'd favored me with earlier.

"In relation to each other." I grabbed her London Bridge saltshaker. "If this is the man who was urinating, where is his friend?"

She set the matching pepper shaker close to the saltshaker. Very close.

"He was facing his friend?"

"Yes," she said. "They were quite near."

A man facing another man whose pants were at his ankles? Urinating men don't watch each other. Unless . . .

"What about their heights?"

She inhaled sharply and shook her head. "Oh, it was dark. And once I saw what they were up to, I tried to give them privacy. How awful to be caught doing that in public by an old woman." She smiled at me.

She had no idea how embarrassing.

"The one urinating was tall, like you. But the other one. Well, he knelt down as I passed by. Tying his shoe maybe. So I couldn't tell his height."

The man facing his pantsless friend knelt in front of him. And she thought he was tying his shoe? Wow.

"Oh, but the other one. The tall one. He had a big belt buckle. Shiny. Like cowboys wear on the telly. I saw it resting on his sneakers."

"A big belt buckle." I repeated the detail as I wrote it down. "Anything else?"

Shasta was nearing my leg from behind. A new angle of attack. I lifted my heel, ready to counter.

"No," she said. "That's all I saw. Perhaps the men saw something that night, but then again perhaps they'd be ashamed to come forward. Because of what they'd done to the course."

"Yes," I said. I thought they might be afraid to come forward. One pantsless man and another kneeling before him.

"Did the men hear you or the dogs?" I asked.

"I don't think so. Shasta was exhausted. I was carrying him home, and Samson was tracking something. Squirrel most likely. Lots of them in the trees."

"One last question. Why did you wait to call us?"

She put her hand to her chest. "Oh. Yes. You see, I only got home yesterday. I left town early Sunday morning to go visit my friend, Barbara. She's not been well. And I stayed until yesterday. When I got home, I heard the news and realized. So I called the station. Do you think it will help catch whoever did it?"

"Perhaps. Thank you, Mrs. Ashworth. If you think of anything else—" I gave her my card and stood. The dogs yipped. "I'll just see myself out."

"Oh!" she said as I made my escape. "But you haven't drunk your tea!"

## 1430 HOURS

I was parked in Suds's lot. I had the car door open and my left foot planted on the ground. The building's eaves dripped rain onto the sizzling gravel. The humid air felt heavy. My hand was on the door handle, but my mind was two miles away, on the golf course. Could one of the two men Mrs. Ashworth spotted be Cecilia North's killer? Or were they witnesses to the crime?

I got out of the car and stretched. My sticky shirt chafed my middle. I walked to the window and peeked inside. Nate stood behind the bar. No Donna. I entered. Nate did a double take. Morning coffees and dinners I ate at Suds, regular. But lunches? Never. "What'll it be?" he asked.

"Grilled cheese with tomato and a side salad, please." It wouldn't do me wrong to eat more greens. I didn't want to look like Stoughton. I'd seen him once. His belly looked like he was expecting twins.

Next door, the washing machines and driers created a symphony of white noise I enjoyed. In Idyll, the noise was all nature: hoots and growls and unexpected chirps. Give me sirens or car horns or whirring machinery any day.

I needed to find those two men from the golf course. But all I had was a vague physical description and a belt buckle. Oh, and they were gay.

The bar had few other customers. One left his stool to approach me. He was of average height and weight, with thinning brown hair. Joe Average. "Still working that murder?" he asked. His voice was reedy and had a twang.

My stare made him back up a step. "Yes."

"Doesn't seem like there's been much progress."

The other nearby faces turned away from the TV to watch the drama nearer them.

"And you know that how, Mr.—?"

"Lyle," he said. He cleared his throat. "Mr. Lyle."

"Are you a medical examiner, Mr. Lyle?"

He rubbed his nose. "No."

"Detective?"

"No."

"Eyewitness to the murder?"

He shook his head.

"So you don't have any pertinent information for me," I said. Someone behind my new friend snickered.

"No, I just thought—"

"No, you didn't, Mr. Lyle. I think you've proven that. If you'll excuse me, I have a lunch to eat. I'm getting to it a bit late because I was out *working* a murder."

Mr. Lyle returned to his stool. His friend laughed at him.

Nate set a plate before me. "House dressing okay?" He set a gravy boat at my elbow.

"Sure."

Nate shook his head. "You getting a lot of this?" He looked Mr. Lyle's way.

"Not much." I thought about Billy. "My men are probably getting the brunt of it."

I dressed my salad and stared at the booze bottles as I ate. What to do next? I had new information, if Mrs. Ashworth was to be believed. But given the climate in Idyll, did I want to mention that the men were gay? I could only imagine how ham-fisted Wright's interview would be. I needed more information. And I didn't trust my men to get it without potentially outing men whose only crime had been to try to get it on in public. A thing I knew something about.

"Everything okay?" Nate eyed my plate. I'd only eaten the salad.

"Fine." I lowered my voice to just above a whisper. "Hey, Nate, is the Nipmuc Golf Course a spot where people meet to um . . ." How to phrase this?

"Get intimate?" He dried a glass. Held it up and examined it for spots. "Nah. The woods above the golf course. And the old cabin, owned by the Sutter guy near Hought's Pond." Christ. Why bother with my detectives? Nate was better informed.

"What if the couple were, say, alternative in lifestyle?"

He leaned against the bar, his ponytail tickling the taps. "Gay?" He chuckled. "Not much of a scene in Idyll. New Haven, yeah. They've got a club there. Gotham Citi. Just opened up." He was better than a detective. "This have anything to do with the murder?" He was also too quick by half.

"Naw. Just some local color."

I suspected he knew better, but he didn't argue. He dried another glass. "If you want to know more about that scene, you should talk to Elmore Fenworth."

"The guy who writes about the aliens he claims we're hiding in the station?"

He set the glass down. "That's Elmore. He has passions. But he also pays attention, lots of attention. Just don't mention JFK to him, or he'll never stop talking."

"Got it. Thanks." I paid my bill. "My laundry ready?" My bag was navy-blue canvas and had a red tag. I often picked it up and left money on the counter.

"Lucy's in there," he said. Lucy was the part-time help and Idyll's contribution to the Goth movement. She had purple hair, a powdered kabuki face, and torn fishnets, and she wore all the black eye makeup sold at Washerman's Drug.

I walked into the Laundromat and found her reading *Beyond Good and Evil*. "Nietzsche fan?" I asked.

She shrugged, exposing a bit of freckled shoulder. "Everyone thinks he's the 'God is dead' guy."

"He is." I pointed to my bag.

She hefted it up with a grunt. "He wrote other stuff, too."

My father had taught Nietzsche, though he wasn't a fan. "'Madness is something rare in individuals—but in groups, parties, peoples, ages, it is the rule,'" I said. It had resonated when I began policing. Madness seemed common to groups.

"You know Nietzsche?" She was young beneath that makeup, impressionable too.

"I'm the police chief. I know lots of things."

She snapped her gum. "There was a problem with your laundry." She pulled a hanger off the rod behind her. "Your jacket. It had a stain. Wouldn't come out. I tried everything." On the shoulder were three tiny brown spots. "Blood, right?" she said. "I tried cold water, dishwashing liquid, peroxide. It wouldn't come clean."

"Thanks for trying. How much do I owe?"

She gave me a number. I handed her a bill and said, "Keep the change." Her wide smile cracked her white mask.

I exited the laundry. The rain was a damp memory, the world shining anew. I glanced at my jacket. Cecilia North's blood couldn't be removed. Why wasn't I surprised?

At the station, everyone but Finnegan was present, sorting through Cecilia North's life. "We've got new information," I said. That got their attention. Billy, hovering at the edge of the pen like a lovesick schoolboy, perked up. I waved him over. "A Mrs. Ashworth was walking her dogs the night of the murder. She saw two men on the golf course."

Revere whistled.

"The description isn't great. Two white men, one tall, and the other probably medium height. The tall man had a large belt buckle, the kind cowboys wore on the telly." I gave an impression of her accent on the last five words.

"She British?" Revere asked.

I nodded.

"Ooh, laddie, your accent's shite," he said. His was better. Show-off.

"Mrs. Ashworth just got back into town. She'd left the morning we found Miss North. So that explains the delay."

"Two white men. One with a big belt buckle," Wright said. He cracked his fingers. "Needles in a fucking haystack."

"So find me the needles," I said.

"She mention a gun?" Revere asked.

"No. Her look at them was brief. She claimed one of them was urinating on the course."

"What?" Billy asked.

I passed on Mrs. Ashworth's information, skipping the shoe-tying bit. If they figured the men were gay, they'd start hunting.

"So, drunk perhaps?" Revere asked.

"Maybe."

"How do we find them?" Billy asked.

Revere shook his head. "Lots of legwork, kid."

"More door-to-doors?"

Wright groaned. "You got it." Under his breath, "Fucking needles in a haystack."

# SATURDAY, AUGUST 16TH
## 2145 HOURS

'd left work an hour ago. And I'd been driving since, heading down roads not yet explored. Idyll was small, population-wise, but the town covered forty square miles, almost twice Manhattan's size. You could spend a lot of time turning down random roads. My mind did its cop thing: assessing threats as I drove. There were few. Most of them in the form of potholes.

Wright had taken Billy with him on door-to-doors today, looking for anyone who saw our two men on or near the golf course. When they'd returned, I'd had to listen to Wright bitch about the town's blind and deaf population. And about how Billy kept slowing the investigation down with his good manners. No cup of coffee refused. No picture of a child or grandchild left unadmired. Revere offered to take Billy with him on the next outing. Mostly to silence Wright.

I could narrow the search, if I told them what I knew. That the two men they were searching for, their needles in a haystack, weren't as common as they thought. But what would the response be? And were the men stronger suspects than Gary Clark, our victim's co-worker? He had an alibi, but so did two dozen men I'd put away over the years.

*You don't have to protect those men.* I could hear Rick in my head. *They're grown-ups. They didn't have to go outside for fun and games.*

I wouldn't be persuaded by his ghost. Not yet. If we didn't find them by the week's end, I'd give the men more information. Maybe let Finnegan talk to Mrs. Ashworth. He'd connect the dots.

It was time to go home. But I didn't want to. I drove down a rutted

road they didn't feature on town postcards. Skinner Street. Why did I
know that name? It came to me. Because Luke Johnson and his mother
lived on it. I could make good on my curfew threat. I parked halfway
in the driveway of number 116. I couldn't go farther. A rusting boat
dominated the space, abandoned to the pitted land of the Johnson
plot. The dirt yard was decorated with appliances. The ranch's shut-
ters were in the process of falling off, and the windows boasted cur-
tains that resembled beach towels. Probably were beach towels. A light
outside each door attracted moths. I stood underneath the front one
and rang the doorbell. Silence. I waited and pushed it again. Nothing.
I opened the screen door and knuckled the wooden one behind. Mrs.
Johnson opened the door. She clutched a ratty pink bathrobe at the
neck. Her eye makeup had migrated south, flecks of black like a trail of
ants marching toward her cheeks.

"Good evening, Mrs. Johnson. I'm here to check on Luke." She
loosened her grip. Under her robe, she wore a stained tank top and
tiny, pink shorts that had lost their elastic grip. She'd had a C-section.
I looked away.

"You really meant it about his curfew, huh?" she asked.

"I did. Is he here?" The air smelled bad. Like burnt tomato soup.

"Luke!" She yelled, not bothering to aim her shout inside. "Luke!"
Her beer breath assaulted me.

"If he's not here, I'll send someone to take him to juvenile court
tomorrow."

She smoothed her limp hair. "He's here."

And lo and behold, he appeared behind her. "What?" he said. He
rubbed his eyes.

"Police," she said.

"Seriously?" He peered around her. "I didn't do nothing." The
words were automatic. He looked behind him, quickly, and then back
at me.

"Hi there, Luke. Remember me?"

He glanced behind him, and I peered around his mother to see
what had him so anxious. I didn't see any drugs or alcohol. Just a mess

of clothes and a sloppy pile of unread textbooks. Beside them a pair of muddy boots and a baseball bat. "What do you want now?" he asked.

"Just checking that you're obeying your curfew."

His shoulders fell, and he relaxed his stance. "Yeah, well, here I am. Stuck at home, again. Playing video games I've played a million times before because someone drank my birthday-present money. Again."

Mrs. Johnson turned to him and said, "Enough about that. I told you I'd buy you a game next week."

"It's always *next* week."

Before I became embroiled in a family counseling session, I bid them good night and returned to my car. It smelled of food. I'd spent more time in it lately. If I weren't careful, it would start looking like Finnegan's. The mayor wouldn't like that. What was it he'd said? I was supposed to treat my car like a lady. Little did he know that my usual approach with women was to ignore them.

What now? I could grab a drink at Suds. But lately the locals had gotten chatty. Who were we investigating for the murder? When would it be wrapped up? Did I favor gun-restriction laws? Did I like those black-and-white cookies they ate in New York? And Donna often worked nights. I couldn't handle her flirting.

I could drive a few towns over, watch a movie, and enjoy the anonymous shared darkness and silence. But it felt like giving up. I had to go home sometime.

My house had become contaminated with too much thinking. Too many memories. My mind kept reaching for Rick. I'd unlock my gun safe and see his key ring and the guilt would consume me. If I'd gotten Rick clean, if I'd had a gentle word with our super, maybe we could've quietly sent him to a facility. Rehab. More cops than you know go. And relapse. But it would have been worth a shot. Instead, I kept my lips sealed.

Why did I keep Rick's secret? Simple. He kept mine. He had my back. So when he slipped up, what was I supposed to do? Narc him out? No. Not me.

And when he stole drugs from a crime scene. Why did I stay silent?

Not so simple. Part of me worried he'd retaliate if I told. Tit for tat. I wanted to believe he wouldn't betray me. But I wasn't dealing with Rick. I was dealing with a guy inches away from junkiehood.

First rule of junkies: they only care about getting high.

Why did I remain silent in the face of his worsening addiction? Because it would bring about the end. Our partnership wouldn't survive that much truth. Out in the open. Exposed. The both of us.

He might be alive if I'd gone to our super and told him what Rick was doing. But I kept Rick's secret and managed to believe I was doing him a favor.

It's amazing the lies we tell ourselves. Amazing what we'll believe.

# MONDAY, AUGUST 18TH
## 1400 HOURS

The funeral day was sunny and eighty-seven degrees. A breeze stirred the heat and brought the smell of cow dung closer. The cemetery was filled with people fanning church programs near their faces. The living almost outnumbered the dead. Sudden deaths attract people who don't show at regular funerals: hairdressers, grocery clerks, and the librarian who'd once helped with a school research project.

A cow mooed, long and low. I surveyed the onlookers: white, middle-class people staring at the minister, the casket, or anywhere but. The family huddled together, shoulders touching. Sad and strange that all four of Cecilia's grandparents had outlived her. The grandmother who'd had hip surgery used her husband as a crutch, her face collapsing as she cried. Snuffling noises emerged from behind her lace-edged hankie. Cecilia's mother and sister cried too, silently. Tears slid down their faces. Dripped onto their dress collars. Had Cecilia cried like her grandmother or like her sister and mother? Billy might know. He stood near the family in his dress uniform, hands at his waist, grim-faced.

The mourners returned to their cars. I followed the last of the stragglers to the Norths' home and stepped past knots of people on the lawn. In the living room, Cecilia's sister, Renee, stood in a huddle of her peers. She was Cecilia's height, but blond. Her eyes were brown, half hidden by swollen eyelids, like raisins poked into dough.

Voices were low, but there was a speed to the conversation. People speculated about who had killed her. I recognized a sharp-faced young man wearing a well-cut, dark suit. The ex-boyfriend, Matthew Dillard. Now that he was alibied, he had my sympathy.

People gave me wide berth as I passed through rooms, looking for the bathroom. A line of women stood outside it. I turned back and went to the dining room. A long row of casseroles sat on the buffet. Oversized plates of cold cuts crowded the room's giant wooden table. Bread loaves were squished between supersize containers of mayo and mustard. The lemonade dispenser sweat giant water beads. The Norths had air-conditioning, but it wasn't strong enough to withstand this crowd. I'd put money on someone fainting before this ended.

A thin, middle-aged woman in a black-and-white checked dress came through the rear door and stabbed a casserole with a slotted spoon. "Help you?" she said when she saw me watching. Her tone implied she'd rather not.

"Hello, I'm Police Chief Lynch."

Her lips formed a thin line. She said, "I'm May Hanover, Susan's sister." Ah, the aunt. She looked a bit like Mrs. North and Cecilia. The symmetry of the features, mostly. Her eyes were dark brown, like her hair.

"You live nearby?" I asked.

"No. Maryland." She checked the other food. Stirred some veggie dip.

"Did you see Cecilia much?"

"Every Thanksgiving. I'd travel up here and see the girls." She adjusted a container of toothpicks near the cheese plate. The cheese looked near melting. God, it was hot. Was her dress wool? It looked it.

"Would you like to step outside?" I asked.

"I should—" She glanced at the food. There was too much of it. "Just a second." She came back twenty seconds later, armed with cigarettes and a lighter. She led me to the backyard. It looked like my own, shaggy and untended. We walked until we reached the edge, marked by a tall wooden fence decorated with bird silhouettes. We stood below a cutout hawk. She snapped her lighter, lit her cigarette, and took a long drag. "Cecilia smoked," I said.

"Did she?" Her voice implied ignorance, but her face wasn't up to the lie.

"You knew."

She blew smoke toward an overhanging tree. There was a nest inside the crook of its branches. The nest was made of straw, and contained a bright-red string. A ribbon?

"I knew," she said, "but her parents didn't."

"What else didn't they know?" The nest. Were there baby birds inside? Should we be standing so close? If the parents thought we'd tainted the chicks, they might abandon them. I'd read that somewhere.

"They're good parents." Her lips flattened again.

"Yes, they are." The Norths had never struck me as otherwise. "So Cecilia told you secrets?" I asked.

"Not exactly. I used to be the cool aunt, but I've aged out of that." She patted her skin, calling attention to wrinkles. She looked good for a woman her age. "But she'd sometimes ask for advice."

"Such as?"

"Anyone ever tell you that you ask a lot of questions?" Was she joking? She finished her cigarette and dropped it to the ground. "She'd been unhappy at work." She looked at the others gathered on the lawn. They sipped from plastic cups and broke into sudden fits of sharp laughter.

"No one else mentioned this."

She shrugged. "I doubt she told anyone. She was good with secrets."

"Did she say why she was unhappy?"

She pushed her chin forward. "Her supervisor sounded like a pill, and there might have been something—I don't know."

"Something?"

She lit a second cigarette. "I got the impression she thought that not everything at the company was on the up and up." She inhaled and held the smoke.

"And you didn't mention this because . . . ?"

She exhaled a cloudy stream. "You think she was killed by an insurance company because she knew too much? Give me a break. She was a Human Resources assistant. If I'd thought for a minute she'd been in danger, I'd have said something."

"So you don't think her death had anything to do with her job?"

"No." She stomped on the half-smoked cigarette.

"What then?"

She flicked her thumb over her lighter, creating a spark and a flame. "I think she was in the wrong place at the wrong time."

"A golf course at midnight is a strange place to be."

"Tell me something I don't know." She rubbed her lips. "I need to brush my teeth. I don't even like cigarettes. The taste, like kissing an ashtray. But the calm, you know?" She stared at the house. "Cecilia actually liked smoking. But then, she was young." Her tears trembled on her lower lids. "She was a sweet kid." The tears fell.

She shook herself. "I'd better get inside. Check on the food." She touched my arm, and the heat of her hand felt unpleasant, like a burn.

Above us, a bird cheeped. Returned to the nest? Or safely tucked inside all this time?

"I'm sorry for your loss," I said.

"Thank you." She left.

I stood and surveyed the crowd. Our victim had a lot of friends. But the one I'd hoped to see, the man from the cabin, was absent. I thought about Cecilia, cadging smokes and sneaking out to meet an older, married man at night. We weren't dissimilar, she and I. She had been scrappy, not one to back down from a fight.

I stayed another half hour, cruising the Norths' house, overhearing stories about Cecilia. Things I learned:

1. She liked to sing but was tone deaf.
2. She'd asked for a unicorn two Christmases in a row until she received a note from Santa that explained that unicorns were mythical creatures.
3. She responded to Santa's note with a dictated letter of her own saying she'd heard rumors that *he* wasn't real, but she believed in

him and so maybe he should look into the unicorn thing more closely.

4. She loved animals and was always rescuing strays and convincing people to adopt pets, including salamanders and rats.

5. She'd told her sister she'd already picked out the song she'd dance to at her wedding, but she wouldn't say what it was in case it jinxed things.

I reviewed this list as I drove home, the air conditioner blowing chill air at my groin and hands.

At home I contemplated watching the game. The Yankees were playing tonight. Maybe I'd go to Suds. Or maybe I'd stay home and watch *Apollo 13*. I liked Ed Harris. He had the bluest eyes.

I removed my suit and headed for the shower. Its black and pink tiles a reminder of how little I'd altered this house. But renovating a bathroom was costly and inconvenient. And I could ignore the colors. Though it was still hot, I took a scalding shower. Tried to cleanse myself of the funeral, of the weeping family, and of the people who pointed as I walked past. Did they think we were taking too long to solve the murder? Did they have any idea what was involved? I rubbed harder. Then I soaped lower. My cock was up for some exercise. I pictured Ed Harris. Ran my hand along my dick and imagined his tongue was my fingers. Stroked with one hand while the other pressed the pink and black tiles, keeping me upright. Ed Harris, Ed Harris, his mouth wet and hot and Ed Harris, Ed Harris, Dr. Saunders. I grunted and convulsed. My cum hit the metal faucet, the drops white and viscous, like glue. I rinsed myself front to back, breathing hard, pleasantly empty-minded for the first time in weeks.

The bathroom's wheezy ceiling fan didn't remove much moisture. I hummed along with its loud mechanical breaths. The mirror was steamed over, drips streaking the glass. I toweled my hair as I walked to the bedroom.

Dressed in boxers and a fresh T-shirt, I sat in my recliner. I reached to my side and opened the file I'd copied at the station, my eyes peeled for witnesses. It's not good practice to make copies of in-progress case files and bring them home. I'd punish anyone I caught doing it. But I owed it to Cecilia North to close her case, and if bringing files home was the way to do it, so be it.

*It is better to beg forgiveness.* Rick's words echoed in my head.

"Amen, Leprechaun," I said, looking toward the gun safe, where his key ring was. I looked down and began reading the crime-scene notes. "Amen."

# TUESDAY, AUGUST 19TH
## 0730 HOURS

**S**uds was closed at 5:30 a.m., when I'd begun my day, so I'd had to get coffee from Dunkin' Donuts. Two large cups with sugar. "With sugar" meant they put Brazil's total export into the foam cups. But it ensured my eyes were open two hours later when Mayor Mitchell opened my door. He wore a polo embroidered with the Nipmuc Golf Course logo. Interesting fashion choice.

"Good morning, Mayor." I didn't stand.

"There was a robbery, out by Lenox Road," he said. No good mornings today.

Ah, so that's why he was here, and why he was annoyed. "Yes," I said. Another baby burglary. So called because they'd stolen the video-game system, again. And eaten all the junk food. We were betting some juvies were the criminal masterminds behind it all. This time our baby burglars had also gotten hold of a private video of the owners' "intimate relations." That had peaked my men's interest. They claimed Mrs. Peterson was super hot. I doubted Mr. Peterson would see his video-tape before some shmuck here checked its authenticity. "I'm aware of the burglary."

He always called them robberies, though the residents were never home when they occurred.

"This is the fourth in six months!" He neared my desk and stared at its chaos. "What are you doing about it?"

"My men are investigating. So far we don't have a lot to work with." A thought became a stone in my hand. A way to kill two birds. "I'll

111

assign another cop. William Thompson." I'd been looking for a way to eject Billy from the murder ever since his snow-blower joke.

"Good. Now, I know you have a murder, but we can't let the crime rate increase because we're focused on one case."

"We'll close them," I said. "Soon."

"Right, then. I'll see you at the Idyll Days committee review."

"Uh huh." No idea what he was talking about.

He asked, "You growing a beard?"

I hadn't shaved. "Maybe," I said, though I didn't plan to. "Ladies love a beard."

He waved good-bye, missing the joke. Rick would've loved that one.

The quiet lasted five minutes. My next guest was Revere. His buzz cut was freshly trimmed and his shoes polished. "Found something I thought you'd like to see." He handed me faxed pages, curled at the ends. A theft report for a Smith & Wesson .45. "Douglas Browning reported this?" I asked after I'd read the topmost fields. Donny's father. "He owned the same type of gun used in our murder?"

"He did. Before he reported it stolen."

"In 1993." Four years ago. "You found this?"

"Thought I'd check state-wide thefts."

"You having the resources." He must've called in some favors.

"Me having the resources." He relaxed his stance.

"So he owned a gun." Douglas Browning's gun was one Smith & Wesson. 45. Just one. And yet his son had seen the victim hours before her death. But the store tape showed him there for his whole shift, and the tech boys said the tape hadn't been doctored. Still, it was odd. I didn't like odd. "They have any leads on who stole it?"

"Browning blamed his cleaners. I swung by to see them. They're still upset about it. Two tiny Polish ladies." He hunched his shoulders, "They don't seem likely."

I bit my thumb. "Could be a coincidence."

"Could be."

"I hate coincidences."

He took a ballpoint pen from my desk. "They're troublesome," he said. He unscrewed the bottom cap and pulled out the ink barrel. Then rotated it. This was how he thought. He fidgeted with office supplies, like Finnegan's paperclip. Perhaps Revere was human after all.

"Let's keep this under our hats for now." I didn't need Wright haring after Douglas Browning, Esquire. Getting us embroiled in a lawsuit that bankrupted the town a second time. "Check if there's a connection between Mr. Browning and our vic. But keep it discreet."

"Sure thing." He set the reassembled pen on my desk. "You hear any more on Gary Clark's alibi?"

"Solid." Finnegan had checked it out. "All of his poker buddies said he'd been present at the game. The host's wife confirmed it, and Finnegan says she didn't like Gary much."

Revere said, "Your shirt's buttoned wrong." I looked down. The fabric on my shirt gaped. I'd matched buttons to the wrong holes. The mayor must've noticed. Great.

"Thanks. Have you seen Billy?"

"He's by the board, talking sports with Finnegan." That's all he said and all he had to. Revere thought Billy was too young. Well, I was about to make Revere happy.

"Send him in." While he fetched Billy, I fixed my shirt, and fingered my stubble. I'd shave this evening. Get tidied up.

Billy came in looking like an advertisement for milk. He had a slight sunburn. "Good morning, Chief."

"Billy, I'm reassigning you."

"What?" All his puppyish good cheer disappeared.

"I need the burglaries wrapped up. Now. You'll report to Hopkins."

"But I—"

"No buts. Report to Hopkins."

He crossed his arms. "Did I do something wrong, Chief? I know I don't have much experience, but I think I can—"

"Hoops," I said. I'd never called him that before. "Report to Hopkins."

He closed my door so quietly I didn't hear it click.

I visited the gents and pissed away half of my coffee. Then I decided to take a closer look at the gun-theft report. When I opened the door to my office, I saw I had another visitor. Mrs. Dunsmore looked at a paper, her ample hip brushing the edge of my desk.

"You've got an interview with Mr. Kelly at ten a.m. today." She stared, expectant. When I didn't reply, she said, "Patrol supervisor. Remember?"

"What's the date?" I asked. Stalling. I noticed she'd colored outside the lines today with her lipstick.

"The nineteenth. Why?"

"The nineteenth?" I blurted, my voice loud and sharp to my own ears. Shit. I'd forgotten. Rick's anniversary. How had I forgotten?

"Is something wrong?" Mrs. Dunsmore eyed me as if she suspected I'd lie.

"Fine," I said. "Everything's fine."

A year ago today, Rick and I had gotten a tip that Apollo St. James was dealing near 171st and Fort Washington Ave. We wanted to talk to him. About where he'd been when his cousin, Bertie, had died from multiple stab wounds. We'd heard rumors Apollo had been there and had seen who'd killed his cousin.

I drove, because I'd won the coin toss. Rick gave me shit about it. "Tommy, you know what the difference is between your and my grand-mother's driving skills, God rest her soul? She had balls." He laughed his crazy-high laugh until we spotted Apollo St. James.

And surprise, surprise, he was leaning into a shiny black Audi. The car faced us, idling in the northbound bus lane. Apollo's hand out-stretched. This was our lucky day. We'd have leverage. Apollo had been inside twice. This was his third strike.

I parked on the opposite side of the street, facing south. Rick and I exited the patrol car, hands at our guns' butts. "Apollo!" I shouted. He jerked out of the car.

"Hands up!" Rick yelled. "Hands up!"

The asshole driving the Audi jerked ahead and U-turned at us. Rick, midstreet, spun away from the car. I turned to catch its number as it sped away. And while I was staring at the New York plate, committing its numbers and letters to memory, Apollo was pulling the gun from his waistband.

I turned. Rick was yelling at Apollo to put the weapon down, now! I grabbed my gun. Apollo's face was sweaty. His hands shook. I looked at Rick. His mouth twitched, but his hands were steady. He hadn't used today, then. Oh, God. I hoped he hadn't.

"We just want to talk. Put the gun down." Rick kept his gun trained on Apollo's midsection. Center mass. That's where you shoot. Rick had never had to. I had. Before we were partnered.

Apollo said, "I ain't going back, man! Not for this!"

"Don't be stupid. We just want to talk."

Rick held steady and I calculated distance and collateral. There were people nearby. A young girl stood behind Apollo. A shot could easily hit her. Shit. And what if Apollo shoots? Doesn't miss? If Rick gets wounded, I'd get a new partner. Same thing if I get hurt. It would be that much easier to stay with the new guy. We'd have cases in progress. Rick would be fine. He'd be okay. But no, that wouldn't—

Is that idiot moving?

*Bam!* The sound tore my ears apart. Rick stumbled backward. *Bam!* Rick fired. I saw the smoke. *Bam!* Apollo, shooting again. People screamed, running for doors, ducking behind cars. Rick fell. I trained my gun on Apollo. *Bam!* Where had my bullet gone? He was running and I took another shot, but my hand was shaking and he was gone, around the corner, out of sight. And Rick was on the ground, bleeding. His freckles were dark against his pale skin, his breathing jagged like there was something between him and oxygen. I got on the damp asphalt beside him. "Rick! It's gonna be okay. Hang on." He coughed. That sound. I'd heard it at my grandfather's bedside. Death rattle.

I radioed for help, tripping over the words. Rick's right hand clenched closed, then opened. "Tommy?" he said.

"Easy, easy." I palmed his skull and lifted it so he could see me. His red hair was dry in my hands. His eyes greener than ever. My leprechaun partner. Sirens tore the air into pieces. I'd never been so happy to hear them.

"Rick, hang tight. They're coming. Hear them?"

But he didn't hear them. He never heard them. His heartbeat was gone and the EMTs couldn't get it back, no matter how I yelled at them. And after they declared him dead, over my protests of, "Can't you try again? Just wait! He isn't dead!" I wondered. Wondered what would have happened if I hadn't turned to look at the license plate. What if I'd been thinking more about the present and less about a future without Rick? Because that's what I got. A future without Rick.

That night I called it in on the police radio. "Station to Number 891." Rick's badge number. I heard nothing but static. "Station to Number 891." The static spiked. "Station to Number 891." No answer. "Detective Richard Coughlin is 10-7. Gone but never forgotten."

10-7 is the code for retired equipment. It's also the code for officers killed in the line of duty. You call their badge number once, twice, three times, and then declare them 10-7. Because they never answer.

"Chief Lynch," Mrs. Dunsmore said. "Chief, the applicant will be here soon."

Her words were cold water, abrupt and stinging. I blinked. "We're going to have to reschedule," I said.

Her granny glasses slid. She pushed them up and demanded to know why.

"I've got a lead on a suspect," I lied. "I can't meet the applicant."

She said, "But we've already rescheduled Mr. Kelly once."

I grabbed a notepad. "Can't be helped. Maybe someone else can interview him." There was no way I could. Not today. Not on Rick's anniversary.

# FRIDAY, AUGUST 22ND
## 0900 HOURS

**M**y next-door neighbor, Mr. Sands, asked if I had plans to put in some lettuce. He pointed with his newspaper at the weedy plot under my bedroom window.

Lettuce? Why would I stick a head of lettuce there?

"Got yourself a bit of a project there." He waved at my lawn. "We always thought a dogwood would look nice near the road, by your mailbox." He'd been mentally landscaping my lawn? "Maybe some hostas by the front porch where it's a little bare. Hostas don't take much work."

"I'll consider it," I said. Anything to get this guy away from my lawn.

"Great!" He grinned. "I told the others you were busy getting settled, and what with the murder, you hadn't had time to work out a lawn plan."

The others? The neighborhood was talking smack about my lawn? And what the fuck was a lawn plan? "Yeah, it's been very busy for such a small town."

He didn't notice the way I threw the last two words like rocks. He said, "How is the murder coming? Any leads? The missus was saying perhaps the state police ought to be brought in. You know, because of their experience with these sorts of crimes."

I looked to the house I'd wanted to escape this morning. I regretted that impulse now. "We're pursuing several lines of inquiry. And we have a state police detective assisting us with our efforts."

He saluted me with his newspaper. "Great. That's great. Well, have a wonderful day, Chief Lynch. And if you need any help with your lawn plan . . ."

"You'll be the first person I call."

He walked toward his lush lawn, cut to regulation length. There was a garden gnome near his mailbox. Now, why would I take advice from a man who liked gnomes?

Mrs. Dunsmore handed me a fresh pile of bureaucracy before I'd completed my lap around the station. One of the folders was marked "Idyll Days." Hands full, I detoured to the pen and stared at the crime board. It hadn't changed much. The Browning gun theft had led nowhere. No new connections found between Browning Senior or Junior to our victim. The Meriden crime similar to ours had no other links we could uncover. We were treading water.

Wright came and stood near my left shoulder. "I got a line." His breath smelled of stale coffee. "Anthony Fergus wasn't home watching telly when our vic died."

"You're still on Anthony Fergus?" I turned.

Wright puffer-fished his cheeks, then said, "Yes. He's scum. He likes hurting women."

"One woman. His wife. Drop it."

His phone rang. He didn't look at me. Just answered the phone with, "Idyll Police. Detective Wright." His wary face relaxed as soon as his caller spoke. "Oh, yeah. Sure, hon. When?" He extended his wrist and jangled his watch loose from his shirt's cuff. "I think so. How's he feeling? Good. See you later."

"My wife," he said. "I need to drop by the elementary school later."

"You catch the baby burglars?" I said, offering a joke.

"Nah. We finally got our kids in Idyll schools." He sounded proud. "Much better than where they are now."

"I thought you lived in Bloomfield." I'd heard him bitch about his commute.

"Moving next week. Finally found a place I can afford on what you pay me." He looked at his family photo.

I didn't say what I was thinking. Bloomfield was one of the few black towns in the state. I'd met exactly seven black people, including Wright, since I'd been living in Idyll. This town was whiter than Wonder Bread. His kids were going to be as exotic as giraffes in their new school. It's not wonderful being the odd kid out.

I cleared my throat. "Anything more on our case?"

"I have a witness who says Anthony Fergus was at Suds an hour before our victim died." He stood and walked toward the board.

"I'm sure there were plenty of people at Suds on Saturday night. Anthony Fergus isn't our guy. He had no known links to our victim. His gun is a Colt. And he isn't—" Shit. I'd almost said "the man from the cabin."

"Isn't what?" He rested his hand on Finnegan's desk. Cursed and pulled it away. Something sticky remained on the desk. He grabbed a tissue and scrubbed at his fingers.

"He isn't our guy."

"What makes you so sure? You know something we don't?"

"Wright—"

"You're not holding out on us, are you?"

He couldn't know about the cabin. He didn't. Still, I felt clammy.

"If I find out you've talked to Anthony Fergus, or so much as looked in his direction, I'll discipline you. Focus on *this* case, not the one you couldn't nail before."

He picked bits of tissue from his hand. "'Discipline,' huh?" He sat at his desk and straightened his family photo. "Don't remember hearing any discipline threats when your lapdog Billy danced around the crime scene. Or when that faggot ME conducted ballistics checks without authorization."

"Billy is a fucking rookie. You're not. Now get your goddamn head in the game or you're off the case."

Finnegan walked in, catching the last of my words. "Problem?" he said. He looked at me as he said it. Making his loyalties clear.

"Not anymore." I walked away. And under his breath I heard Wright mutter, "Racist asshole."

"What did you say?" I stomped back to his desk.

"Nothing." He leaned back in his chair, eyes wide.

"Don't you *ever* excuse your poor performance with an accusation of racism. Got it? I don't care what your skin color is or how many gods you believe in or what you like to wear at home. But I do care that you do the job and do it well."

He looked scared. Maybe because I'd gotten close while I laid it all out for him. Maybe because he could see the vein throbbing near my temple. I could feel it, threatening to pop like an overinflated balloon. I got out of there before I forgot my parents' advice about violence not being the answer to my problems.

I stayed in my office, reading the folders Mrs. Dunsmore had given me. Not that I absorbed any of the words. I was losing my grip. I'd nearly hit Wright, and before that I'd nearly told him about the cabin. I rubbed my eyes, but when I opened them nothing had changed. Maybe I'd just stay here, silent, unresponsive. How long until they sent someone inside to check on me? Hours? Days?

Someone knocked on my door. Loudly.

"Come in."

Billy and Hopkins walked in, smiling like they'd won the lottery. "We caught 'em," Hopkins said. "The baby burglars. They're getting processed now."

"Nice work," I said. "Let's have a look-see."

I followed them to the fingerprint area. Two men on the wrong side of twenty were having their fingers rolled in ink. Hopkins said, "We caught them coming out of 119 Elm, arms full of things that didn't belong to them."

"Says you," one of the men said. His bare arms were a mosaic of bad tattoos. He even had a dancing hula girl. Her lips were crooked. When I looked closer, I saw that all of her was crooked. He deserved a refund for that tat.

"Says the owner of the house," Hopkins said.

Billy said, "You were right, Chief. About them working at the houses. These guys did landscaping. They cased the homes, learned the owners' schedules, and then robbed them."

Days ago, I'd suggested they check into workers who'd had access to the robbed houses over the past year. Seems like I was capable of detective work, after all.

I clapped him on the shoulder. "Good work. By the way, did you find the videotape?" The Petersons were quite anxious that their sex tape remain private.

"No," Billy said. "But these guys have a storage unit. Hasn't been searched yet."

Hopkins stayed with the suspects. Billy followed me. "Now that I helped solve the robberies . . ." he said.

I could continue punishing him for offending me. Or I could let it go. He was young. Stupid. Maybe he'd learn. Probably not. I said, "Process them, and go home and shower. Eat something. Come back at seven."

"I can help?" he asked.

I nodded. Christ knew I could use more manpower. Revere and Wright could deal with having him underfoot. Finnegan didn't seem to mind him much.

"Thanks, Chief."

"And I mean it about the shower. Mrs. Dunsmore is complaining about our smell." Which was surprising, given her heavy-handed application of lavender perfume.

So the burglaries were closed. Now if only I could clear our homicide. I picked up the Idyll Days folder. The first page was the poster I'd seen hanging in every local business window. A picture of a family: parents with two blond, blue-eyed kids, picking apples. The title, "Idyll Days," printed in big, white letters. "September 12–14, 1997. Hay Rides! Apple Picking! Pony Rides! Crafts Fair! Bake Sale!" Everything deserved an exclamation point, including free parking. The blond family reminded me of Wright's accusation. Confronted by this poster every step, working in a station with no other minorities, was it any wonder he felt threatened? But he didn't need to lay that at my door.

My phone was blinking. Messages. I sighed. So much for Dunsmore doing her job. I hit the button.

"Chief Lynch, Doug Martin here." Revere's boss. Or his boss's boss. "Seems you're having some trouble with the girl's murder."

"Thanks, Captain Obvious," I said. I pulled out my lower desk drawer.

"We pride ourselves on having one of the highest murder-solve rates in the country."

I rooted below a pile of papers. My hand found the crinkly cellophane package. I tugged it up.

"Revere's a sharp detective. I hope you're putting him to good use. Please call me and give me an update. We'd like this one closed, stat."

I shook a cigarette free from the pack and said, "What the fuck do you think I want? A pony? Shit heel." I rummaged in the drawer for a lighter and lit the cigarette.

I smoked when I first joined the force. Everyone did. But after a few months I found it harder to breathe and, the truth was, I never took to it. So I stopped. But I still keep a pack on me. I say it's for suspects. You'd be amazed what you can get out of a guy when you offer a ciggie. But the truth is some days I need one. I feel the pull of longing under my skin. It must be something like what Rick had felt, only his need had been a thousand times worse.

I inhaled deeply, and then coughed. Shit. I sounded like Finnegan. I smacked my chest and took a shallow hit from the cigarette. The tar and nicotine and rat poison and whatever else they put in cigarettes made me feel light-headed. But calm. Calm for the first time in weeks. Maybe I should take up smoking again. Maybe then the boys here would accept me as one of their own. And maybe the moon was made of cheese.

I walked over to the window. Looked at the little plant, still struggling bravely to live. I tapped some ash onto it.

A trip of raps on my door. I heaved up the window sash and exhaled a stream of smoke into the muggy summer air. Shit. She'd smell it. I crushed out the cigarette and tossed it below. It hit some schmuck's car. Not mine.

"Just a second!" I said. I waved armfuls of air into the room. Then I walked to my desk, hid my cigarettes, and said, "Come in."

Mrs. Dunsmore entered, carrying a folder and a cup. She sniffed. "Have you been smoking?" My anti-smoking policy was the one thing we agreed on.

"What?" I said. "No."

She handed me the folder. "This is last year's Idyll Days roster. You'll need it for planning purposes." She brought her cup to the sill and said, "This plant looks dreadful." I waited for her to find the ash on it. She tipped the cup over the plant and said, "Maybe less direct sun." And moved the pot a few inches.

I exhaled. My stupid chest betrayed me, and I was racked by a series of coughs.

She narrowed her eyes. "You ought to see a doctor. You sound like Finnegan."

I nodded. She left. I wiped my hand across my mouth and vowed never to smoke again. It wasn't worth the trouble.

Determined to salvage this dog of a day, I'd check in with the detectives. Tell them we'd solved the burglaries. Maybe mend a fence post with Wright. Then we'd get on the gun. Surely we could find it. When I got near the pen, I heard Wright say my name. He said it low, like you do when you're talking shit. I stopped.

"Why'd he come here then? No way some big-city detective packs it in for this place unless he's dirty."

Finnegan said, "My money's on drugs."

More murmuring, but I couldn't pick apart the sentences. Yankowitz approached. His eyes widened when he saw me, but he held his ground. "Afternoon, Chief," he said. "Need help?"

I lurked near a file cabinet. "No, thanks." Luckily, the cabinet had a calendar featuring half-naked women. "Wrong month," I said. I flipped the pages over from May to August.

"Oh," he said. "We know. But we like Miss May best."

"I see." I let the pages fall back to Miss May, who was washing a sports car with more enthusiasm than accuracy. The suds were all over her red bikini, not the car.

Yankowitz moved on, and I took half a step closer.

"He think he's going to get some sort of medal for solving this case?" Wright asked.

Finnegan said, "Dunno. Hasn't solved it so far."

And then they started to rip into city cops. How we thought we were tougher, smarter, and better than everyone else. I pushed away from the cabinet, ready to go.

Wright said, "How many drug tests does a cop have to fail to be sent here?" Like he was setting up a joke.

Finnegan said, "How many?"

"All of them."

They laughed until Finnegan went into tubercular-attack mode. I made a beeline for the exit.

"Chief, you got a call from DPW," the desk sergeant said. "Someone's been messing with their trucks."

"I'll get back to them." I didn't break stride. I walked out the door and headed for my car, away from whispers and speculation. I'd run before, from New York to here. Tired of the guesses about what had happened that awful day between Apollo and Rick and me. Of regretting what Rick and I had talked about the prior week. My request for a transfer, away from the station and his habit.

"I heard you requested a transfer." Rick laced his shoes and double-knotted them. Just as he did each night before we left the station. He claimed his father told him a story of a cop who tripped over his laces and discharged his weapon into a Sunday church crowd. So he always double-knotted his laces. Superstitious to the last.

"Closer to home," I said. I zipped the lower half of my jacket, checked that my gun wasn't bulging. It's harder to dress a gun than it looks.

He said nothing. Just put on his sunglasses and said, "So it's the location?"

"Yup."

"Not the company?" His voice peaked. I couldn't see his eyes behind his mirrored shades. Only saw myself keeping to myself.

"Company?" I said, as if the thought had just occurred. "Of course not, Leprechaun. Don't be crazy."

He adjusted his loose belt. "Right," he said. He scratched his nose and clapped his hands, fast and hard. The noise made me jump, but I covered it by slamming my locker closed.

"Ready?" I asked.

"Always."

When we got outside, I realized why his gesture had bothered me. Rick scratched his nose when suspects told him lies. "I'll drive," he said. And he drove us to talk to Vince Reginald, the man who would lead us to Apollo St. James.

# MONDAY, AUGUST 25TH
## 1030 HOURS

Cecilia North's sister, Renee, didn't want to meet at the police station. I let her propose a spot. She picked Dunkin' Donuts. When I pulled into the lot, she was in her car, staring through the windshield at nothing. She didn't see me, so I knocked on the driver's window. She jumped. Then she opened the door. "Sorry. I must have zoned out."

We walked inside. Two customers stood in line. A couple in the corner bickered about rent payment, and the mother of two small kids wiped their faces free of sugar with thin napkins.

"What'll you have?" the young girl with the Dunkin' cap asked me.

"Coffee, black, small." I turned to Renee. "Large hazelnut iced coffee," she said. "And a plain bagel, toasted with butter." She told me, "I forgot to eat this morning."

We took our drinks and her bagel to the corner table farthest from the fighting couple. We sat facing each other. Renee's eyes darted on and around me. She tucked a strand of hair behind her ear. A gold hoop hung from it.

"You had more questions?" she asked. Finnegan had interviewed her, weeks ago. I hoped to get more from her. She sipped her drink. Renee looked more like Cecilia's cousin, her family resemblance diluted. Renee was taller, blonder, and had more oomph—as the boys liked to say. Rick used to say that when we were out, driving. "Would you look at that? That girl got some oomph!"

"It seems that your sister planned to meet someone the night she died." I kept my voice low. I didn't need the town gossip wagon hitching a ride. "Did she mention anything to you?"

"No. I didn't talk to her that day. I saw her the weekend before." She took another sip of her drink, set it down, and said, "Who was she meeting?"

"I don't know. I was hoping you might have an idea."

"Her friends would have mentioned it if they'd met her that night." She gripped her drink. "You don't think—" Her face gave it away. She thought I might consider one of Cecilia's friends to be the killer.

"No. I don't."

"Then who?"

"We're looking into it. If Cecilia had been going to meet someone and she wanted to keep the meeting private, where would she go?"

Renee broke off pieces of bagel, but she didn't eat them. "Depends. If it was a guy, maybe the woods, or Sutter's cabin. She used to meet her boyfriend, Rob, there when she was a sophomore in high school. I told her about it. It's pretty private." She bit her lip. "Rob was a good guy. I wouldn't have let her go out with someone . . ."

"It's okay. The cabin. That's a good idea." Finally, someone had mentioned the cabin in connection with Cecilia. Now I could share it with the men as a tip from the deceased's sister. We didn't have any news about the soda cans I'd submitted from there to the techs. The men still regarded the cabin as low on the list of places she might have gone before she was killed.

"Do you know if she was seeing someone?"

She assessed me. "She'd broken up with her boyfriend."

"But?" I said.

She leaned in. "I thought in July that maybe she had started seeing someone."

"Why's that?"

"She kept singing. She couldn't carry a tune if it had a handle, but she loved to sing. And she always got more singy when she was interested in a guy."

"And she was like that in July?"

"Yes, but when I asked her about it, she laughed and told me I was reading too much into it. Said she was just in a good mood. And she stopped doing it so much after that. So I thought maybe I'd guessed wrong. She never mentioned any guys." Her eyes darted toward my hand. Checking for a ring. I suspected I was getting more information not because I was a better interviewer than Finnegan but because I was better looking.

"I see. What did she sing?"

She put her hand to her forehead. "Oh, God. Songs from musicals and pop ballads. She really did have the worst voice." She squished her bagel bits into one messy ball. Butter leaked out. She wiped her hands on her jeans.

"Is it possible she was seeing a co-worker?"

Renee shook her cup. The ice rattled. "Maybe."

"Would your sister have dated someone who was married?"

Her laughter wasn't the happy sort. "Yes, sad to say. Cecilia was very trusting, and she had terrible taste in people. Really. She always assumed people were telling her the truth." She tapped her fingers. "I can see her falling for a guy with an 'unhappy marriage' no problem."

Gary Clark. Had he fed her a line about his troubled marriage? Sure, he had an alibi, but he'd also spent a lot of time in her office. Too much time.

She set her hands on her thighs. "Cecilia was sweet. But not super bright. God, that sounds bitchy. Sorry. But—" She shrugged. "We all knew it, Cecilia most of all. Poor thing. When she got to school, all her teachers were like, 'You're Renee's sister' and then, because I'd done so well, they expected the same of her. Wasn't fair, really. And my parents, they sometimes expected more of her too. They kept talking about her job like it was a stepping-stone, but I'm not sure it was. Cecilia didn't have any job passions, expect maybe for animals."

I felt a kinship to my murder victim. Her childhood sounded a bit like my own, only in reverse. John's teachers were surprised and delighted to discover that Thomas Lynch's brother did his homework without complaint and never got into fistfights.

"But she'd never have become a vet," Renee said. She rolled her straw wrapper into a tight sphere. "Veterinary school's tougher to get into than med school, and she didn't have the grades."

"Right." I was done hearing about Cecilia's academic failures. "About her job. Any trouble there?"

"Not much. I think it was kind of boring. And her boss seemed like a bitch."

"One last thing. Do you remember if Cecilia was sick this summer?"

"Sick? I doubt it. Cecilia never got sick. I'm the one who catches every cold."

"She called in sick to her job on July thirty-first."

Renee finished her iced coffee with a loud slurp. "You could ask my parents. I wasn't home all summer, just weekends mostly. I should go back to my apartment soon, but . . . I feel like as soon as I go, that will be it. It will mean she's really gone. Which is stupid, I know. She *is* really gone. But as soon as I leave, the next time I come back . . ." She lifted her head and stared at me. Her eyes were damp. She forced a smile. "I'll have to go back soon. Or the food will start leaving the apartment," she paused, "on its own feet."

"Thanks for your help," I said.

"Do you think you'll catch whoever killed her?" she asked. "I mean, do you? You don't have to say you will because I'm her sister or anything."

"Yes. I'll catch the killer."

"Good."

"Do me a favor?" I sweetened my words with a smile. "Please don't mention what we talked about to anyone, not even your parents."

"Sure. If they get too pushy, I'll lie. I'm pretty good at it, if I have time to prepare." She thought for a moment. "Cecilia was the same way."

I walked her to the parking lot, where she waved me off. Then she got in her car and sat, staring at nothing again.

When I shared my new intel, the reaction was underwhelming.

"Why'd you talk to the sister?" Finnegan asked. He tugged his tie. Annoyed.

"I wanted to see if she recalled Cecilia being sick this summer. Also, see if Cecilia told Renee about any summertime romance, if she'd had one."

"I asked her that," he said. He kicked the bottom of his desk. It had a dent from years of such abuse.

"I know. But not about her being sick. And we didn't know much about Gary Clark then."

"His alibi's still waterproof." He pointed at the board.

"Yeah," Wright said. "Anyone else you interviewing?"

"Why?"

Revere, silent until now, chimed in. "It helps to know whom you're planning to interview as part of the ongoing investigation, sir."

They all stared at me.

"It's kind of hard, not knowing what you're up to," Finnegan said. "One day you're at the autopsy—"

"I didn't see any other volunteers," I said. These fuckers. Piling on me for doing my job.

"And the next you and Billy are out bagging evidence. No word to any of us," Finnegan said. "It feels like we're competing, not cooperating."

He had a good point.

"Plus you dismiss any theories other than your own," Wright said.

"Like your harebrained scheme about Anthony Fergus?" I said.

Revere formed a "t" with his hands. Time out. "Chief, maybe if you just kept us abreast of your inquiries . . ." He let it hang there.

"Sure," I said. "I'll stop by and inform you of my movements every morning."

They weren't sure how to take this. Wright made the mistake of accepting it at face value. "Great."

"When hell freezes over," I said. "If we're going to complain, how about starting with the fact that my detectives disappear for hours and can't be raised, when major tips come to light? Wright you didn't answer when called about Mrs. Ashworth. That's why I ended up taking her statement. And Revere, while you're grabbing info from your statie pals, Billy's left to try to match gun-theft reports on his own. Something you were supposed to supervise."

"Hold on," Revere said.

"No. You hold on. You're a guest at this station. I didn't request your assistance. Now if you'd like to second-guess my work, go ahead. But do it silently."

Wright said, "My kid broke his ankle. I had to take him to the ER that day."

"You should've called in," I said. I took a few steps. Paused. Turned. "And he sprained his ankle. He didn't break it. Don't lie to me, again."

I left them to curse me. Lord knows I'd done it to my supers over the years. But I'd trusted and respected them. I had no such illusions that these men felt that way about me. They thought I was dirty. My mind walked through the woods to the Sutter cabin. The place I'd pretended never to have visited. Where I'd never seen Cecilia North the night she died. They were right. I was dirty.

# TUESDAY, AUGUST 26TH
## 1200 HOURS

Elmore Fenworth's home didn't look as though it belonged to a crazy person. It was a large, gray Victorian boasting a blue plaque that informed me it was on the register of historic places. A colorful garden surrounded his wraparound porch. His lawn would've made my neighbor, Mr. Sands, envious. Elmore sat in a rocker on the porch. I'd expected wild hair, thick glasses, and shabby clothing. He had a close beard and gray eyes. He wore khakis and a white dress shirt. "Good afternoon, Chief Lynch." He rose from his rocker. "How are you?"

"It's a pleasure to meet you, Mr. Fenworth." I extended my hand. He paused before he grasped it. His hand was dirty. No, not dirty. Stained with newsprint. Newspapers were stacked beside his rocker, a foot-tall pile of them.

"You have a nice home." Potted flowers were arranged by the front door.

"Thank you. You live up near Hilltop Avenue, don't you?"

"Yes." I wondered how, and why, he knew that.

"You should get a water filter." He held the front door open for me.

"Why's that?" Inside, the temperature fell twenty degrees. The hall was lined with photos. There was one of John Paul II and one of John F. Kennedy. So Elmore was a good, old-school Catholic. And then I recalled Nate's warning. *Don't ask him about JFK.*

"Used to be a printing press a few miles north of your place, back in the sixties. They dumped toxic stuff up there. People think it's all gone now, and that their well water's unaffected." He rotated a finger near his ear. Universal symbol for crazy. "People believe what suits them."

"What sort of toxic stuff?"

"Toluene, methyl ethyl ketone, tetrachloroethylene, and some others. Buy a filter. Put it on your kitchen tap. Bathroom tap too."

We'd arrived at the parlor. Built-in bookshelves occupied two of the four walls. Historic landscapes and framed maps hung on the others. The room wouldn't have looked out of place in a furniture catalog. Did Elmore write us letters as a joke? Surely the man who lived here didn't believe in aliens.

"Would you like some iced tea?" he asked.

"Yes, please."

He left to fetch it, and I began to snoop. I started with the books. Not one on aliens or UFOs or even space travel. Then I looked at the framed photographs. They were of a family, presumably his. There was nothing odd about them.

"Here we are." He sat and poured a stream of amber liquid into a tall glass filled with crushed ice. "I make my own. It's strong. You can add sugar if you like."

"Thanks." I sipped from the cold glass. *Strong* was not the word. *Lethal* was. I reached for the sugar spoon and kept reaching until there was a quarter inch of sugar silt at the bottom of my glass.

"I'm guessing this isn't a social call." He drank his iced tea straight.

"No. I heard you might be able to help me, with an investigation." I'd debated coming here. Sure, he might know things about Idyll's gay scene. But was he reliable? And could he be trusted to keep his mouth shut?

"What sort of investigation?" he asked. He picked up a pen and pad of paper.

I breathed in and out. "I have information that two homosexual males—"

He guffawed. "You mean gays? No need for polite cop-speak here, Chief."

I rotated my shoulders down and back. "They might have witnessed something pertinent. But I'm not familiar with the area's gay scene."

He said, "Gays 'round here keep to themselves. Idyll's not exactly queer-friendly. People like to talk liberal, but talk's easy. Cheap too." He finished half of his tea. "That cop of yours, Wright. He ever tell you what happened when he started to work here? The station got calls every day for weeks that a black man had stolen a police cruiser. They had to run a front-page story about him in the *Register* so people would know he was a cop."

Christ. No wonder Wright had a chip on his shoulder.

"About my problem," I said. "I don't know where to begin looking." I held up my hand. "I don't intend to persecute anyone."

"Of course not. You hardly would, now would you?" What did *that* mean? He set his glass down and stood. "Just a moment."

He returned with an oversized, leather-bound album. He handed it to me. Heavy. And old. The leather flaked in patches. He said, "Turn to the middle bit." I turned pages until I'd reached roughly the middle. Found an illustration of a spacecraft. Turned the page. A list of alien-abduction reports, beginning in 1912. Turned the page. In flowery script was a list of names. At the top it read: "Idyll Defense Troops." I scanned the list.

"This list says 'Idyll Defense Troops,'" I said.

He chaffed his hands. "So it is! You see, homosexuals will be the first line of defense against an alien attack. Gay men are immune to their pheromone-based persuasion."

"'Pheromone-based persuasion'?" I asked.

"You know, chemicals given off to indicate sexual availability and genotype information. That's what they'll use to subdue people. Gay men aren't susceptible to them in the same way as heterosexuals. They've done studies, in Sweden."

He was crazy as a shit-house rat. "So this is a list of all of the gay people in Idyll?" Maybe he'd made some lucky guesses. But half of the list was probably useless.

"Able-bodied gay men in the local area," he said. "Quite frankly, gentlemen of Major Allen's age won't be much help to us."

Major Allen? The tottering WWI vet they'd paraded down Main

Street on Memorial Day? Why did Elmore think he was gay? "How do you know—?"

"That he's gay? Well, he had a longtime friend with whom he used to go birding and fishing every month for nearly thirty years. He never brought back a fish and couldn't tell the difference between a house sparrow and a Carolina wren. Honestly. Plus, he used to order gentlemen's magazines from Europe. They were always marked as academic journals. Lucky goose never got caught. Good thing, too. He's too kind a soul to have survived it."

"How do you know about the journals?" I asked.

"Mrs. Wilton, who runs the post office, is a close friend." Wonderful. The postmistress was feeding the local nutter private information.

I said, "This list is of able-bodied men. So, young?"

"Under sixty-five and physically fit. Though Bert Lawrence is on there and he's seventy-two. He makes Jack LaLanne look like a wimp."

Mrs. Ashworth hadn't guessed the golf-course men's ages. But able-bodied and under sixty-five was a good place to start. I'd exclude Bert Lawrence. Fit or no, I doubted he was up to midnight golf-course exploits.

I scanned the list. Mr. Gallagher and Mr. Evans, the owners of the local candy store. Anyone could've guessed their sexual preference. More names. Some I recognized. Officer Klein was on here. Some I didn't. All these people. A charge ran through me. So many names. It couldn't be right. Elmore was crazy. But if it was . . . I felt a low hum of delight. I wasn't alone in Idyll. Not by a long shot.

Dr. Saunders was near the bottom of the page. His name had an asterisk after it. A footnote explained that Dr. Saunders wasn't "local."

"Dr. Saunders?" I said.

"As a medical examiner, he'll be invaluable. He can do alien autopsies."

I scanned the room again. This time for weapons. Always best to know whether the lunatic across from you might be armed. No guns in sight and no fire pokers, either.

I flipped the page. The list ran to two sheets. My heart stopped

when I reached the bottom of the second one. My name. Thomas
Lynch.

"This list," I said. "Where do you keep it?" Visions of his house
being burgled, of this book made public, made my heart race. My
printed name grew bolder and darker on the page. Jesus. The damage
this list could do.

"In a safe, hidden. It would do me as much harm as you if this got
out."

"How so?"

"People would be angry, and it would utterly ruin my defense
plans."

My chest tightened. Was this what a heart attack felt like? "Why
am I on this list?"

He smiled. "You're gay." He templed his fingers.

"What makes you think that?"

He held up his index finger. "You're forty-four years old. Never
been engaged or married. No serious girlfriends, aside from Helen
what's-her-name in high school."

How the hell did he know about Helen Mayes?

He lifted another finger. "You read *Men's Health*, presumably 'for
the articles.'"

He'd been checking me out. Like I was a perp. He raised his hand.
"I have more conclusive evidence, but I don't think we need to get into
that."

"You have copies of this evidence?" I set the book down.

He held up his hand. "Chief, you have it all wrong. We're on the
same side. I'll make you a copy of the list, for your investigation." He
paused. "But I want something in return."

"Why should I believe this list is anything more than your imagination run amok?"

"Because you do believe it, don't you?"

I did. Gut feeling. And seeing my name. "What do you want?"

"Tell me about what's stored in the basement of the police station."

Oh, God, the alien remains. "I've only been down there twice."

I helped myself to more iced tea. The taste had grown on me. "I was fetching buckets to put throughout the station. The roof leaks."

"I know." Of course he did. He probably had the station's floor plans tacked to his bedroom wall. Where he could study them before he fell asleep each night.

"There was a large collection of rusting bicycles, some tools, and a few dog cages. I didn't see much else down there."

"Any signs?" he said. "Road-works signs?"

"Yes. The kind they put up for emergency detours."

"Aha!" He wrote a note on his pad of paper. "As I suspected." He reached for the leather album. "I'll need a tour, of course."

"A tour?"

"Of the station."

Mrs. Dunsmore would have a conniption. She thought Elmore was a public nuisance. "But—" I said.

He closed the album. "You want something and I want something." He reminded me of a boy from grade school who'd made me trade my Ernie Banks baseball card just for the chance to use his Satellite Shoes.

"Okay, but it'll have to be late." After Mrs. Dunsmore was gone.

He stuck his hand out. The newsprint stains were gone. He must've washed up earlier. I squeezed harder than necessary. He smiled and stood. "I'll bring your copy to the station," he said. "When shall we meet?"

Crafty fucker. Didn't trust me to do my part. "Ten p.m. Come to the rear of the building."

He saluted me. "I look forward to it." He stood. "Might I say you're a vast improvement on the last police chief?"

"Really?" I smoothed my shirt as I rose from my chair.

He snorted. "That one chased every skirt his stubby arms could reach. He'd have been no use at all during an invasion."

## 2345 HOURS

I opened my kitchen door and stepped inside. My shoe struck an ant trap. It skittered across the floor and smacked the trashcan. Lately, objects kept appearing where I didn't recall placing them. My badge on the counter, not beside my recliner. Rick's key ring outside my gun safe. This stupid ant trap. Maybe I'd moved it. I didn't know.

I'd never been the smart one, not in my family. But I'd always trusted my gut. Cops respect that. Intuition. Mine was flawed now, suspect to second guesses. It reminded me of those last months with Rick, my eyes on him at crime scenes, checking him for twitches, grabby hands, or speedy talk. My mind divided in half by worry. I couldn't survive that again.

I opened the refrigerator and pulled out a beer. After my tour of the station's basement with Elmore, my well of patience had run dry. He'd insisted I open every cobwebbed door so he could peer inside. He took pages of notes. And we'd seen nothing more exciting than a mouse. But he'd seemed pleased. That made one of us.

For my troubles, I had his list. I sucked down a mouthful of beer. I wouldn't look at it. Not tonight. It made me anxious. But I planned to use it. To see if any of the listed men could've been on the Nipmuc Golf Course the night of August 9th. Figure out if they owned or had access to a Smith & Wesson .45. Put that way, it didn't sound bad. It sounded like police work. So why did I feel like drinking the remaining seven beers now?

I'd locked the list up, once I'd traded my uniform for sweats and a fresh tee. Mine smelled like I'd been running, for days.

My answering machine blinked. I debated hitting the delete button. Curiosity overcame caution.

"Chief Lynch? It's Renee North. I, um, didn't catch you at the station. I hope you don't mind me calling you at home. I, um, I found something. Cecilia wrote the name Gary in her diary. Seems like she'd been seeing him since June. So I was right. She was dating somebody."

I grabbed a pen and wrote her number as soon as she got to it. It was late, but her call had come only twenty minutes ago. I dialed the number.

"Renee?" I said. "Chief Lynch. You still have the diary?"

She didn't want to give it up. She felt guilt-wracked having read it. She cried. I waited her out, and then I told her how helpful the diary would be, how it would help us put her sister's killer behind bars. I didn't point out that her sister was past feeling embarrassment, or any other emotion. Dehumanizing her sister was no way to win Renee's cooperation.

She agreed to meet me at my house, despite the hour. When she showed up, her face was puffy. She held the diary to her chest, her feet planted on the threshold. "Come in," I said, waving her toward my living room. She walked slowly, looking around. When she spotted my recliner, she said, "So you *are* a bachelor." As if she'd had a bet with someone about my romantic status.

"How'd you guess?" I pointed to the recliner. "My sister-in-law keeps threatening to burn it someday."

She glanced at the flower-print loveseat. "You picked this out?" She sat on its very edge, not making herself at home.

"It came with the place." I ran my hand down its armrest. "I'm thinking it might come back in fashion."

Her eyes widened, and then she laughed. "Oh, God, I thought you were serious for a second." Her grip on the diary relaxed.

"I grew up in New York, so I've always lived in an apartment. I wasn't ready to furnish a whole house."

"Huh," she said. "How long have you lived here?"

"Seven months." Seven months. Seemed incredible. Felt like I'd arrived two weeks ago.

"Seven months?" She tapped the arm of the loveseat, holding the diary in one crooked arm. "Maybe you ought to upgrade." She scuffed her sneakers against the mostly clean beige carpet.

"Maybe," I said. "Décor isn't my strong suit."

She let the diary fall to her lap. "Well, beige carpeting went out last decade, and your recliner was never in fashion."

I pretended to take notes. "Thanks for those helpful hints. Now, may I?" I extended my hand.

She covered the diary with both hands. "I'm sorry," she said. "It's just . . . I feel like I'm betraying her. I know it's stupid."

"It's not stupid," I said. "Come into the kitchen. Want a drink?"

"Sure," she said. "What do you have?"

I opened the fridge. "Water, milk, orange juice, and beer."

"That's two more beverages than I would've bet you had." She peered over my shoulder. "Is that a vegetable I see?"

"My desk sergeant keeps pushing farm goods on me. And I keep putting them in the fridge. Waiting them out."

She sat at the kitchen table. Moved aside a stack of junk mail and set the diary down. "You can eat them, vegetables. They make you big and strong." She blushed.

"So I hear. Water?"

"Make it a beer."

I grabbed two bottles and opened them using a Yankees gadget John gave me for my birthday. She pointed to it. "Be careful. That could get you beaten up 'round here."

I cocked a brow. "You think I'll get beat up?" I flexed a bicep.

She blushed redder. "There are some rabid Red Sox fans who aren't very bright. They might try to start something." Her eyes returned to my bare arms.

I handed her the beer. She took a ladylike sip. I sat down, and slid the diary to me. "Where am I looking?" I asked.

She exhaled so hard her hair fluttered. "Late June. The twenty-sixth," she said.

As I flipped pages, I asked, "So where did you find this?"

"There's a loose panel in her closet. We used to store stuff there as kids. Treasure. Candy, mostly, and some cheap jewelry. Stuff from our Easter baskets." She smiled at a memory. I paged through April and May. Cecilia didn't keep a daily account of her activities. "Anyway, Mom was talking about cleaning out some of Cecilia's things, and I thought I'd check the panel, just in case there was something there she wouldn't want found."

"She has a vibrator hidden beneath her mattress." I didn't look up.

"How did you know that?"

"I checked her room, looking for clues. It's a common hiding spot."

"Thanks," she said. I imagined she'd clear it out soon, before her parents stripped the bed and washed the sheets. It could take them months, years. But better safe than sorry.

And the idea of it brought me back to Rick, lacing up his shoes. Double-knotting them. We were talking of our deaths. Our last wishes. Normal stuff. And I said, "Hey, if I bite it, go to my apartment and empty the blue waste bin."

"Why?"

"My porn is there."

He tapped my forehead. "Bright boy. Will do." And he'd meant it. If I'd taken a bullet, he would've rushed to my place and found that waste bin, tucked beneath a rolling cart. He would've disposed of the magazines, the videos, and the incriminating, large dildo.

My stash was now tucked in that same bin at the back of the guest-bedroom closet. But there was no one to empty it for me now. My family, perhaps. But no friend.

"June twenty-sixth," Renee said, interrupting my vision of my brother looking at the dildo, surprise all over his face.

"Right."

I found the page.

## JUNE 26, 1997

Processed five new employees today. One of them was handsome, but a jerk. He complained about his parking spot. As if I control the assignments. Ms. O'Donnell made a comment about the length of my skirt today. I think she's a deeply unhappy woman.

Renee was right. Cecilia was generous in her assessments of others. I'd have classified Ms. O'Donnell as a jealous bitch.

## JULY 1, 1997

Good day! Got a free bagel this morning. Think the coffee-counter guy likes me. And someone else, maybe. Gary, the hot new guy, apologized for his behavior last week. Says he's going through a rough patch but that he shouldn't have taken it out on me. Promised to make it up to me sometime. Ate lunch with Jenna today. She's so funny. I asked her what actor she'd pick to marry and she had no idea! Mine's Brad Pitt. I kept listing actors, but she kept saying she didn't know them and they wouldn't marry her anyway. She takes things too seriously.

## JULY 4, 1997

Watched the fireworks with Mom, Dad, and Renee. Felt like we were kids, especially when Mom warned me and Renee to watch out for traffic. I swear, she still thinks we're in grade school. Saw Will Thompson in uniform. Renee teased me. Kept saying, "Look, your boyfriend!" I smacked her arm to get her to stop pointing. Will's handsome, but he seems young. I think I'm into older men now.

"Your sister liked Will Thompson?" Billy. Our Billy.

Renee said, "She used to follow him like a puppy when she was young. Watched him practice his skateboard tricks for hours. Poor Will. He was always so nice, but she was just his kid sister's friend, you know?"

So Cecilia had a crush on Billy. And he knew. No wonder he wanted on the case.

## JULY 7, 1997

Gary asked me out for a drink after work! I said yes. What will I wear? I don't want another lecture from Ms. O'Donnell on the length of my skirt.

## JULY 9, 1997

Work boring. Mr. Smythe cannot remember any of his passwords. Seemed like forever til the day ended. I waited a bit for Gary to be done. We drove in our own cars to a place in Vernon. I had a glass of red wine. He paid. Said it was the least he could do. He told me he's married. I knew that from his file. (Yes. I snooped.) His wife was his college sweetheart. But now they can't have kids and she blames him. He says they barely speak to each other at all anymore. He's lonely. Now that he's got a new job, he hardly knows anyone. I said I could show him around, and he said I was the nicest person he's met in ages. He stared at me the whole time. His eyes are like the ocean.

I skimmed, turning pages. Three days later, she slept with him. Instead of an ecstatic description, she wrote: "Not what I expected. He was fast in bed."

I chuckled.

"You get to her sexual critique?" Renee asked.

"Sorry."

She waved her hand. "Don't be. It made me laugh, too. Cecilia could always make me laugh. She did great impressions. That's probably another reason the teachers didn't love her. Got caught imitating them once too often."

"I had disciplinary problems in school," I said. I took a long pull from my bottle.

"Bully?" she asked.

"Anti-bully. I beat them up so they'd stop picking on the little ones."

"Ah, so you were born to be a cop, to do good."

"I don't think my teachers saw it that way. They thought I had self-control issues."

"Do you?"

"No." I tilted forward on my chair. "I'm a self-controlled, functional member of society."

"Who really needs to rehab his house. I didn't even know they still made fridges that color," she said.

"I don't think they do. It's the last of its kind."

"Thank God."

"Hey, now," I said, all indignation.

"Sorry. I'll stop picking on your abominable taste in furnishing as soon as I ask what is up with your coat rack?"

"I think a child made it."

"A dim-witted one with poor motor skills?" She slapped her hands over her mouth to stifle her laughs. "I'm sorry." Her laughter turned to hiccups.

"Probably."

Her hiccups evolved into tears. Some hard-asses at the old precinct melted under a woman's tears. Me? I just fetched toilet paper from the bathroom and offered it to her.

"Thanks," she said. She blew her nose.

I sat and waited. She settled in two minutes. Took another sip of beer. "God, I'm sick of crying. My nose is going to fall off soon. Just secede from the rest of me if I keep it up." She patted it. It was a good nose. And she knew it.

"I doubt that will happen." I glanced at the clock. "It's late." It was. Half past two in the morning. I'd convinced her to drive over right away. Not very chivalrous of me.

She yawned. Nodded. "Yup. So it is. Hope I'm okay to drive."

She'd only drunk a third of her beer.

"I'll vouch for you," I said, taking her elbow and tugging upward.

"Don't suppose you have a guest room?" She was half slurring her words now. Over reaching. She was confusing our intimacy for the sexual kind.

"I do. It's filled with boxes."

She subtly resisted my forward push, but I was stronger. "Thank you," I said. "You did the right thing, bringing the diary to me."

Her face collapsed, as if it had sprung a leak of air. "Every day I feel like I'm losing more of her. It's stupid because she's dead and I can't lose her more. But I guess I mean that soon I'll wake up and I won't even forget to remember she's not alive." She leaned into me. I let her. I rubbed circles onto her jean-jacket-clad back.

"I know," I said. And I did. Because I could still remember the morning I woke up and thought, "Rick's dead," and there was no hesitation or doubt. I'd thrown the nearest thing to hand against a wall. It had been an alarm clock. The breaking plastic did little to console me.

"Is it stupid to want the hurt to last?" she asked. Her eyes were pink-rimmed.

I opened the door. The night air was cool. The moon, a half circle in the sky. It always looked sadder when half full. I walked Renee to her car. Closed her door. Watched her drive away.

I stood, my arms prickled with cold, and whispered, "If it's stupid to want the hurt to last, I'm the world's biggest idiot."

# WEDNESDAY, AUGUST 27TH
## 0835 HOURS

**M**rs. Dunsmore had rearranged my desk. Folders were stacked in piles. Atop one was a sticky note that read URGENT. I glanced inside. Idyll Days stuff. Should I draft a memo to her defining *urgency*? I could list examples including fire, plague, and masked gunmen.

"Chief Lynch?" A male voice interrupted my daydream. The man with his hand raised to knock on my open door was Mr. North. He wore a flannel shirt that made his hazel eyes browner. Cecilia's eyes. It's a little disorienting, seeing the features of the dead repeated in the living.

"How may I help you, Mr. North?" I gestured to a chair, but he didn't sit. Had Renee told him about the diary?

"I wanted to know how the case is coming. My daughter's murder investigation." His hands moved convulsively. He glanced at my desk. I was grateful for Mrs. Dunsmore's tidying. There were no autopsy or crime-scene photos on display.

"Mr. North, we're continuing our investigation. Pursuing leads. I can't share the details with you." I used my patient tone. He was grieving. He wanted answers. And not the kind I had. But I wasn't the only one withholding information. Apparently Renee hadn't mentioned our conversation to her father.

"I'm her father."

"I can't share details of an investigation with family members. I'm sorry."

"Can you at least tell me if you have a suspect?"

"No."

His mouth twitched. "No, you can't tell me, or no, you don't have a suspect?"

"I can't. I'm sorry."

"Sorry?" He moved closer. "Everyone says nothing has happened, that you haven't questioned one person in connection with her murder. Instead, you've run around town chasing men who steal video games."

"Sir, I understand that you're upset." I kept my tone low, even. He'd run out of steam, soon enough. They all did, eventually.

"Upset? My daughter is dead. And the person who shot her is still out there." He waved his arm toward the open door. "And he's happy! Because he got away with it. Don't tell me you understand. Tell me you've found her killer."

Through the doorway I saw a small crowd had assembled. Damn gawkers. "Sir, I think perhaps you should go home."

He said, "I think you should—"

"Mr. North?" Mrs. Dunsmore appeared at his elbow, a steaming cup in her hands. "Would you care for a cup of coffee? I was just having some. I could pour you another."

He started and looked down at her creased face. Then he brushed his shirtfront and said, "No, I, no, thank you." He left the room and the spectators scuttled.

"Poor man," she said. We watched him walk away. His posture had slackened, his head and shoulders bowed low.

"Thanks," I said. Her timing had been impeccable.

Mrs. Dunsmore turned to me. "Word has it you paid Elmore Fenworth a visit."

"Yes." Small town. I should've known word would get out.

"What about?" she asked.

None of your damn business.

She continued. "I hope you've managed to convince him we're not hiding the remains of extraterrestrials."

I don't think I had. Though there was no evidence of aliens in our basement, Elmore had seemed encouraged by his visit.

Annoyed by my silence, she huffed and said, "Have you reviewed the folders? The Idyll Days review committee meets tonight. Seven p.m., Porter Room, Town Hall. You'd better be up to speed."

Was she serious? I sighed. "You heard Mr. North. You think I should spend hours reading about the pony-ride location rather than work his daughter's murder?"

She blew at the steam escaping her coffee cup. "Very well. You solve the murder, and I'll create the work detail." She picked up the folders.

"Deal."

So Dunsmore knew I'd visited Elmore. What other visits had she and the town gossips logged? I tugged at a hangnail. If they paid careful attention, they'd notice a pattern soon. All men. Mostly single. With one common denominator. Shit. I tugged harder, and the hangnail came loose. Blood welled in the exposed slit of raw skin.

"Oh, here," she said, handing me a pink message slip. "Techs called earlier. Something about a button."

A button? She was gone by the time I remembered. The button from the cabin. I'd grabbed it along with the Coke cans. I swung by the pen. Wright was on the phone. He looked up when I came in, then back down. I hadn't forgotten what he'd said about me being dirty. Revere sat, tracing an area map, muttering under his breath.

They didn't like me. So what?

I set Cecilia North's diary on Revere's desk. He glanced at it. "What's this?"

"Victim's diary. Her sister brought it to me last night."

He cracked the cover. "Anything good?"

Wright had the phone to his ear, but he was listening to us.

"Just the details of her affair with Gary Clark."

"No shit," Wright said. Whoever was on the phone heard him. "Sorry. I have to go. Call you back." He hung up.

"Get Finnegan in," I said. "Start reviewing Clark's alibi. I'm going to visit the techs. Seems they might have some info on the button I found at the cabin."

"Bring them sugar," Revere advised, looking up from the diary.

"They live off it." His words were warmer. Maybe we weren't friends. But we were no longer enemies.

I followed his advice and picked up two boxes of donuts, bear claws, and crullers. Sure enough, the techs loved it. They mumbled their thanks through full mouths.

When I asked about my button, I was directed to a dark-eyed man who looked like a lumberjack. He gave me a once-over and said, "New here?" He was fit. Had nice teeth. He needed a haircut, though.

"A recent addition to Idyll," I said.

He gave me another going over, eyes lingering on my groin. "Welcome to the neighborhood. I'm Mike Shannon."

"Thomas Lynch."

We shook hands. As I pulled away, he ran his middle finger across my palm. A jolt shot through me.

"A pleasure." My pants were tight. I adjusted my stance. "Now, about my report?"

"You want Dave." He pointed to a corner. "Good luck." His tone implied I'd need it.

The corner was an alternate universe. Cartoons featuring crime scenes covered two walls. Star Wars figures were arranged in rows on a low bench. Dave, a pale man in a lab coat, fiddled with a microscope and ignored me. His mug had a chemical equation on it I didn't understand. Beside it, six nutrition bars were stacked.

"Do you want something, or do you enjoy hovering over people while they work?" He turned. He had a face full of freckles and wore glasses thicker than double-paned windows. The freckles formed shapes. Near his right eye, I saw a bear.

"Cruller?" I offered the last of the treats.

"You know what's in that thing?" He reached for a nutrition bar. "Six grams of saturated plus trans fat. That's a third of your day's worth." He unwrapped his bar. "Whereas this little bar has twenty percent of my protein and only three grams of fat." Perhaps, but it looked like raisin-studded feces.

"You did a report for me, on a button found at the Sutter cabin?" I asked.

"Which?"

I had the report request. I recited the number for him.

His eyes got bigger behind his lenses. "Ah, right. It came from a pale-blue Ralph Lauren man's dress shirt. Style 4281906."

"You sure?"

He rolled his eyes. "No, I just guessed." He slapped his palm to his forehead. "Of course, I'm sure. We have a guy in the office with a similar shirt. From there it was just a matter of search and match."

"That's great. What about the soda cans?"

"No joy. Your girl's prints weren't on either can."

Shit. I couldn't place her at the cabin without saying I'd seen her there.

He bit his bar. Whatever it was made of, it required lots of chewing. He swallowed. He swiveled his chair and rolled it to a file cabinet. A magnet on it read THE NERDS WILL INHERIT THE EARTH. He looked at the files. "Here." He pulled one out. "You thought the victim was near Hought's Pond. The gravel in her sneakers is conclusive. They have a special type of rock, imported when they first landscaped the area, ages ago. The only other place she would've encountered it would be in Vermont."

"That's great!" From the pond to the cabin was a logical leap. I'd have preferred fingerprints on the soda can, but this would do.

He said, "You want the fiber report too?"

I checked my report. "There's nothing about fibers in here."

"You didn't ask. I thought of that myself. The cabin and the golf course are miles apart. I figured if she was in a car, maybe her clothes had fibers from it. Her shoes were unlikely. Fibers only stay there between five and thirty minutes. After that—" he closed his hand and then opened his fingers, "*poof!* Gone."

"Did you find car fibers on her clothes?"

"Yup." He bit the bar and took his time chewing. He was enjoying this little power play.

"And?" I said.

He picked up a pen. Clicked and unclicked the end. "She had fibers on the seat of her pants and the left arm of her shirt."

"Can you match it to a car type?"

"I can do better than that. Using polarized light, cross-sectioning, and dye extraction, I found your car." He pushed his glasses up. "It's a Honda Accord. Gray. Brand-new model. That gave me some trouble. I was checking the ninety-sixes. They changed the upholstery in the new model."

"You're sure?"

He brushed a crumb from his lab coat. "Dye extraction doesn't lie."

"Can I have a copy of that report?"

"Sure."

I tucked the warm copy papers inside my jacket and dialed Jenna Dash from a phone in the lab's hallway. She was surprised to hear from me. Even more surprised by my lunch invitation. We agreed to meet at a small Italian place she recommended near her work.

⁝⁝⁝

I was sitting at an off-balance table, deciding between chicken parmigiana and gnocchi, when she came in. She smelled of pencil shavings and her hair was down.

"So," she said, picking up her menu.

"Relax," I said. "Take a minute. Get a drink. Place your order." When our server arrived, he welcomed Jenna and asked what we'd have. She ordered a Caesar salad. I chose the gnocchi. "You ought to have more than a salad," he said to Jenna. "You're gonna disappear. You don't eat enough protein." She turned red and said she was fine. She leaned against the table and it tipped toward her. The waiter apologized and stuck a matchbook under one of the legs. He said sorry again and left, looking over his shoulder. He liked her. Her face showed no recognition. She didn't realize. Civvies are so damn unobservant.

I told Jenna about Gary and Cecilia's relationship.

"Oh," she said, eyes glued to the waterproof, gingham tablecloth. "I wondered. I mean, he was *very* familiar with her. But she never said, so I didn't want to speculate."

Then I told her how Gary had lied to us. She'd been in his car the night she died. Jenna listened, her hands folded in her lap. When I'd finished, she said, "How can I help?"

"Has anyone else been talking about him at work? Any gossip?"

"I don't really mingle at work." She tucked her hair behind her ears. Right. She'd said as much, before.

"Maybe you can see if everything seems kosher. Any complaints from other female staff, that sort of thing."

"I don't have access to HR stuff. In fact, I only have access to the studies I run, except—" She bit her lip. "I could review his accounts. I shouldn't be able to, but I got access months ago for a report I was running and they forgot to close me out. The IT guys are too busy playing around in chat rooms to monitor that stuff." I couldn't ask her to look at his private files. She said, "I doubt it will be of help, but I'll take a look tonight. You think he killed her?"

"He was having an affair with her. He lied about it, and now she's dead. We call that a one-plus-one where I work."

She considered it. "A one-plus-one. Huh."

I didn't talk about the case after our food came. I asked about her background and whether she thought she'd stay in insurance. She said it was good for now, but she might like to get her Master's in information science. "Don't suppose you'd like to be a cop?" I asked.

Her hair fanned out as she shook her head. "Um, no. It seems kind of macho, and besides—"

"Yes?"

"I'd look terrible in the uniform."

I lowered my voice. "Here's a secret. All cops look terrible in uniform. That's why everyone wants to be a detective. So they don't have to wear one."

"You look good in your uniform." She coughed. "I mean, it suits you."

"Thanks, but even I wanted to be a detective to get out of it." Both true and not. One of my happier days was putting on a uniform the day I graduated the academy. But I'd enjoyed trading the required polyester blend for a bad shirt of my own. Was happy to move from busting check kiters and spouse abusers to locking up killers. It felt grander, more important. Just doing this: getting background on Gary Clark, felt right. I hadn't prevented Cecilia North's death. I might have precipitated it with my cabin intrusion. But I could nail the son of a bitch who'd killed her. Earn back my uniform.

## 1600 HOURS

When I reached the station, I went straight to the pen. Billy was sorting messages from the tip line into piles labeled: Follow up, Maybe, and Crazy Town. So they'd found a use for him. "Hi, Chief," he said. "How's things?" Apparently he didn't think I was dirty. Not with that smile.

"As I'm sure you know, the victim's father paid a visit to our station today," I said. Everyone but Revere straightened. Finnegan pulled at his lapels; making his suit skew to the right. "He was upset, and he had a right to be."

Billy said, "That's not fair."

Revere said, "Yes, it is. We've got bupkis. No murder weapon. No forensics to tie to a suspect."

"We have forensics now." I told them about the dress-shirt button. "Plus, lab rats found fibers on Cecilia's clothes. They came from a gray 1997 Honda Accord."

"Holy shit," Finnegan said. He knew what Gary drove, thanks to his car-accident story. "She was in Gary Clark's car?"

"The night she died," I said. "So let's get everything we can on him. Pronto. Billy, stop playing with those papers. Help Wright."

"With what?" Wright asked.

"With Clark's work history. Any accusations of sexual harassment? Cecilia probably wasn't his first office romance. How's his home life? What's the wife do?"

Revere asked, "What should I do?"

"Check to see if he owns or has access to a gun."

"You gonna pull him in?" Revere picked up a rubber band. Began stretching it.

"I'd like more evidence before we tip our hand."

"He's got an alibi," Wright said. He hadn't moved an inch. Billy watched him, awaiting orders.

"I'm going to bust it. Finnegan, you got the names and addresses of his poker buddies?"

He did. He gave me the list.

"What makes you think you're gonna break his alibi?" Wright asked. He had that tone he'd used on Revere. The one that asked, why do you think you're better than me? God, he had a complex. And I was tired of coddling it and him.

"One of these guys will recant his statement. Once I apply some pressure."

He made a noise. Not quite a snort. Not quite a cough. "Wright, you got something you want to say?" I asked.

He said, "No."

I took a step closer to his desk. "Didn't think so. You're the kind that prefers to talk behind a man's back. Accuse a cop of being dirty, but never ask him outright." His eyes got big. Finnegan wriggled in his chair, like a worm on a hook.

Revere looked from one to the other. "You guys thought he was dirty?" He pointed to me. Billy stared, open-mouthed. They said nothing. Revere gave an aw-shucks shake of his head. "You could've asked me," he said. "I'd have told you he wasn't." Under his breath he said, "You think I didn't check?"

"How were we—" Wright began.

"Shut up," Finnegan said. "Sorry, Chief." His face got extra bulldog jowly as he offered the apology.

"Right. Have any of Clark's friends done time?" I asked him.

Finnegan tugged his earlobe. "Nah. They're a clean-cut bunch. Nine-to-fivers with mortgages and families." He sounded relieved I'd brought the talk back to business.

"Any of them divorced?" I asked.

"One, I think. Pat Davenport."

"Custody issues?"

He said, "No idea. Didn't come up. Why?"

Why? Because I was looking for leverage. I needed a weakness to exploit. And a man's custody privileges are a good bet. Assuming he loves his kids.

Pat Davenport loved his kids. He had photos of them all over his office. It appeared that his gap-toothed daughter fancied T-ball, and his toddler son enjoyed drooling.

He had a corner office on a used-car lot. Giant banners outside advertised once-in-a-lifetime sales and crazy-low financing. The banners shifted and swayed in the wind.

"Detective," he said.

"Chief of police," I said.

"Chief." He sat after I did. "How may I help you?"

"Your kids?" I pointed to a picture of the two, leaning drunkenly into each other beneath an over-decorated Christmas tree.

His eyes flicked to the photo. His face relaxed. "Yeah."

"Must be a handful."

He looked away from the photo. "They can be."

I looked outside, where a balloon arch swayed over a row of Jeeps. "How's business?"

His face tightened. "Good. Look, Chief, can I help you with something?" He arranged objects on his desk, trying to look casual. Failing big time.

"You know what the punishment for obstruction of justice is?" I said. His whole body tensed. "I don't. Sentencing isn't really my area. But I can tell you this. Men who have every-other-weekend custody of their kids often find they have no custody after they've been charged with a crime." I drummed my fingers on his desktop. "Sad how society always favors mothers in these cases, isn't it?"

"Why are you threatening me?" Sweat dotted his upper lip.

"I'm not threatening you, Mr. Davenport. We found out that Gary Clark wasn't playing poker with you as you testified. There will be consequences. But hey, no custody means you'll have a lot of free time, am I right? You can play poker all weekend."

"I don't have anything to say." His hands weren't steady. He was on the edge and just needed a tiny nudge.

"You know, before I file a report, maybe I'll call your ex-wife. Let her know what you've been up to. Family court is really the proper place to rearrange custody-visitation issues, right?"

"All right!" He held up his hands. "Okay! Gary left the game early."

A surge of energy made it hard to remain sitting. "So when did he leave?" My foot tapped the floor.

"Nine p.m. Sometime around then. We'd barely eaten the pizzas when he got a call and told us he had to go."

"Did he say why?"

"No."

"But you knew." I drummed my fingers.

He winced. "Yeah. We all did. He was seeing a girl from his office. He asked us to keep our mouths shut, so we did."

"Even when you knew the girl had been murdered."

He ran his hands through his receding hair. "Look! Gary isn't violent. I swear. He wouldn't hurt a fly."

"You'll need to come to the station and make a statement."

He cleared his throat. "Am I in trouble? Do I need a lawyer?"

"Not if you tell the truth. And you might encourage your friends to do the same." I stood and stretched, my arms wider than his desk. "Oh, and not a word to Gary. I hear you tipped him off, and you'll be lucky to see your kids for one hour on holidays."

## 1730 HOURS

Mrs. Dunsmore handed me a folder and said, "For tonight's meeting."

"Tonight's meeting," I repeated.

"The Idyll Days planning committee," she said, reading my echo as ignorance. "You have to go." She cut off my mutinous reply and handed me a folder. "Here's the work detail. Plus the fines schedules. Give the mayor one copy and his assistant two because he'll lose his."

"You know we're closing in on a suspect, right?" I asked her. "In the murder investigation."

She sniffed. "That's what the detectives are here for, Chief." She emphasized my title. Putting me in my place.

I stood outside the Porter Room, staring at Isaiah's portrait. He looked constipated. Mr. Neilly, a selectman, mistook my stare for interest. "Isaiah was quite a visionary. Have you toured his home?" he asked.

"Ah, no." I'd not set foot inside one historic town site. And I wasn't looking to break that record.

"He was a talented silversmith. You can see some of his bowls at the house." He tapped the portrait's gilt frame with a gnarled finger. "Idyll Days is a tribute to his pioneering spirit." Sure, except they'd named the festival after the town name they chose over Porter's original, Wheaton. What kind of tribute was that?

"Come inside, Chief," he urged. "Things are about to get underway."

Inside, it looked like a science fair and a yard sale had mated. Against three of the room's walls were long tables, each draped with a yellow or orange cloth. Poster-board displays and dioramas were assembled on the tables. A television in the corner played video of former Idyll Days.

Mrs. Kettle, the town's lone selectwoman, sidled up to me. "Lovely, isn't it?" Before I could agree, she said, "Every committee member has presented a portion of the program in a visual display." Her bangles jingled as she pointed to a poster board showing tents and thatched huts. "That's the arts-and-crafts display, headed by Mrs. Mullen. And that," her bangles jangled, "is the apple-orchard tours, organized by Mr. and Mrs. Whitmore." She was a one-woman percussion section as she led me through the room, her hand on my arm, pointing out each "attraction area." She stopped before the end of a yellow-skirted table. "And here you are." An 8 ×11 paper marked IDYLL POLICE occupied the only bare space in sight.

"I brought handouts." I held up my folder.

She removed her hand from my arm. "Oh. Handouts. How efficient."

I'd hoped the displays meant I could observe, feign attention, hand out my copies, and be on my way. But Mr. Neilly torched that happy idea. "Let's all have a seat," he said, pointing to the grouped chairs. "It's time to get started." Started? I'd already spent fifteen minutes admiring handwoven wreaths and scary apple-peel dolls.

Mr. Neilly talked about the history of Idyll Days, interrupted now and again by his aged colleague, Mr. Sousa. Then we had to go around the room and discuss our plans. Mrs. Prior, in charge of the bake sale, spoke first. "This year, we've decided not to sell the Mother Lodes." Whispers from the group. She adjusted her bejeweled glasses and said, "Or the caramel apples with nuts." The group revolted with cries of "Why?"

"What are Mother Lodes?" I asked. The room fell silent. Like I'd farted in church.

"Pretzel rods coated with chocolate and dipped in caramel chips, toffee bits, and nuts. They're to die for," Mrs. Mullen said. "And they sell like hotcakes."

"Helen, why not sell them?" Mr. Anderson pled.

"Last year we had a lot of concern from parents of children with allergies. Remember that boy with the peanut allergy whose face blew up like a balloon? He had to be ambulanced to the hospital."

"*Pshaw,*" Mr. Sousa said. He waved her concern aside with his liver-spotted hand. "In my day, no one was allergic to nuts."

It took a half hour to resolve the nuts-in-baked-goods crisis. And then it was my turn. I handed out copies of the papers Mrs. Dunsmore had drawn up. "Here's all the information needed from the police station."

The mayor looked at the papers and said, "Parking fines are the same as last year."

"Yes, they are." I didn't elaborate.

"Who's manning the emergency-care station?" he asked.

Inside my folder was an underlined note from Mrs. Dunsmore. "EMERGENCY CARE IS THE FIRE DEPARTMENT'S REPONSIBILITY!!!"

"That's the Fire Department's responsibility. And where is Captain Hirsch?" I asked.

"He doesn't attend the committee meetings," Mr. Neilly said. "Busy putting out fires." He chuckled at his wit.

"Right. Any other questions?" I asked.

"You only have two men assigned to the arts-and-crafts areas," Mrs. Mullen said. She worried the tail of her gray braid. "But we need more support! There's thousands of dollars in merchandise. Some booths aren't well staffed."

"I'm afraid two officers are all we can manage."

"But—"

"Now, Mrs. Mullen," said Mr. Neilly. "This is Chief Lynch's first Idyll Days. He's not familiar with the procedures. I'm sure he'll incorporate our feedback and give us revised copies of his plans at the next meeting."

"There's another meeting?" The circle of faces looked at me, astonished at my ignorance.

"Next week. Same date and time," the mayor said.

"I'm sorry, but I can't make it."

"What?" Mrs. Kettle asked. Her bangles sounded the alarm as she raised her arms. "Now, Chief," she began.

"Look, I'll provide police support for this large and important town event. But I have other work. I'm running a murder investigation.

I'm sorry, but I can't attend more meetings. My proposals are based on prior years' needs and this year's estimated attendance. And they're final."

A woman came into the room. "Chief Lynch? You've got a phone call from the police station. He said it's urgent."

"Excuse me." My chair scraped backward. I followed her to a cramped office dominated by stacks of telephone books. She pointed to the phone and left.

"Hello?" I said. "Lynch here."

"Hi, Chief," Billy said. "You still there?" I'd had the foresight to tell him to call me at Town Hall, just in case I was trapped there after an hour.

"Just leaving. Thanks."

"You need anything else?" he asked.

"No, thanks. Have a good night." I hung up and looked around. Phone books. I had one for Idyll, but not for neighboring towns. They'd come in handy for the names on Elmore's list.

*You don't need Elmore's list. You've got Gary Clark.*

But did I? I wanted him to be our man. No one wanted it more.

Perhaps the men on the course were witnesses.

The gay men could've fled after the shots were fired. Scared. Afraid to come forward, to admit why they were there, what they were doing. Any defense attorney would love to get at those witnesses. Perverts committing filthy acts on a golf course? It would be a slam-dunk. No wonder they hadn't come forward, volunteered what they knew. Would I in that situation?

I picked up three area phone books. Just in case.

# THURSDAY, AUGUST 28TH
## 1130 HOURS

The air in the station was charged, like the atmosphere before a thunderstorm. The men crackled with purpose. Even Yankowitz strode with his chest out, shoulders back, as he carried his ticketing booklet. Everyone knew we had a man in our sights.

Our arguments were forgotten, for now. Wright reported to me, without attitude, that Mr. and Mrs. Gary Clark owned a home in Cheshire and a cottage on Nantucket. Mrs. Clark came from money. Poor Gary had to earn his. At his last job, he'd gotten into hot water. A sexual-harassment complaint was filed. He'd left the company and gone to Liberty Insurance. Where Cecilia let him harass her. Finnegan said that all of Clark's poker buddies had recanted their prior statements. Revere told me that Gary didn't own a registered gun, but his wife did. Not our model. That didn't sink our hopes. He could have bought one illegally. Borrowed one.

I was reaching for the phone when it rang.

"Hi, Chief, it's Jenna Dash. I just finished reviewing his files. There's something you might be interested in." I noticed she didn't mention Gary Clark by name. Did she think we taped our calls?

"I'm all ears," I said.

"Do you know anything about STOLIs?"

"Isn't that vodka?"

"Um, yes, but STOLI is also short for stranger-originated life insurance."

"Not familiar with it." I grabbed my notepad.

"STOLIs represent when someone offers another person a life-insurance policy and says, 'Hey, you don't have to pay the premiums or the interest on this. I'll take care of it for you, for say, two or three years.' Then at the end of that period, the payer asks the insured person if they want to pay the accrued interest and principal."

"Okay," I understood this, sort of.

"But most older folks are on fixed incomes. They can't afford a large policy. So whoever's been paying keeps doing so, and when the insured person dies, the payer get the money. And since most STOLIs are targeted to the elderly, they don't wait too long for payday."

"Is this common?" It seemed like betting, only on death rather than on dogs or horses. Death was a surer proposition.

"It's becoming more so, and it's worrisome. If an elderly person has a STOLI taken out on him, he can't purchase another life-insurance policy, and if he can't afford the one that's been taken out on him, then he's pretty much screwed."

"And that's legal?"

"Yes, but it's not best practice."

"And Gary Clark was offering these policies?"

"He's handled policies where the insured party is not the same person paying the premium. And the payee doesn't appear to be a spouse or family member. I'm going from what I can see on my computer. The paper files would have more information."

"But if it's not illegal, he wouldn't be in trouble, right?"

"Yes and no. Legally, he's within bounds, but six months ago, Liberty Insurance issued a memo to all agents insisting they not handle STOLIs. The company is being sued by a couple who claim we defrauded their father by offering him a STOLI. Until that's settled, agents shouldn't complete these deals."

"Could he be fired?"

"Yes."

"Could Cecilia have known?"

She gave it some thought and said, "She couldn't have seen his caseload, and, honestly, even if she had, I don't think she'd have known how to interpret this stuff."

"But he might have told her."

"Maybe," she said. "If they were close, like you said."

I asked a few more questions about the policies. "Don't suppose there's any way the company is likely to let me peek at those files?"

"Not without a warrant," she said.

"Then I'll get one."

"You really think he killed her? Over STOLIs?" she asked.

"I'm not sure why he killed her, but he's looking better and better for it. Thanks for your help, Jenna."

"Don't mention it. Please. I don't think my employer would be happy about my helping you."

"Mum's the word."

Did Cecilia and Gary Clark fight the night she died? Had she threatened him? Made him fear for his job? How badly did he need to work? His wife had money. Or was Cecilia unhappy about being the mistress? Had she wanted more?

Time to share what I'd learned. The pen was dim with smoke, the air thick with testosterone. I explained about the STOLIs. I didn't tell them how I knew, even when asked. I wanted to keep Jenna's job safe.

"You think our victim found out about the policies?" Revere asked.

"He might've told her."

"How did he plan to keep them secret? Wouldn't they eventually be found?" Billy asked. Good question.

I repeated what Jenna had told me. "The files appear to be pending, though they're months old. Maybe he hoped to keep them like that until Liberty settled its STOLI lawsuit."

"Seems dangerous," Wright said. "What if Liberty ends up paying through the nose and banning all future STOLIs?"

"I'm told it's unlikely. STOLIs generate revenue, and no court has faulted an insurance company for offering the policy. Most likely, he'll be in the clear."

"He killed her because of insurance?" Billy asked.

"Maybe not. Maybe she threatened to tell his wife."

He crossed his arms. "I don't think she'd have done that." Everything about his body said he wanted to believe Cecilia was a good girl. And good girls didn't sleep with married men. But he'd seen the diary.

"Billy, if you can't keep an open mind about the victim, say so now."

He uncrossed his arms. "I can. It just doesn't fit her profile."

Finnegan exhaled cigarette smoke in circles that expanded and wobbled through the air. Billy, easily distracted from his anger, clapped. Wright said, "You should be in the circus."

"Time to pick Clark up. Who wants the honor?" I asked.

Billy shot his hand up in the air. We all pretended we hadn't seen him. After a few seconds, he lowered it and said, "Oh."

"Wright?" I said. He probably wasn't the smartest choice. He was the type to bump Gary Clark's head into the cruiser door while saying, "Watch your head." But I needed to make a peace gesture, and I didn't much care if our suspect got a bruise on his way in.

He grabbed his keys and said, "Time to get the bad guy." He hummed as he left.

Revere said, "What's with him?" He asked Finnegan, "He has a hard-on for men who hurt women?"

"How'd you know?" Finnegan asked.

I recalled Anthony Fergus. How Wright had wanted to fit him up for this killing.

Finnegan stubbed out his cigarette butt. "His mother got knocked around some when Wright was growing up. Makes him a bit zealous when it comes to guys like that."

I felt a flare of anger. That I hadn't known this. It would've helped. I would've understood why Wright wanted Anthony Fergus so badly. But then, I hadn't made much of an effort to understand. Too busy playing solitaire in my office, staying away from my men. Not getting too close, as I had with Rick. People can't hurt you if you don't let them near.

Revere offered to fetch the warrants. Said he knew the judge on roster. "So we want his home and car, right?" he said. He ran his hand over his buzz cut.

"I want access to his work files too."

"That's gonna be a tough sell. Privacy concerns for the clients, yada yada."

"Sway the judge to our side. If the files don't pertain to the case, I'll gladly return them. But the victim told her aunt she suspected something wasn't right at the company. If Mr. Clark knew she'd talked—"

He interrupted with, "Did he kill her because of his job or because he didn't want her talking to his wife? Pick a motive and stick to it. I don't want to be arguing two separate cases."

"Get me a warrant for the files, his car, and his home, and I'll get you one solid motive."

Revere huffed, but he said, "I'll try," before he walked to his much newer, nicer patrol vehicle.

While I'd jawed with Revere, Billy had updated the board. Gary Clark was front and center, and a picture of his car was pinned to a town map.

"Has anyone been able to establish that he and the victim were together the day he lied about his car accident and she called in sick?" I asked.

Finnegan said, "Her mother said Cecilia was out most of the day. Said she went out to return library books and to get medicine. Her mother offered to do both, but Cecilia insisted."

"Did she return the books?"

"Yup. Two of 'em. I checked with the library."

"Did she get medicine?"

"No. When her mother asked, Cecilia got upset and said she didn't know what to buy since she wasn't sure if she had a summer cold or some other bug."

"So she makes it to the library but not the drugstore," I said.

"You think she met him after the library?" Billy asked.

"It's possible. But where? The cabin isn't the safest bet during daytime," Finnegan said.

We thought about it but had no answers.

"Come to me when you've got a confession," I said as I walked to my office. I needed to be out of sight when Gary Clark came in. Just in case he recognized me.

I passed an hour moving papers on my desk. Trying to figure out where he might've dumped the gun. When I couldn't stand the sound of my own breathing, I did twenty push-ups. It helped. But not enough. So I cracked the door and yelled Billy's name.

He arrived, flushed. "Yeah?"

"How's it going?" I pointed to the interview room.

He worked a piece of chewing gum, hard. "Finnegan and Wright are tag-teaming him. Clark spent his call on his wife. He told her he was working late tonight."

"How long they been in there?"

He glanced at his watch. "Forty minutes."

"Keep me updated."

He nodded. "Will do."

The next few hours were torture. I wanted to be in that room, getting in Clark's face, pushing his buttons. I was good at it. Rick used to call me "Secret Spanish," as in the Inquisition. First time we handled a murder, I got the killer to confess in less than two hours.

"Damn, Tommy, that was fucking A-one stuff!" Rick had high-fived me, his hand small against mine. "At this rate, we'll have all the killers in this precinct locked up by Christmas!"

We didn't. Of course we didn't. But our solve rate was better than average. At least until things started to sour. I don't know why he first tried the stuff. He'd always been a booze guy. The great Irish way. But I knew when he started because no one visits the john that often unless they've got problems. He had a problem. He was developing a cocaine habit.

"Chief?" Wright stood outside my door, ajar just enough for me to see any major activity.

I rubbed my forehead, as if I could massage it empty of troubled thoughts. "Come in."

His shirt was creased. Damp under the armpits. The interview room was hot. We kept it that way. Wright rubbed his graying hair and said, "He's admitted to seeing her, even said they were at that cabin by Hought's Pond. But he swears he dropped her off near the golf course and never saw her again."

"Convenient."

"Plus, he's got this story about two guys at the cabin."

My stomach fell six stories.

"Two guys?"

"Yeah. He says he and the victim were 'getting intimate' and these two guys stormed inside the cabin. Accused him and Cecilia of trespassing. So he and the victim left. But now he's saying maybe it was these two guys who followed them, and after Cecilia got on the golf course, maybe they shot her."

"He give a description of these men?"

He smiled. "He says one was a cop. Claims he had a badge. The other guy was smaller and older." He scratched the back of his neck. "I swear, he's going to say he saw Jimmy Hoffa there next."

I forced my mouth into a smile. "Great. He lawyered-up yet?"

"Yes." He tapped his belt. "But I didn't recognize the name."

I got up and stood in the doorway. Finnegan was smoking, talking to Revere. Revere started laughing. I should be happy. And I couldn't be.

Wright said, "We got Billy calling the lawyer now. Figured he earned it by fingering the cabin for their meeting place first."

Billy. Not me. Right. I said, "Has Clark said anything else damning?"

Wright scratched his chin stubble. "Other than that he's the last person to have seen her alive and he dropped her at the murder site? Nope."

"What about the STOLIs?"

"Oh, man. He about wet himself when we mentioned those. Kept saying, 'I could lose my job' over and over. Like that's his big worry. I swear, this guy . . ." He shook his head, confounded by our suspect's priorities.

"Great. Let him sweat, then give him his lawyer."

Ten minutes later, Billy recounted the conversation with Clark's lawyer for us. The guy was a real-estate attorney who knew Mr. Clark through insurance work. When called, he went into shock. "Gary's

accused of what?" followed by denial, "But I can't handle this!" And
then anger. "Why would he pull me into this?" He quickly moved on
to acceptance, the kind that involved passing the buck. "I'll call my
friend, Lou," he said. "He's done some criminal law."

Wright looked forward to informing Mr. Clark that his lawyer had
referred him to a man who'd practiced "some criminal law." He estimated that Gary would produce another half cup of sweat after this
news. I smiled because it was expected. But inside I was furious. At
myself. I wasn't going to get near Gary Clark now. Not after he'd told
Wright there was a cop in the cabin. I was going to have to be careful,
to make sure Gary only ever saw my back.

I took one last look at the board and said, "Right. Good luck, boys.
I'm headed home. Call if you need me."

Revere looked stunned, Finnegan puzzled. Billy said, "You're not
staying? But we've got him here."

"And my detectives are interviewing him. Order some supper and
enjoy. I'll see you tomorrow for the searches. Be prepared. I want so
much evidence even a blind and deaf jury couldn't acquit."

"Here, here," Finnegan said.

Billy watched me zip my jacket, still agape. Wright, on break from
interrogating, wished me good night. He hummed a happy tune.

Outside, I rounded the corner, took a deep breath, and punched the
station's wall. Fuck! My knuckles throbbed. I shook my hand, inhaled
deeply, and leaned my forehead against the cool bricks. I wanted to
make Clark confess. And I should've had the chance. But my stupid
dick had done my thinking and led me to that cabin. And now I had
to stay away, keep out of sight as if I were the criminal. Starting my car,
I wondered if this was how Rick felt, when he knew he was spiraling
down, endangering his career, unable to stop. And for the first time
in over a year, I felt something more than anger at Rick. I felt pity and
something like sympathy.

# 2145 HOURS

I drove to Suds. I was too upset to go home. By the car's interior light, I examined my injured hand. Below my knuckles, the skin was abraded and crusted. I sucked on the dried blood, the taste dark and salty. Then I went inside. The scent of laundry detergent was smothered by beer and fried food. Half the town was inside. I looked behind, at the door. Funny that a crowd should make me hesitate. I grew up on an island crammed with people. It wasn't that. I just didn't want to talk about Idyll Days, the murder, or, God forbid, my lawn plan.

"Hi, Chief," Nate said, busy at the taps. "What can I get you?"

"Scotch."

He reached for the bottle of Laphroaig. Within a minute I had a glass in my hand containing one ice cube and a generous amount of liquid gold. I slid a bill onto the counter and nodded my thanks.

I eyed the room for a space large enough to hold my drink and me. Someone touched my elbow. Brown hair, brown eyes, mustache, and beard. He half shouted, "Hello, Thomas." The lumberjack tech from yesterday.

"Mike," I said. Mike Shannon. "You live nearby?"

"Not really." He led me to a table hidden by papers covered with equations and formulas.

"Work?" I asked, taking a seat.

"No. I use these to discourage people from sitting."

"Clever." I checked him out. His hair still needed cutting, but he had full lips and ruddy cheeks. He was a total bear.

"Hoped I might see you here," he said.

"Really?" He knew I was from Idyll. So he took a gamble, visiting the only bar in town. Not much of a gamble. Though if I'd been able to interview Gary Clark, he'd have been out of luck. But I couldn't. I could only worry about how it was going.

"Tough day?" he asked.

I'd been silently thinking for who knows how long. "Sorry," I said. "Big break in our murder case. Your colleague, Dave, helped. Found us some fibers."

"Ah, Dave. Very bright boy. Very bad socially."

"Yeah, I got that."

"I was just about to leave," he said.

"Oh?" His appearance had lifted me from my self-directed anger. Once he left, I'd be right back to it.

"You staying?" He set his glass down with a thump.

"It's a bit crowded here." I leaned forward. "You know some place quieter?"

He picked up his papers. "I'm driving a blue truck. Follow me." He gathered his things and left. I sat and finished my drink, not too fast. Then I headed outside.

In my car, I waited until his blue truck made a U-turn in the lot and pulled out. I reversed. What if he headed east, for Hought's Pond? I couldn't return to the cabin. I wouldn't. It had cost me my place in that interview room with Gary Clark. But his truck turned left, headed west. I cracked the window and drove steady at 45 miles per hour. Was he taking me to his house? He hadn't said where he lived. I imagined a log cabin with a wood-burning stove. He slowed six miles outside town, and turned left again, driving into and through an industrial lot, filled with low-slung cement buildings. He parked at the end of a block and stepped down from his truck cab. The lot was vacant.

He stood outside, waiting. Stupid, but I was nervous. I pocketed my keys and got out. Noticed that the building before us had a large sign on it. Mike's Woodshop. He walked to the front. "Yours?" I said.

He didn't glance behind him. "Mine. Come on." He used a key on a recessed door. I followed him in. I smelled wood shavings and polyurethane. He turned the lights on. Inside the large, high-ceilinged space were workbenches, tools, and several canoes in various stages of completion. He walked straight to the back. I stopped to stroke the smooth side of a finished canoe, and then followed.

At the end of the large space was a small room with a bed, a three-legged table, a wooden chest, and shelves built into the wall. There was a water glass on the table beside a Frank Lloyd Wright biography. The shelves had photos of men fishing. Some books. He stepped closer, blocking my view. "I didn't bring you here for décor tips," he said.

"Good thing." I unbuttoned my shirt. "You'd regret it."

He took off his polo. His chest was wide, barrel-shaped, and tan. His skin was smooth and fatty. Muscles rippled below as he moved. He lifted my undershirt above my head and leaned in to lick my neck. My cock stiffened. He struggled out of his pants, hopping to disentangle his foot from the cuff. I stripped. We stood, nude, facing each other. He wasn't as big as I'd expected, but he certainly was ready.

He spat into his hand. My cock swelled. Then he rubbed his saliva over my dick. I groaned and thrust into his hand. He rubbed until I backed away, too near climax. I sat on the bed and pulled him near, stuck my head near his groin and breathed deeply. He smelled like sweat and cotton and man. I took him into my mouth. He sighed low and long. I licked him from tip to stem. Then into my mouth again, where I hummed a little as I worked him over.

"Ah, ah," he said. He rocked into me. I loved this. Having power over someone's pleasure. Their joy dependent upon me. It had been too long.

I stood and said, "What'll it be?" I stroked his ass and kissed him long and slow.

He bent over and offered himself. Generous. "Lube's in the trunk."

Under several shirts and a stash of dirty magazines, I found the bottle. I worked the cold gel inside him. He gurgled and thrust his backside nearer. I used the lube on myself, enjoying his whimpers of impatience. Then I rolled a condom onto my stiff dick. Lubed it up.

"Now!" he said. I slid my cock into him by half inches. His ass throbbed, milking me. I pulled out.

"More!"

I pushed back in and he gasped. We rocked and groaned. I fingered his fuzzy balls. Harder, faster, my pelvis slapped his ass, until I shouted and squeezed his balls. He yelled and shuddered beneath me.

After a few moments, he leaned forward and my cock fell out of him. "Bathroom?" I asked. He pointed. I went. A small room adjoined to the workshop held a toilet, a tiny shower, and a pedestal sink. I turned the shower tap and it blasted a jet of cold water. I adjusted the lever and got the water hot. I stepped inside and soaped myself lightly, still sensitive. With a too-small towel I dried myself to dampness.

He lay in bed, on his side, waiting for me. "Okay?"

"Fine. You?" I asked.

He smiled and rubbed his chest. "Never better."

"You'll keep this," I drew a line between us, "to yourself?"

He said, "Of course. Wouldn't want to upset the status quo, would we?" He grabbed my hand.

"What time is it?" I asked.

He glanced at an alarm clock on his shelf. "Eleven thirty. You have to be somewhere?" His voice aimed for teasing but fell short.

I pulled my hand free. "No, but I've got an early morning." I sat on the bed. It bowed under our weight. "Have to search a suspect's home."

"So, no round two?" His breath tickled my ear. He drew a line down my back. My dick stirred, rousing from its nap. I needed to go home and sleep. Tomorrow was a big day. I needed to be alert. I couldn't let sex come between this case and me. Not again.

"I can't." I stepped into my underwear. Over my shoulder I said, "But I'd like to."

He pushed himself up. "Maybe some other time?"

"Sounds good." I poked my head though my undershirt. "I'll show myself out."

The road was dark and empty of other cars. The air smelled sweet, like flowers. I reached for the radio knob, ready to sing along in my off-key voice. Cecilia North and I had something else in common. Ahead, two shiny orbs hung at hood height. Too late, I realized what they were. Eyes. I stomped on the brake and cut the wheel, skidding into the other lane. The deer, startled, ran forward, in front of the car. I saw its face, its white muzzle. We collided. My head snapped back. Metal crunched. My body slammed forward, hard into the wheel. I blinked. The car, stopped, sounded like an angry hornet. I shook my head. Pain. I touched my forehead. No blood. Good.

In front of me was the dark road. No deer. I opened my door with shaking hands. Adrenaline. My chest felt sore. I stood, holding on to the car frame. The deer's crumpled body visible ahead. I walked forward. It lay on its side, back legs kicking. Its eyes frantic. The front grill of the car done in. The sounds of its flailing hooves on the blacktop made me wince. I rubbed my sore chest and looked away.

I needed help, so I got the radio. Called it in. What was the code for a hit deer? Or animal? "Hey, it's Lynch. I've just hit a deer."

The dickhead on dispatch thought I was joking. A prank pulled by patrol.

"No, it's me. Listen. Listen! If I don't get some assistance, I'll have you suspended for a week without pay. Got it?"

Now he believed me. He asked about the deer. I told him it was seriously injured. Bleeding at the mouth, but moving its back legs. He asked about the accident. I rambled. Too many words. Still shaken.

"It's gonna have to be put down," he said, when I'd finished talking.

"Put down."

"Shot," he said. "You got your gun?"

"You want me to shoot it?" Somehow I hadn't considered this. I thought they'd send animal control. Try to rescue it. Release it back into the wild.

"I can send someone to help you remove it from the road."

But he expected me to kill it.

"Okay," I said.

I wondered if I ought to have a rifle, but it didn't matter because I didn't. Just my .40 Glock. I walked to the deer, hoping it had recovered. Had by some miracle found the strength to regain its legs and hobble to the woods.

"Don't make me do this," I said. The deer's eyes weren't fearful. They were blank. But its legs twitched, and I knew it wasn't gone. That it needed me to put it out of its misery.

I hadn't fired my gun since Rick died. Since I'd tried to shoot Apollo St. James and missed. Maybe that's why I was so reluctant. I didn't want to inhabit that space again. But the dying animal before me, its side moving up with each panted breath, wasn't going to let me forget. I pulled my gun from my belt. Took the safety off. Positioned myself. Aimed at its slender head, its marble eyes seeing something I could not.

"I'm sorry," I said and I fired once, twice, three times. My eyes closing reflexively after each shot. The noise splitting the night in half.

I opened them. Blood streamed toward my feet. The deer dead. I looked up at the stars and waited for sirens. Forgetting for a moment when, and where, I was.

# FRIDAY, AUGUST 29TH
## 0815 HOURS

**N**ate had given me a plaid thermos when I'd asked for a to-go coffee container from Suds. The guys at the station started in on me as soon as they saw it. "Mommy pack you soup?" Lots of laughs. High spirits. They were amped, excited to search Gary Clark's stuff. I recalled the feeling.

"You got a matching lunch box?" Revere asked.

"Hey, Chief," Billy said. He handed me a folder. "Mrs. D. said for me to give you this first thing." Billy got away with calling Mrs. Dunsmore by a nickname. I'd have been flayed for that offense. The folder was marked URGENT. I groaned and set it down.

"She said you should read it before we go." He bit his lower lip.

I rolled my eyes, and flipped it open. Citizen's complaint. I sighed. Scanned the form. Name: Jane Doe. I squinted.

Was Revere giggling near me?

Address was listed as 1512 Woodsy Lane.

What?

Officer's name listed was Thomas Lynch.

What the fuck?

On the night of August 27th, Chief Thomas Lynch drove his police cruiser (like a lunatic) into me, causing me to fall. I sustained grievous injuries. Not satisfied with this, he then took out his gun, and, without provocation, shot me multiple times. His aim was as good as that of a blind, elderly woman. My child, Bambi, will now suffer as an orphan.

I looked up from the report. Billy had his hand to his mouth, his eyes crinkled with pent-up laughter. Finnegan lifted his mug in salute and asked, "How's your car?"

Wright laughed, and Revere let out some more unsettling giggles. Jesus. He sounded like a twelve-year-old girl.

"Undriveable," I said. After help had arrived and moved the deer corpse from the road, I discovered my car wouldn't start. It had been towed to a repair shop. I had a loaner patrol car now. Its suspension was a memory and the brakes a danger to myself and the general population.

"Welcome to Idyll," Wright said, toasting me with half a bagel. "Where Mother Nature is much more dangerous than the citizenry."

They were having fun at my expense. Until someone yanked your chain, you were outside the tribe. I knew that. But it was hard to treat the deer's death as a joke. Because of Rick. They didn't know.

"We really ought to put up some signs," I said, deadpan. There were, in fact, signs warning drivers about deer. They were the first things I noticed when I'd moved here.

"Good idea. Signs," Finnegan said. He framed a sign with his hands. "Watch out for Police Chief. Next ten miles."

I gave him a grin and a middle finger. He was as delighted as if I'd handed him a twenty.

"So, how'd we make out last night?" I asked, hoping to leave Jane Doe behind.

Revere and Finnegan reported that Gary Clark had gone silent on the advice of his lawyer. So they'd moved him to a cell, to await transfer. Finnegan said he'd cried all the way to his new digs. "If you can't handle the crime, don't pull the fucking trigger," he said. He stubbed out another half-smoked cigarette; too wired to finish smoking one.

We had warrants for his car, office, and home. We weren't allowed to remove files from Liberty Insurance, but we could review them. I assigned Revere to it, along with two helpers. Finnegan would ride with him, to check out Clark's car. And Wright and I would handle the house. I needed to work on repairing my relationship with my lead detective.

Wright drove. We listened to the news as we sped down the highway. "You believe this?" He pointed to the radio. "These guys think that opening a casino will have all these wonderful benefits for the Pequot tribe."

"Hasn't it?" From what I'd heard, Foxwoods Casino pulled in tons of money. And it paid subsidies to all people who could prove they had Pequot blood.

"Sure. For now. But casinos are trouble. Ask any poor cop stuck in a casino city. Crime skyrockets. And this whole 'we'll regain out cultural heritage through slot nickels'? I'm not buying it."

"So you'd rather they stay dirt poor?" I asked.

"I'd rather they didn't sugarcoat that what they've done is finagle the law so they can run a gambling empire." He switched stations until he landed on some Top 40 nonsense. Some man was mumbling quickly to a beat borrowed from Diana Ross's "I'm Coming Out," that old standby of pride parades and gay clubs everywhere. Wright was oblivious, tapping the wheel and matching the song word for word.

"You like this?" I asked.

"What?" He spared me a glance. "Notorious B.I.G.? Or rap music, in general?" He looked at my face and laughed. "I'm not as old as you."

"How can you understand what they're saying?"

He grinned and tapped his right ear. "Again. *Not old.*" He turned up the volume. "Better?"

I had a glimpse of how Wright was outside the station. Looser, funnier, less quick to offense. I turned down the volume, and he said, "Guess we can test this song's theory."

"Which is?"

"More money, more problems."

"Sounds like something rich people made up," I said.

He agreed and checked the rearview. "I'm guessing Mrs. Clark might be worried about her husband, seeing as how he didn't come home last night."

"Maybe she's used to him being out all night," I said.

Mrs. Gary Clark wasn't used to her husband being out all night. She opened the door before we'd pushed the bell, which was a shame. I'm sure the *bing-bong* would have been terrific, bouncing off marble surfaces and mirrors wider than I was tall.

"Where is he? Are you here about Gary? Is he hurt? Is he dead?" She was tall, blond, and pretty, though we weren't seeing her at her best. The hollows under her blue eyes were violet. Her pale skin was pink in patches. She wore a soft-gray sweater that reached her knees. I bet it was cashmere. Oh, she had money. Only the rich, accustomed to central air-conditioning, would wear cashmere in late August.

"Ma'am, I'm Police Chief Lynch of the Idyll Police. This is Detective Wright. Your husband, Gary, is in police custody."

"Custody?"

"We've arrested him on suspicion of murder."

She looked to Wright as if he might refute what I'd said. "Murder?" she said. "What are you talking about?"

"Ma'am, we have a warrant to search your home." I showed her the papers.

She snatched them out of my hand. "You can't! I want to talk to my husband!" She tossed the papers. I bent to catch them.

Wright said, "Mrs. Clark, your husband is in custody. If you'd like, you may call his lawyer, Mr. Louis Jacob."

"Who's Louis Jacob? I've never heard of him. He's not our lawyer." Her pale skin got pinker with each word. She looked behind us, as if her husband might be in view.

"Your lawyer doesn't handle criminal cases, so he recommended Mr. Jacob," I said. "Excuse me." I stepped past her into the house. Wright followed. I said, "We'll be removing items from the house. You'll get an inventory receipt." Two cars pulled into the driveway. Officers emerged.

"All of these people are going to search my house?" Her eyes were as wide as half dollars.

"With a house this size, we need the men." I wasn't kidding. You could fit three of my houses inside this one, and still have room to spare. This was going to take all day, unless we found the gun, a signed confession, and some bloody clothes in the first closet we checked.

"Whoa," Billy said when he crossed the threshold. He looked up at the sparkling underside of a crystal chandelier. "This place is like a castle."

Mrs. Clark said, "I'm calling the lawyer. Don't touch anything until I get back." She hurried out of the room, her light steps leaving echoes behind in the vast entryway.

I said, "Billy, Hopkins, and Clyde, you're upstairs. Wright and Smith, take the downstairs. I'll check the garage and outside."

The garage housed a silver Mercedes Benz. Garden tools were arranged neatly on a pegboard. A shining, metal garbage bin stood near the retractable doors. Other than a broom, bucket, and cleaning cloths, there wasn't much else. I checked the cloths, but they were spotless. I sniffed them. No bleach or detergent. New. Not freshly laundered.

I left the garage and walked around the house, poking in and out of rose bushes. I overturned small statues but found nothing but worms. The lawn was less vast than I'd feared. But it still took hours to walk the property, searching for evidence of fire or recent digging. Any signs that someone had attempted to destroy evidence. Nothing. I'd nearly returned to the front door when I spotted it. A bit of paper stuck near the house's foundation, obscured by a tall hedge. I crouched and grabbed it with gloved hands. A paper packet. Yes! I pulled it close, avoiding twigs. And read the print on back. It was a seed packet. Nasturtiums. Not Pop Rocks. I dropped it.

"Chief?" Wright yelled.

I jogged around the side and found him calling for me near the garage. "Find anything?" I asked.

He held up a dress shirt. "Found this hidden in the back."

Mrs. Clark called from the doorway, "It needs mending. Clara was going to bring it to the tailor."

I walked to where I could read the label. Ralph Lauren. "Let me guess," I said to Mrs. Clark. "It's missing a button."

"Yes." She scowled at me.

"Anything else?" I asked Wright.

His eyebrows pinched together. "We found a note from the victim, arranging to meet him at work. But aside from that—" he kicked the ground, "nothing. No weapon."

Mrs. Clark moved indoors, where she began complaining about a rug.

Wright flexed his hands together. Knuckles cracked. "She's been scolding the men every time they move something." He rolled his eyes. "I understand why her husband went looking for company." He didn't bother to lower his voice.

"Chief!" Hopkins stood in the doorway, waving. His gut wobbled.

I hurried to him. "What is it?" Please let it have DNA. Great big blobs of DNA.

"Phone call." He handed me a mobile phone, like the one the selectmen had said I should own, so I could be reached at all times. I'd promised I'd look into it. I hadn't.

"Yeah?" I hoped it was Revere or Finnegan about to report a major find.

"Chief Lynch?" an unknown voice said.

"Speaking."

"This is Dan Bergen from the forensic laboratory. We got footprint matches from your golf course. Mike Shannon said I should phone you." Looked like last night's adventure had scored multiple payoffs. "Frigging miracle we retrieved them, given what the scene looked like. We lifted two prints around the scene and her body. Men's. A work boot, size eight and a half, and a sneaker, size eleven and a half. The sneaker's a partial, but it's fairly distinct. We're checking treads to see if we can ID the brand and style."

"Great. Thanks." Two footprints. Two men. The ones Mrs. Ashworth saw? Maybe not. They could've been made earlier. Or perhaps the techs hadn't excluded everyone from our squad. Still, two prints— it made my stomach feel sour. Never a good sign. My stomach went sour before a suspect pushed me down a stairwell sixteen years ago. I'd bumped my way down three flights. One of those bruised vertebrae can now predict rainstorms.

"Where are Clark's shoes?" I asked Hopkins. Might as well check them.

"Upstairs." He stepped inside and walked past Mrs. Clark, who said, "Slow down! That's a Tiffany vase there!" I followed him up the stairs to the second floor, down a hall lit with frosted-glass fixtures, and into a bedroom the size of my own. That's where the similarities ended. It was done up in gold and army green. The furniture glowed. Someone spent time polishing it. I doubted it was either of the Clarks. "He has his own bedroom?" Everything in it was masculine.

"Yup. She has her own. You should see the closet. And they have a shared master bedroom. This place is nuts."

I approached the open closet. Suits hung on cedar hangers, the scent strong enough to scare moths miles away. Below were his shoes. Nine pairs. I picked up a pair of loafers. Size 10.

Hopkins asked, "Is it a match for something?"

"No." Shit. "Are all of his shoes size ten?"

We lifted each pair and checked the numbers. "These are ten and a half." Hopkins held up a pair of shearling slippers.

I saw no boots. And only one pair of sneakers, which were so white I doubted he'd ever worn them. He favored dress shoes and loafers.

"Come on," I said. We went downstairs, where Mrs. Clark threatened Wright with legal retribution if he didn't have the place professionally cleaned after we left.

I interrupted her fantasy to ask him, "Are we finished inside?"

Wright nodded. "All but the putting everything back exactly as it was and dusting." His voice was level, but his eyes laughed at the thought.

"That's not going to happen," I said. Mrs. Clark sputtered. I ignored her. "Let's pack it in. Bring what we've got and we'll see how Finnegan and Revere did."

They hadn't done better. Techs had found brunette hairs that might belong to Cecilia in Clark's car. But no gun and no visible blood in the car's interior. And while it was clean, it didn't look "too clean" according to Finnegan. "If he tidied, he's a fucking pro." He crushed an empty pack of cigarettes and tossed into the trash. "Clark doesn't seem like a pro."

No, he didn't.

"So he leaves the car, shoots her on the course, wipes down, gets back in," Wright said. "Problem solved."

"Where are his clothes? Where's the gun?" Revere asked. "Where's anything that can put the nail in his coffin?"

"I don't fucking know. We've got the shirt missing the button," Wright said. "We know she was in his car. A jury could buy that."

But they easily might not. His feet didn't fit our too-big and too-small shoe prints. Maybe Gary Clark wasn't our Cinderella.

"Keep searching for the gun," I said. "Finnegan, check on his club memberships." We'd heard that some of the clubs Clark belonged to had shooting ranges. We hoped he was a regular at one of them.

Mrs. Dunsmore approached. "Chief? You have a call. From the mayor." She waved her hand at the thick cigarette smoke and pursed her lips at Finnegan, the chief generator. He scowled at her, and then grinned. He liked the old bat. They had a long-standing truce.

"I bet your lungs are half tar," she said.

"Probably so," he said. "Want to place any bets on my liver?"

She walked away. I went to my office to find out what the mayor wanted.

"Congratulations!" His hearty voice nearly knocked me to the floor.

"Pardon?" I said. Maybe he'd dialed the wrong number.

"Heard you searched the son of a bitch's house." Where was he getting this information?

"We executed searches today."

"That's great. Get this mess sorted before the celebration."

"We didn't find the weapon." I needed him to temper his expectations.

"You'll find it," he said. "Or you won't need it. Maybe he'll confess now that you've got his shirt."

Okay. Who the fuck told him about the shirt? "How'd you know about that?"

"I like to keep informed." Cagey bastard. Knew better then to tell me. "Well, just wanted to wish you the best, though it doesn't seem you need it. Bye."

The buzz of the phone matched the dull buzz in my head as I worried. Who was talking to the mayor? And what if Clark wasn't our man? I couldn't put it off any longer. I was going to have to pursue Elmore's list.

# SATURDAY, AUGUST 30TH
## 1430 HOURS

A bell tinkled as I entered Sweet Dreams. A kid, elbow deep in a glass jar of Tootsie Rolls, looked up, assessed me, and went back to filling his bag with candy. The place was very clean, very white, and occupied by kids with an occasional adult thrown in for variety. Near the scale where sweets were weighed stood a tall man in his fifties, wearing rimless specs and a pristine apron. "May I help you?" he asked me.

"Mr. Evans?" I said.

"Mr. Gallagher." He smiled as if used to the confusion.

"Pardon me."

He asked if I'd like anything. He had some nice truffles from Vermont, filled with maple cream. I told him I hadn't come for candy.

A child stomped to the counter and said, "Where are the gummy worms?"

"Next to the Atomic Fireballs," Mr. Gallagher said, pointing. The kid hurried to the spot, bag swinging at his side. "Sorry, Chief, how might I help you?"

So he recognized me out of uniform.

"You live on Durham Street?" I asked.

He nodded. Durham was two blocks over from Cecilia's house. Close to the golf course. "Did you hear anything the night of August ninth? We're double-checking reports of loud noises."

"Oh, I'm sorry." He knew why I was asking. Everyone knew what that night meant. No way to be sly about it. "We were out of town that weekend. Confectioners' conference. Kansas City. David and I go every year. When we got back we heard about—" he checked that there were no children nearby, "the murder. Terrible thing. Sorry I can't help."

The interrupting child in search of gummy worms slapped his bag onto the counter and said, "Ring me up."

"Please," I said.

"Please what?" the kid said.

I leaned down and said, "It's polite to say please when you ask for something."

"You sound like my Nana," the kid said. He told Mr. Gallagher, "Please ring me up." Mr. Gallagher weighed the bag and tallied the total. The kid handed Mr. Gallagher a five-dollar bill, accepted his change, and walked out the door.

More kids, hopped up on sugar, raced past me. "That's gross!" and "No, that is!" they shouted.

"I couldn't do your job," I said.

"Charles?" A man emerged from a red curtain behind the counter. He was squinting at a calculator. Mr. Evans, no doubt. "Oh," he said, looking up. "I'm sorry. Didn't mean to interrupt." He stared at me and at his partner. If looks could kill, we'd both be bagged and tagged.

Mr. Gallagher said, "David, this is Police Chief Lynch. He was asking if we'd heard anything on the night of the accident." A trio of small children lurked near the chocolates.

"Oh." David put his small hand to his chest. "I see." He smiled, and a dimple appeared in each cheek, perfectly symmetrical. "We were traveling. Confectioners' conference."

"So I heard. Sorry to disturb you."

"Not at all," he said. "It's a pleasure to meet you. Would you care for a sample?"

Mr. Gallagher and I exchanged a look. Mine said, "He always this jealous?" and his said, "Yes, but I keep him anyway."

"No, thank you." I patted my abdomen. "Trying to stay in shape."

"You're doing an excellent job," Mr. Gallagher said, smiling. Mr. Evans swatted his ass. The kids didn't see it, but I did.

I stopped by the post office on the pretense of investigating a package I was expecting. Mr. Nichols, the gay postman, was only too happy to help. He was too short to be the man Mrs. Ashworth had seen standing on the course, but perhaps he was the other. The 8.5-size boots. In between his questions about ship dates, I looked at his small feet. He wore graying sneakers. "Are those comfortable?" I asked. "I need new sneakers."

"These?" he pointed. "Absolutely. Need good shoes in my line of work. Of course finding my size is tough." He grimaced. "I'm a six. Tough to come by. I had to special-order these from Massachusetts."

Not everyone I spoke to was so forthcoming. Mr. Sidorov, who ran the lumberyard outside town, squinted at me when I asked about his boots. "My boots?" he said. "They're okay. Steel-toed." He jerked his head toward the stacks of wood. "Save your foot if you drop a plank." I'd said I was thinking about reflooring my kitchen. Which was true. In a way. I thought about it every time I noticed the linoleum was peeling upward in bigger patches.

"Are those Timberlands?" I asked, checking his feet. Our crime-scene boots were.

Mr. Sidorov looked at me like I was soft in the head. "Yeah. You like oak? Or maybe walnut?" He gestured to different woods, and I pretended to consider them.

"Maybe walnut," I said. "Are the boots good in snow? Do you need to size up? Or are they true to size?"

He chafed his chin stubble. "Fine for snow. I wear an eleven. Always eleven. This maple is good. Probably fit your kitchen. Your house was built when? Fifties? I can cut you a deal."

I told him I'd think about it and then retreated to my car, where I sat, thinking. I wasn't getting anywhere. One more conversation like this, and the town would think I had a foot fetish.

Then again, there were worse things they could think about me, or know.

Back at the station, I did some math. I'd winnowed Elmore's list by fifteen names so far. Not bad. Time to see if my detectives had made any progress. In the pen, Revere sat alone, rereading the fibers report.

"Any word?" I asked, hoping against hope that Gary Clark had confessed while I was away.

He shook the report. Slapped it onto his desk and said, "Nothing. He's sticking to his story. He dropped her off. She walked away. He drove away. She got shot and died. He knows nothing."

"You believe him?" I asked.

He gave me a look like I'd offered to sell him the Brooklyn Bridge. "No," he said. "But what I wouldn't give for the gun."

"Any progress on our needles?" I asked, adopting Wright's description of the two men on the course Mrs. Ashworth had told us about. The ones I'd been systematically eliminating from Elmore's list.

Revere rubbed under his eyes. "Based on the old lady's stunning descriptions?"

I took that as a no.

He grabbed an apple from his desk, polished it on his shirt. Then he strolled to the board and looked at our case, such as it was. "So why'd you become a cop?" Revere asked. He tossed the apple up, let it fall to hip height, and caught it.

Guess we were through discussing our lack of progress. That suited me fine.

"You know, my father offered me two grand not to join," I said.

He whistled. "Adjusting for inflation, that must've been what? A million dollars?"

I crumpled a ball of paper and, without leaning forward, tossed it at his head. It nailed his cheek. "You're no spring chicken, Grandpa," I said.

"I'm a toddler compared to you," he said. "So why was your father so set against you being a cop?"

"It just wasn't what he or my mother wanted for me. They wanted me in some safe, boring job they could brag to their friends about."

"Such as?" He tossed the apple up again. His grip made me think he'd played a bit of ball, back in the day.

"Professor of ecology, like my brother."

He whistled again. "Fancy." He set the apple down on Finnegan's desk. Where it would likely go unnoticed until it rotted and attracted flies. "My whole family is cops or firemen. And the women are nurses or they stay at home."

"I had a partner like that." Except all the women in Rick's family stayed at home, working their rosaries and ovens with equal diligence.

He looked right at me. "The one who died?"

I nodded.

"Sorry to hear about that."

"Why? You don't even know if I liked the son of a bitch."

He said, "Did you?"

"More than my brother."

Revere chuckled. "A least you've got just the one. I've got five."

"Sweet Jesus."

He pointed at me. "That's right. We're good old-fashioned Irish Catholics, being fruitful and multiplying, unlike you and yours. What, just the two kids?"

"Yeah. My parents didn't go in for housefuls of children."

He tsk-tsked, shaking his head. "No wonder you're such a crap copper, with an example like that. I blame your parents."

I lobbed another ball of paper, but he ducked it.

"Crap aim too," he said.

I laughed and challenged him to a game of wastebasket ball. We paced out ten feet. First shooter to make three shots wins. It was cute the way he trash-talked. What was cuter was how I won, three to one. What I hadn't told Revere was that I hadn't just played wastepaper ball for years. I was on the all-star team.

# TUESDAY, SEPTEMBER 2ND
## 1650 HOURS

Billy stormed into my open office. "You let Clark go? Why?"

I recalled what Renee had said about Cecilia's crush on him. Thought about what this meant for him. How it looked to him. And kept my voice low. "We don't have enough on him. The DA wasn't satisfied."

"But he admits she was in his car! Right before she was killed! Who else could have done it?"

"I don't know," I said. "But his feet don't match the prints on the golf course. And he has no motive. No gun."

"The affair?"

"His wife knew he was up to his old tricks. And she's not divorcing him. Far from it. She's paying through the nose for a new lawyer. Telling his wife wouldn't have incited him to kill Cecilia."

"The STOLIs?" He wanted to put Clark in the frame. But Clark's pretty mug wouldn't fit. I'd seen more seasoned cops refuse to see the truth staring them in the face. And Billy was a class-one rookie.

"Gary Clark is going home," I said.

Billy clenched his jaw. "You didn't know her. Not like me. She deserves better."

"Billy?" I rubbed my sandpaper jaw. Squinted at him. "You been talking to the mayor lately?"

He shrugged. "Sometimes. He's my uncle. My mom's brother."

That explained everything.

"You've got to stop telling him details of the case."

He said, "But I thought since he's the mayor . . ."

"No one outside the station should know details. No one. Not the mayor, not the president. Capisce?"

"Am I off the case again?" He looked prepared for disappointment.

"No. Just don't talk about the case outside of these four walls."

"Chief Lynch?" A man in pinstripes and wing tips rapped on my door. Billy moved away from him, farther into my office. Why? "I'm Harold Jenkins." Ah, Gary Clark's new attorney. The one his wife had hired after meeting Louis Jacob and declaring him "unfit to try a pizza."

"Good afternoon, Mr. Jenkins." What did he want? His client had been transferred to Osborn Correctional. That's where he could fetch him. I'd already made the call to have him released.

"It seems Mr. Clark's possessions weren't transferred. He'd like them now."

"Fine." I wondered how much he charged his client for this bit of fetch-and-carry.

"He's here now."

Gary Clark walked into my doorway.

My chest got tight. I held my breath. He looked right at me.

"Where are my things?" he asked his lawyer. His voice was low. The skin under his eyes sagged, and his hair looked grayer than in his photos. His brief jail stint hadn't improved his looks.

"Billy, go ask Hopkins where Mr. Clark's personal effects are, will you?" I coughed. Any second now, Clark would tell his lawyer that I was the man he'd been ranting about. The one from the cabin with the badge. The one Wright and the other detectives had laughed off. Billy left. Thank God. He wouldn't witness this.

"Can I go home after this?" Gary Clark's voice shook.

We'd both be going home soon. And neither of us would return. What station would hire me after this? None. I'd become a mall cop. No. Not that. I couldn't be that.

His lawyer gripped his arm and squeezed. "Yes, we'll take you home."

"Good." He shrugged his shoulders. "I'm going to take a long, hot shower when I get there." He looked at me. My body was frozen, waiting for the ax. He quickly looked away. He'd developed a fear of cops. Not surprising.

"You might keep an eye out for a lawsuit," Mr. Jenkins said to me. "Violating my client's civil rights."

"You might too." I wasn't going to be threatened by some three-hundred-dollar-an-hour suit. Even if I was about to be outed by his client. Civil rights, my foot. "Your client obstructed our case."

Billy returned. "His stuff is at the front desk, Chief." He ignored the two men near him.

Mr. Jenkins sniffed. "Good afternoon," he said.

They both turned and left. Gary Clark didn't look back. I exhaled. He hadn't recognized me.

Then it sank in. The weight was like liquid cement that had settled to stone within me. He hadn't made me. He might never have been able to pick me out of a lineup. Which meant that I'd wasted precious hours and days staying out of sight, avoiding work. If I'd not been hiding I might've seen sooner that Clark wasn't our man. I'd have been looking for the size 8.5 and 11.5 killers earlier. They say hindsight is twenty-twenty. It's more like a hard punch to the head.

# MONDAY, SEPTEMBER 8TH
## 2100 HOURS

**D**onna set a plate before me. On it was a cheeseburger and fries. The burger's bun was to its side. On its cheesy surface, someone had ketchuped a smiley face. "What the hell?" I pointed.

She said, "You looked like you needed cheering up." I smooshed the face with the bun and bit it, hard. She took the hint and left me to my meal.

I looked depressed? Well, why not? I'd let Gary Clark go. My team was pissed at me. Finnegan wondered aloud if Clark would've cracked if we'd left him in custody longer. Wright bitched about why did we need to gift wrap perps in order to prosecute them. Revere worried every office item within reach, leaving a trail of broken binder clips and autopsied pens in his wake. And Billy offered up unlikely scenarios. His latest was wiring one of Clark's poker buddies and sending him to have a chat with Gary about how Cecilia's murder had gone down. I hadn't wasted breath shooting down that idea.

Meanwhile, I'd spent the past few days working my list. All I'd done was eliminate people. The one person I'd spoken to who wore size 8.5 shoes was Dr. Ghentz, and he'd been delivering a baby at Rockville General Hospital the night Cecilia was killed.

The detectives had also looked at the footprints and harassed the techs for information on brands or styles. So far the techs were being shits. The only thing they'd offered us was advice: don't trample the crime scene and you might get better prints.

I'd spent bleary-eyed mornings sorting through the tips, reading suggestions from the citizenry. Most were cranks, clueless, or crazy. As expected. One or two had offered up cars they'd seen in the area. But nothing about two men.

I'd eaten all of my happy-face burger when a finger tapped me on the shoulder. Mike Shannon? I swiveled and found myself staring at the tall and thin Dr. Saunders. "Hello, Chief," he said.

I asked how he was. "Well, thanks," he said.

Donna came over and said hello. Asked the doctor what he'd have. "In-and-out martini," he said.

She took my plate and walked away, with just a little extra wiggle. I sipped my drink and waited for him to speak. The last time I'd thought of him had been while masturbating in my shower. That cut short my small talk.

"Heard you got a murder suspect," he said.

I took another swallow. "We had to let him go."

Donna set his drink down. "You a friend of his?" she asked him.

He took in the bosomy wonder of Donna. "Is there a correct answer?" he asked me.

"Work colleague," I told her.

"Get him to loosen up, will ya?" she said, before heeding the cry of another patron.

"That's Donna," I said. "She means well, I think. Why don't you have a seat?" The stools on either side of me were empty. Always the case, unless there was a game on and people had no choice but to sit next to their police chief. Or they wanted to "talk" about their parking tickets. Seems Yankowitz was a hard-ass about those.

"I was keeping an eye on the tables," he said.

"Meeting someone?" Why had I assumed he wanted to talk to me?

"No. I just prefer a table."

"I can probably help you there."

"You know a guy who knows a guy?" He tried saying this with a New York accent. It was terrible. The worst thing I'd ever heard. I barked a laugh. And scouted the tables until I found one where a man nursed the foam in his glass. He read the paper.

I walked over. "Done here?" I asked.

He glanced up, all angry eyebrows, and then he took in my uniform. "Yeah, just about." He gathered his paper and took his glass to the bar. I waved to his empty seat.

"Neat trick," Damien said. He sat.

"Thank you." I hadn't tried this hard to impress someone since my days in the academy.

"You do it often?" he asked.

"Almost never."

He smiled, and the scar on his cheek shortened. "So what do you do when you're not working?" he asked.

"Watch a game or . . ." Shit. Why couldn't I think of anything else? "Or work on my lawn plan."

He coughed and set his martini down. "Your what?" He raised his slender fingers to his mouth as he tried to fight his cough. "Pardon me." He coughed again.

"My lawn plan. It's something the neighbors have. I think it involves cutting grass and planting things. Oh, and watering them."

He smiled. "Not your cup of tea?"

I shrugged. "I grew up in the city. We didn't even have window boxes." We probably could've. My parents had never cared. Too busy with their heads in books to look outside.

"You could hire a lawn service. They'll cut your grass, water the lawn."

"Huh." I'd thought about paying neighborhood kids to mow. But a service. That might bear looking into.

Next to us, a young couple argued about whose turn it was to pay the bill. The man said something about reverse sexism.

I said, "You have a lawn?" Jesus, why was I asking that? What was it about him? When he got near, I turned idiot.

"Sort of. It's a little unconventional."

"Would you like another drink?" If drunk, perhaps he'd find my fumbling charming. His martini glass was a third full. My alcohol was long gone.

"Yes, thank you."

I hummed to myself as I waited for Donna to finish a large order of Jäger shots. Ugh. I'd had those at my retirement party last November. I couldn't drink them again. Ever.

"What'll it be, Chief?" Donna asked.

"Another in-and-out martini and a bourbon, please."

"You got it."

I thought of things to discuss with Damien. How he got into his work? Most people chose the living to practice medicine on. No, maybe sports or cars or—

"Here you are." Donna set the drinks on the bar. "You going to be at Idyll Days?"

"Working," I said.

"Be sure to stop by the kissing booth," she said. "I work a shift on Saturday." I made a mental note to assign Yankowitz there.

Back at the table, I forgot every safe topic I'd identified. So I said, "Can I ask you a question?"

"You bought the drink. Ask away." He adjusted his dress shirt. White with blue stripes. Good-looking, but not flashy.

"Have you ever heard of the Nipmuc Golf Course as a place to cruise?"

"Excuse me?" His voice was coated with frost.

"I don't mean you. But have you ever heard anyone mention it?"

His fingers stopped playing with the base of his drink and fell to the tabletop. "Why do you ask?"

I took a swallow before I answered. "It pertains to a case I'm investigating."

"*You're* investigating?"

"Yes."

He flushed and his scar whitened in contrast. "What's the case?"

"I'm not at liberty to discuss that."

"So you want me to identify gay men who might've mentioned the golf course as a cruising locale so you can, what? Lock them up for public indecency?"

I pushed my drink from me. "No. No, nothing like that."

The couple fighting over the bill was still at it. I worried they'd stop. I didn't need them overhearing this.

He said, "You just want to ask them some questions? Maybe they can help you with your lawn plan, is that it?" His lips thinned. He sounded like Wright did when racial politics came up.

I was making a muck of this. "Look, Damien, I'm sorry if I upset you."

"Not at all. When you want to find a gay, ask the only one you know, right? How long did it take your boys to tell you about me? A week? Or was it your first day?"

"It isn't personal. I needed help, and since you've lived in the area longer, I thought—"

He stood and pushed his chair back. "Yeah, well I'm sorry I can't be your one-man homopages, but I don't provide directory services."

"Wait."

He didn't. He pushed past patrons until he got out the door. I stood there, aware of the eyes on me. At the bar, Donna watched. Fuck it. I left.

His car revved hard. The tires spat gravel. I ran to my crappy loaner. The engine coughed, but I made it respond. He turned out of the lot, and I followed. There was traffic, but I had no problem tailing him. He drove the speed limit and signaled at every intersection. He'd probably seen too many grisly car-accident results to drive recklessly, even when angry.

Fifteen minutes in, it occurred to me that he might be driving to let off steam and I could be shadowing him for hours. But I'd nowhere else to be. And it was important that he understood I wasn't bullying him. I wasn't singling him out because he was gay. I mean I was, but that wasn't it. I could've asked Mike Shannon. I hadn't. Why? Mike wouldn't have gotten angry with me.

A crack of thunder startled me, made me grip the wheel tighter. My backbone ached. I hated driving through storms. But I followed his car's lights. Even though I had to max out my windshield wipers, even though I had to fight the wheel to maintain control after my car went through a tire-high puddle. The car's brakes, iffy on good days, tested the strength of my calves. After nearly an hour, he slowed and turned into a driveway. I parked behind him. The house before me was a two-story flanked by tall trees. It was hard to see much detail. Everything was black and gray. He ran to his door, and I hurried after.

His keys were out when I yelled, "Wait!"

He turned. "What?" He stood beneath the cover of his small porch, sheltered from the blowing rain that soaked me.

I took a few steps closer, to save my voice. "I didn't mean to offend you. I thought you could help. And I didn't ask you because you're the only gay man I know."

"Name another." He sounded tired.

"Mike Shannon." Perhaps I shouldn't have said that.

Damien said something, but a loud rumble muffled the words. I thought one of them was "slut." He fit his key into the lock and used a second key on another lock. Quite the security setup. "Come in," he said.

I walked up three steps, dripping water like a folded umbrella. In the entryway, he flicked a light. Overhead, a tiny, red, metal chandelier lit the space. He kicked off his shoes and laid them on a bench alongside others. He walked deeper into the house. I removed my boots and put them below the bench. Bit my lip. His back was to me. I picked up his shoe and looked for the size. The print on the tongue was worn, unreadable.

"Just put your shoes anywhere," he called. I threw his shoe down, as if it was on fire. Waited. Checked. He'd disappeared. I picked up another, a sneaker. The label said size 12. I exhaled, hard. Size 12. Only half a size larger than the crime-scene sneaker. Best to be sure. Heart racing, I checked a third pair. Size 12.5. Thank God.

I walked into a room with gray walls and minimal furniture. Floating shelves held photographs and knickknacks. A small, carved elephant, a conch shell. The photos showed Damien standing near a small woman who resembled him. Mother. And another of him and a boy, as children. Brother. I was always a little surprised by familial resemblances. John and I were similar only in our gestures and speech.

The furniture was low to the ground. Next to an egg-shaped chair was my table, the metal-and-glass one.

He reappeared, dressed in scrubs. "Here." He tossed me a fluffy, white towel. I caught it. "You're soaking," he said, after I failed to do anything.

"Right." I rubbed my hair.

"Want a drink?" he said.

I'd never wanted one more. Well, that wasn't true. After Rick died, I lived off booze and pretzels for three days. Then I realized I was headed for rock bottom and stopped drinking. Wouldn't let myself touch a drop for two whole months.

"No, thanks. I have to drive home. Where are we, by the way?" I asked. The downpour had made sign reading impossible.

"Avon." He had a bartending set on a sideboard. He looked like he belonged in a Dean Martin movie as he mixed a drink.

"Nice place," I said. "I have that same table." I pointed.

"You have an Eileen Gray side table?" His tone said "liar."

"Um, I don't know the name. But it looks just like that. Only piece in my place that I like much."

He gave me a raised brow. "It's a famous piece. Eileen Gray created the E-1027 table in the 1920s. She was an architect."

"Funny, it looks futuristic." It reminded me of the movie *2001: A Space Odyssey*. A movie I'd never seen all the way through. I stopped rubbing my arms with the towel. I felt conspicuous.

"Is your table a recent reproduction?" he asked.

"I don't know." I could invite him to take a look. No. What would he think when he saw my house? The black and pink bathroom. The seashell lamp. God, no.

He raised his drink. Something in a highball glass. "Cheers to good taste." He took a healthy swallow. We stood, staring at each other. A clock ticked. It was that quiet.

"I just came to apologize," I said. *And to check your shoe size. Make sure you're not a murderer. You understand.*

"No, I should apologize." He sat on the low, beige sofa. "I'm not usually so sensitive. I had a rough day at work."

"Sorry to hear it." I remained standing, towel in hand, unsure where to put it. Everything was so clean.

"Someone messed with one of the toe tags on an unidentified corpse. Wrote the name 'John Homo.'" He massaged his brow with the heel of his hand. "Not even a good joke. I know who did it. The new guy, Wayne."

"Can you fire him?"

He tugged at the knees of his scrubs. "I suppose I could mention it to his supervisor, but," he took another sip of his drink, "I'd rather not. No, I'll handle it my way."

"How's that?"

"I'll give him the worst we see for a month. Babies and burn victims." He swirled his drink. So Damien played rough. Good for him.

"The guys at the station did tell me, about you," I said. "But recently. It wasn't the first thing they mentioned."

He said, "Perhaps Idyll lives up to its name."

No it didn't. The townspeople were just as biased, as stupid, as people anywhere. It's why I kept my private life private. Why most of the men on Elmore's list did the same. Fear of harassment. I shifted my weight. "I should go. I just wanted you to know I wasn't singling you out. Or, I was, but because I thought you'd be sympathetic."

"Sympathetic to what?"

I decided to come clean with him. "I'm looking for two gay men. They were on the golf course the night of the murder. I need to talk to them, and I don't want it to turn into a witch hunt. I haven't told the others."

"Don't trust them?" He set the glass down on the Eileen Gray table.

"Not with this. Not yet."

"I see." He got up and walked to the sideboard. Seemed to consider another drink. "I've never heard about the Nipmuc Golf Course as a cruising spot. Scout's honor." He gave the Scout salute. "Though you should take that with a bucket of salt. I got kicked out of the Scouts."

I didn't ask why. "Where should I put this?" I held out the towel.

He reached for it. Under the damp cotton, I grabbed his hand and held it. And looked into his very blue eyes. "There's something else," I said. "I'm gay."

His scar got white, and he blinked twice, fast. "Oh," he said.

I let go of his hand. "Surprised?"

He held the towel to his chest. "Yes, actually. I thought—Well, you're quite convincing. And my gaydar is broken. I'm always hitting on straight men." He fingered his scar. "Not such a good idea."

He'd been attacked? Years ago, judging by the scar's age. Around here? God, I hoped not. I didn't want to endanger anyone with my investigation, and it seemed I might, if the locals wielded knives this way.

"No one knows at work. Do you mind keeping it secret?" I asked.

"Of course. No. I . . . God, you must think me an idiot." He rubbed his scar. "Accusing you of being a homophobe."

"I didn't, and you didn't." I walked to the entryway to claim my damp shoes. I'd checked his footwear. Just to be sure he wasn't our killer. Rick once told me I'd check my mother's prints if she looked likely for a crime. I'd laughed and said of course I would.

He held the towel. Its dampness had soaked his chest, turning his light-blue scrubs navy. "Maybe we can have a drink sometime. When you're not investigating," he said.

"I'd like that." My heart went thumpity thump.

"Well, good night, Chief."

"You can call me Thomas." Why had I said Thomas? I usually went by Lynch or Tom or Tommy. I got to the door and realized I had no idea how to get home.

He gave me directions I hoped I could remember. Then I left. Outside my car, I looked toward his front door. The rain had stopped. He stood there, towel to his chest. As I drove home, an electric buzz filled me. I turned the radio on and sang along to songs from my youth, now identified as hits from prior decades. Geez. At least they weren't calling them oldies. Not yet.

*I always hit on straight men. My gaydar is broken.* If he'd mistaken me for straight, did that mean he was interested? Had been attracted to me? Maybe I'd invite him to look at my table with the lady's name. After I'd had the place redone, from peeling linoleum to pink and black tiles.

And when I got to my wreck of a house, the first thing I was going to do was dig up Elmore's list and cross Damien Saunders's name off it.

# SUNDAY, SEPTEMBER 14TH
## 1445 HOURS

Idyll Days was hell on earth. The soles of my feet felt as though they'd been beaten with rods. My toes were cramped. I'd not walked this much since I was a rookie, community policing in the Bronx. Today was the last day of events. My constant motto, since I'd risen this morning. Last day. Last day. Last day. I wasn't the only one who felt this way. Locals who didn't make their fortunes this weekend had gotten the hell out of town.

"Too much hustle and bustle," Mr. Yener, a DPW worker, had told me. "There's no parking and everywhere you go there are lines. If I'd wanted that kind of aggravation, I'd live in the city!"

Main Street resembled Herald Square. Hordes overtook the sidewalks and streets. Idyll Days brought four thousand tourists to town. I walked past Idyll Garden, the town's florist shop. "How quaint!" a woman said. She tugged her husband's arm and pointed at a lawn ornament. It looked like an old woman leaning over, exposing her bloomers. Quaint?

"Everything okay?" I asked Billy, as he walked past, supporting a limping woman.

"Bit of a brawl at the wool station," he said. "Just going to the first-aid tent."

"Okay." I'd instructed my men that anyone with so much as a sneeze should be brought to the first-aid tent, manned by the firefighters. This, after I got a call from Captain Hirsch suggesting I lend "support" to the tent. As if my men weren't stretched thin already by this event. Oh, and we had that murder. So far, I'd personally sent a sprained ankle, an asthma attack, a bad sunburn, and two bloody noses their way.

Main Street was closed to cars, both lanes overtaken by booths hawking maple syrup, beeswax candles, and old-fashioned wooden puzzles. I walked the street, mindful of the open cashboxes. So far, no thievery had been reported. The worst incident of the weekend was a superficial head wound suffered by a three-year-old who'd wanted to pet the pony. He'd tripped over his feet and clipped his head on the fence. Thing bled like a sucker and attracted quite a crowd.

My only piece of good luck was that I'd been tied up sorting out a fender bender at the library parking lot yesterday when Donna had her shift at the kissing booth.

"Chief!" Mr. Neilly waved to me from his post at the dunking station. He manned the ticket booth. Currently on the hot seat was Mayor Mitchell.

"Everything okay, Mr. Neilly?" I rotated my ankles, one at a time.

"We're running out of tickets. Could you ask Sandy to send some from the library?" It was five blocks down the road. Contemplating the walk gave me blisters.

"Sure." There was no one in line. "Not many takers?" I asked.

"We just had a group of high schoolers."

"They all had arms like linguini," the mayor called. He kicked his tan legs to and fro. He wore a polo shirt and khaki shorts. Didn't make sense to bundle up, not if he landed in the water. But he was dry and smiling.

"Would you like to try?" Mr. Neilly said, reading my expression. "All proceeds benefit the Idyll Food Pantry."

"How's your car?" the mayor asked. He'd heard of my deer run-in. Had given me grief over it. Like I'd chosen to smash the vehicle.

"Fixed," I said, eyeing the bucket of balls.

"Repairs come out of your budget," the mayor said, as if I didn't know. I was tired of his veiled threats, of his constant shadowing of my work.

"It's for a good cause, right?" I said, handing Neilly a five-dollar bill.

"You didn't happen to play baseball, did you?" the mayor asked. He wiggled on the plastic seat above the tank.

"I did." I took the first ball, held it tightly, and then relaxed my grip. "Don't worry, I didn't pitch." I moved to the right and zeroed in on the bull's-eye. Breathed in, held the breath. Then exhaled hard and hurled the ball. It thwacked the tarp.

The mayor grinned. "What were you, a designated hitter?"

"Nope." I picked up the second ball, adjusted my grip. A small group of tourists had collected behind me. "Shortstop," I said, and let loose. The ball went fast and hit the edge of the bull's-eye, ringing the bell. The mayor's seat upended, and he splashed into the water. The crowd applauded. The mayor stood and sputtered water. His wet hair covered his eyes.

"Nice shot," Mr. Neilly said.

"Thanks. I'll go check on those tickets."

My mood was lighter, but my feet throbbed as I walked past the wool exhibition, where a small pen of lambs was stationed. Nearby was the knitting club. Those women, with their long braids and ever-moving needles, made me nervous. I crossed to the other side of the street, where children were having their faces painted and balloons were being contorted into animal shapes. The squeals of the balloons being twisted made me want to stuff my fingers into my ears. Last day. Last day. Last day.

I reached the library and passed along my message. Sandy grabbed a roll of tickets larger than my head and left for the dunk tank. I stood on the front steps, enjoying the soft weather. Summer was gone, with its wet storms and humid nights. Fall was almost here, tinting the leaves yellow. Making Idyll even more postcard New England. You had to hand it to the natives: they knew when to exploit their local resources for profit.

In front of the columned, brick library, the grassy lawn was covered by the bake-sale and book-sale tables. People browsed books and brownies with equal intent. Inspired by a tug of hunger, I went to the bake-sale tables. Mrs. Prior greeted me absently as she counted change to tourists buying pies. I exchanged a dollar for a Mother Lode. Then it was back down Main Street, where the smell of horse dung mingled with that of roasted nuts, confusing my stomach.

The sounds in town had amplified a thousandfold, and I had to keep checking if the yelling indicated fear, anger, or excitement. People were enthusiastic. About the apples. About the pony rides. About our five-and-dime store, though nothing inside cost five or ten cents. I'd nearly completed my sixth circuit, and the end of my shift, when I heard a familiar voice encouraging people to adopt a cat. Outside the hardware store, Tiffany Haines, my late-night golf-course trespasser, stood next to four cages holding six cats. She had a clipboard, a pen, and a voice that carried. "Bring some love into your home! Adopt a cat! Cats who are not adopted may be euthanized!"

"What's yootamized?" a girl in pigtails asked her mother.

"Let's go see the ponies." The mother tugged her daughter away from Tiffany and her cats.

"Hello, Tiffany," I said.

She said hello quietly. "Do you want a cat?" She pointed to a small, black fur ball. "They're nice pets."

Is this how Cecilia North had been as a kid? Hustling pets for adoption on Idyll's streets? I peered at an orange cat with blue eyes. It stared back at me, then lifted its leg and began licking its bottom. "Sell many cats?" I asked.

"We're not *selling* them. We're giving them away to good homes."

"How do you know the homes are good?"

She tapped her clipboard. "People have to give references, at least two. And we check them. Plus, we ask if they have other pets or small kids, things that might be problematic for the animal."

"But if you're checking references, can people take the pets today?"

"If we can reach their references and do the other checks, yes. If not, they have to come to the Rescue League to pick up the animal."

"Sounds complicated." The orange cat butted its head against a striped cat.

"We want these animals to have good lives. Some came from bad homes where people mistreated them. Some were just dumped by the side of the road. It's terrible."

A woman carrying a bag full of bake-sale goods stopped to peer at the orange cat. She made kissing noises at it. The cat ignored her. "What a dear," she said.

Tiffany sprang into action. "That is a very sweet cat," she said. "And unless we can find a home for him by Wednesday . . ." She made a sad face. "Unfortunately, we can't accommodate so many cats, and the no-kill shelter nearby can't take any more."

"Oh," said the woman. "How awful." She bent to get a better look. "But I already have two cats, Mittens and Puck."

"Oh, this cat loves company! That's why we put him in with a friend!" Within eight minutes, Tiffany had the woman's information, references, and a $50 check to cover veterinary fees.

"Well done," I said.

"I've still got five to go."

"Hey, Cat Lady!"

Tiffany kept her head down and yelled back, "Keep talking, Cowboy."

Another of my trespassers, Christopher Warren, jogged to the cages. His ginger hair glowed in the sun. "How's cat sales?"

"It's not sales," I said. Tiffany smiled.

"Good afternoon, Chief Lynch. Enjoying Idyll Days?" he asked.

"Not really." Both kids looked shocked. By my honesty? Or my failure to appreciate their town's event? "It's not much fun if you're working," I said.

"Gotcha," he said.

"Why'd you call him 'Cowboy'?" I asked Tiffany.

"Mr. Warren here fancies himself a man of the Wild West," she said.

"Shut it," he said.

"He learned how to ride a horse and everything."

"Lots of people ride horses," he said. He bent and meowed at the cats.

"Yes, but most of them don't wear ridiculous horse belt buckles every day."

She held her hands just below her belly button to illustrate her point. "Where is that thing? You haven't worn it in weeks."

A large belt buckle. Mrs. Ashworth had seen a belt buckle on the man who was standing on the golf course the night of the murder. Chris was nearly as tall as me. No. I was reaching.

He said, "Haven't felt like it." He poked a finger into the wire cage, and the black-and-white cat swiped at him. "Fuck!" He pulled his finger back, fast. And then hit the side of the cage. It rattled. The cat mewled.

"Chris!" Tiffany said.

"Look what it did!" He showed his bleeding finger. "Is that cat sick? Will I get an infection?"

"Don't be stupid. They've got all their shots. You'll be fine, you jerk."

He had a quick temper. I looked down. He wore large sneakers. Red and black. I recognized them. Michael Jordan had worn them during his famous Flu Game back in June, leading the Bulls to victory over the Utah Jazz. Bet they had a distinct tread. Large feet. Size 11.5? Possible. Very possible.

"I'm sorry." Chris bent down and addressed the cat. "Sorry," he said, softly. "You scared me."

"Right. And you just delighted the hell out of her," Tiffany said.

"It's a her? How can you tell?" he asked.

"Um, have you heard of genitals?" They both cracked up. Chris bent double, laughing.

When they'd settled down, he asked me, "How's the murder case coming?"

*Funny you should ask.* "I can't discuss it."

"Oh. Well, did you follow up on the flashlight? The one I saw?" he asked.

"Yes." But no one, including Charlie Fisher, had seen it. And wasn't that interesting? Him being the only witness to it.

"I heard about Luke's punishment." He kicked the sidewalk. It made my toes ache just to watch. "Do you really check up on him at his house to see that he's home by nine?"

"Yes, I do."

He nodded to himself. "Probably a good idea. You've met his mom?"

"I have."

"Man, is she nuts or what? Luke's probably gonna wind up in jail like his dad."

"Chris," Tiffany said.

"What?" He pointed to me. "He's the police chief. I'm sure he knows."

"So Luke's dad did time?" That explained a lot.

"Robbing houses mostly. But then he got into a bar fight and knifed a guy. Got off because the guy came at him with a gun. Then he left town. Luke hasn't seen him since. That was five years ago."

"That's unfortunate." I'd heard a lot of stories like that one.

"I think Luke just wants attention," Tiffany said. "It's why he acts out."

Chris said, "Maybe it's genetic." He sucked on his injured finger.

"What is?" I asked.

He looked up. "Being bad. Maybe it's in your blood."

"That's a happy worldview," Tiffany said, dishing out kibble to her furry friends.

Maybe he was just making conversation, but it seemed like he was trying to lead me somewhere. He'd reminded me of Rick earlier. He was doing it again, but the resemblance now was to my lying, drug-addicted partner. The Rick who'd say anything to get what he wanted.

He looked across the way. "Remember when we could ride them?" he said to Tiffany. He stared across the street at the ponies.

Tiffany said, "I remember you trying to ride one two years ago. Nearly broke the poor thing's back."

He said, "Ah, memories. Well, I've got to run. I promised to help out at the dunk tank."

"Going to offer yourself up?" I asked.

He chaffed his hands. "No way. The water is freezing. I'm selling tickets." He loped off, his stride long.

"He play sports?" I asked. His size was right for basketball.

Tiffany said, "Soccer and track. But he's not a jock."

Ah, the classification system of high school. "So what is he?"

She pursed her lips. "Well he's not straight-edge or a nerd or one of the potheads. He's been elected to vice president, but he's not really a student-government kid. I don't know. Chris is just Chris."

But was Chris a killer? Probably not. And yet he was too curious and too helpful about the murder. With large feet and a big belt buckle. I'd keep him in the picture, for now.

## 2015 HOURS

I'd never been so happy to be home. Idyll Days was over, for me. They'd be tearing down tents and cleaning the streets, taking down posters from lampposts and utility poles. But I wouldn't be there. My stomach gurgled. I recalled that I still had the treat I'd bought at the bake sale in my pocket. The famed Mother Lode. I tried to undo the pink ribbon holding its cellophane wrapper together. I couldn't. The knot was tight, and my big fingers couldn't work it apart. I grabbed a pair of scissors, cut the ribbon, and pulled at the crinkly cellophane. This had better be worth it.

I took a bite and chewed. And chewed. And chewed. "Ugh." After a minute of mastication, it felt like half of it was still stuck in my molars. I reached into the fridge. Drank milk from the carton. It helped dampen the sweetness. I tossed the remains of the Mother Lode into the trash. Well, that was one more thing I didn't have in common with the towns-folk. Their taste in sweets was awful.

To get the smell of horse, hay, and small-town fun off me, I show-ered. While I lathered up, I considered my next move on the murder and thought about my conversation with Mike Shannon. I'd asked him a few days earlier if he knew about the golf course as a cruising spot. He'd laughed and said no. Made a joke about a hole in one. Unlike Damien Saunders, he wasn't upset by my assumption he'd know such things. He'd asked if the murder was keeping me busy. A slight prod. Testing the waters to see if I recalled my promise of a rain check.

"That and Idyll Days."

He'd laughed and scratched his beard. "Idyll Days. Where small-town living is a grand adventure!"

I'd said I'd see him after things quieted down. Probably would. He was a nice guy. Fun. Uncomplicated.

I grabbed some fresh clothes from the bedroom, smelling of the fabric softener used at Suds. Then I got dressed and moved to the living room, sat in my recliner, and groaned. My feet. They'd never feel good again. I flexed my toes. Ow.

The talk I'd had with Tiffany and Chris still nagged at me. His belt buckle, unworn in weeks, and his attitude. Something was off. I moved to my gun safe and unlocked it. Grabbed Elmore's list and scanned it for Chris or Christopher. There were three, but none of them with the surname Warren. I squinted at the list again. No one on it was under age twenty-three. I wondered if Elmore subscribed to the opinion that many young men experiment, or if gay was on the decline among Idyll's youth. Either way, Christopher Warren wasn't on the list.

I locked the safe and wandered into the kitchen. The only other person to talk to would be Mrs. Ashworth. I recalled her dogs on my legs. No. I'd call her.

She answered on the fifth ring, when I'd begun to think she must be out. "Oh, Chief Lynch," she said. "I saw you at Idyll Days yesterday!"

"Yes," I said. "I was calling about the murder."

"Did you enjoy yourself?"

I assumed she meant at Idyll Days.

"Very lively. I just wanted to ask—"

"I thought the fireworks show this year was less spectacular than last year's. Lacked a certain . . . oomph."

"Could the man you saw peeing on the golf course have been younger?"

"Than you? Sure." Her rapid answer implied most people were younger. Christ. I was only forty-four. "How young?" she asked.

"A teenager, perhaps?"

"I suppose he could've been." She chuckled. "I bet he got in trouble when he got home. Stumbling drunk at that age."

"I bet. Well, thanks for your time. Have a nice evening." I hung up before she could say another word.

I returned to the living room and sat in my recliner. Rubbed the worn nap of the arm with my finger pads. Closed my eyes and saw images. Cecilia's corpse on the course. The shoe prints. A belt buckle. The gun. Where was the damn gun? How would a teen get one? Did his parents own one?

And without thinking on it hard, I decided I'd pursue this angle alone, for now. I suspected the detectives would scoff. And anyway it was just a small thing to keep to myself. I already had so many secrets. What was one more?

I picked up the copy of Cecilia North's autopsy report. Looked at the wound chart. This was where the bullets entered, this where they exited. Rick had only one entry and exit wound, but it had been enough. And his autopsy, required because of who he was and how he died, was the bullet in my career. The exit wound blew me to pieces.

They found traces of cocaine in his system. His hair showed he'd been using for months. Sometimes at night I still hear my super's voice asking, "Why didn't you tell me, Lynch?" I hear and feel his anger and, worse, his disappointment. I'd been Rick's partner. I should've protected him from everything, including himself.

They didn't formally discipline me. No one wanted to ruin the image of a cop dying on duty with news of his drug habit. But it was understood that I would never be promoted, never be trusted as I had before.

So I left. Came to Idyll. Kept my head down and played by the rules. Until I hadn't. And look where that had gotten me. I couldn't come clean about seeing Cecilia North. I set the autopsy report on the side table and knuckled my brow. Secrets were overrated. The moment I had a real lead, no matter the suspect, I'd share it. Who cared if my men laughed? I'd survived worse.

# THURSDAY, SEPTEMBER 18TH
## 1545 HOURS

I'd sent a description of Christopher Warren's shoes to the forensic lab's tread expert for a comparison to our 11.5 crime-scene print. But the tech went on vacation to Jamaica. Today he was supposed to be at work.

"Where is he?" I said into the phone. I squeezed the stress ball I'd taken from Finnegan's desk. It had sparkly bits inside, like a squishy snow globe.

The receptionist at the forensic lab said, "He hurt his back on the trip home."

"When do you expect him to return to work?" I squeezed again. The gooey ball protruded up and out, over my thumb.

"I couldn't really say."

"And he's the only person who can analyze the shoe treads? Really?"

She said, "Sorry. I'll let him know you called." And hung up.

This is the stuff you don't see on TV crime dramas or cop shows. The tedious, mundane shit. Techs go on vacation, MEs get sick, lawyers die midcase, and you're left to wait until they come back or their work is reassigned to get your results.

Stymied, I went in search of Revere. Maybe he could ask the staties for help with the tread. He was alone, transferring items from his desk to Finnegan's disaster area.

"Little late for spring cleaning," I said.

"They're pulling me back to the Eastern." He picked up cards, pens, maps.

"What?" We'd had him less than six weeks. Surely the Eastern District could spare him longer. "Why?"

"Boss says he can't spare me."

"This case isn't over. We've got the techs working on the footprints. They might have a shoe brand for us tomorrow." Not true. But I was willing to stretch or even abandon the truth, if it meant he'd stay on. "And I've got the budget to dredge Hought's Pond." I'd pushed it through last night. Got Mr. Neilly on board by praising Idyll Days, specifically the Mother Lodes. And I'd won Mrs. Kettle over by asking for gardening tips. "The gun could be there."

"Or it could be at the bottom of the Connecticut River," he said. "It could be anywhere. Look, I'm sorry I can't stay. But there's nothing I can do." He massaged his crew-cut fuzz and said, "The state thinks this one's a goner. And they prefer to keep the stink off them."

"Rather than help solve the case?"

"It's not my call." He tossed his mobile phone and notepad into a duffel and hefted it onto his shoulder. "Good luck, Chief." He held out his hand. I wanted to smack it away. He was a good detective. Knew his stuff. And he was leaving. Taking all his contacts with him. I shook his hand. It was warm and dry.

"And the next time Billy cracks a gay joke, say something." He picked up a takeout container and tossed it into the trash. "You got to nip that shit in the bud."

Why was Revere so passionate on the topic? I looked him over from his crew cut to his shined shoes. No. No way. Revere was straighter than a ruler.

He glanced at the board. There were a few new items, but nothing about Christopher Warren. I couldn't say anything yet. Not until I had one solid piece of evidence.

"I hope you get him," he said. He turned away from the board. "I really hope you do." He left.

A minute later, Billy appeared, two coffees in hand. "Where's Revere gone to? I got his coffee."

"Home," I said.

"Home home or back to his station?"

"Station."

It took a moment for him to process what this meant. "But the case!" His voice cracked.

I left Billy and the board and returned to my office.

I'd review the equipment folder, overdue by a week. If I couldn't solve large problems, I'd manage little ones. Three pages in, I saw that one of our patrol cars had been in an accident. The car was nearly totaled. The driver? Officer Yankowitz. I buzzed Dunsmore and told her to come to my office immediately.

She arrived in five minutes. Her idea of immediate.

"Yankowitz nearly totaled a patrol car. Why is this the first I'm hearing of it?" I pointed to the folder.

Her wrinkled face got more puckered. "I couldn't say." No, she wouldn't say. Wouldn't say, "Gee, Chief, the men don't seem to have warmed to you. Or they'd have told you straightaway about Yankowitz's latest wreck."

"Get him in here," I said.

"He's out sick."

I grunted. Of course he was.

"You shouldn't be too hard on him." She adjusted her pearls. Must be bridge-club night.

"Give me one good reason." I picked up the stress ball. It was sweaty.

"He writes eighty-five percent of our tickets."

"He's the meter maid."

"Yes, and he takes that duty seriously, unlike some I could mention." She pointed to the folder in my hand. "Yankowitz always deals with Caroline Ross." Our cranky bad driver. "He's the only one brave or compassionate enough to take her on. The others just let her park in front of the hydrants or double park in front of the dentist until someone calls to complain."

"Why is she such a pill?" I asked.

"She's Chief Stoughton's ex-wife. The first one."

Huh.

She said, "Yankowitz is a poor driver, but he won't hesitate to ticket other poor drivers. Did you know he paid that ticket you wrote him the day you arrived?"

I said, "He parked in my spot. Two spots, actually."

"Yes. But you didn't actually think he'd pay the ticket, did you?"

"Since I wrote it on a napkin, no, I didn't." I'd been trying to establish my authority, and to lessen the sting I'd played it off as a joke. No one had laughed.

"He put the money into the Widows and Orphans Fund. The others laughed at him for it. But he said he deserved it. Should've been more careful."

Her guilt trip wasn't working. Not entirely. I sighed, "Fine. I won't fire him, yet. But I'm sure as hell removing him from the patrol cars. He can be on bike patrol."

"We don't have a bicycle patrol," she said.

"We do now."

I opened a new folder with my free hand. She could show herself out. "What the hell is this?" I yelled after I'd scanned the first page.

She sighed and said, "What?" I extended the sheet to her. She held it away as far as her arms allowed. She must've left her glasses on her desk. "Oh, this is the estimate from the carpenter. You know, for changing the nameplate."

As if I'd forgotten. "That's what he plans to charge?" I squeezed the stress ball. It made an odd squealing noise.

She pointed to the nameplate. "It's attached with screws. He'll need to remove it, repair the door, and install the new one. Probably resize it too. Your name is shorter."

The stress ball exploded with a splat. Liquid hit my face, torso, and desk. I wiped at my eyes. Opened them. Yuck. Goo covered my desk. Covered me.

"Is that glitter?" she asked.

Small sparkly bits covered my hands. I was a human disco ball.

"Tell you what," I said. I tossed the rubbery shreds of the ball into the trash. "I'm not waiting another damn day for the carpenter." I walked to the equipment room. Took the key from my ring, and unlocked the door. Searched the shelves. Found what I wanted, and walked to where Mrs. Dunsmore stood, arms crossed over her mighty bust.

She saw the crowbar in my hand. "Chief!"

"Look at it this way." I inserted the crowbar's end underneath the "S" of "Stoughton" and pulled toward me. The plate screeched and cracked in half. "This'll save money *and* time." I repositioned the metal bar and pulled. The first half of the nameplate dropped to the carpet along with a chunk of the door.

"Don't worry." I kicked aside the wood. Then I wedged the bar under the remaining part of the nameplate and yanked hard. The plate and its screws fell to the floor. "I'll make a replacement."

She said, "You've ruined it!"

I grabbed a red marker and wrote CHIEF THOMAS LYNCH on a blank sheet of paper. I taped my sign so that it half-covered the damaged area. "There." I set the crowbar against the wall and admired my handiwork. "Good as new."

A few men stood in the hall, drawn by the sounds of my labors. I called, "Hey, fellas! There's a new chief in town. Spread the word." A few clapped. Billy whistled. Mrs. Dunsmore said I'd pay for the repairs and stomped off. Probably to report me to the carpenter or the selectmen. Or both.

"Chief!" Finnegan hustled over, his breathing labored. His pant legs were wet. He glanced at my door and said, "Huh." Then he stared at me for several long seconds and said, "Do you have glitter on your face?"

"Did you know you can explode a stress ball?" I said.

"Nope. Hey, I got something you'll like." Finnegan's idea of "something" could be a donut, a new sports car he could never afford, or a lingerie model he'd pegged to be the next ex–Mrs. Finnegan.

"Yeah?" I picked up the two largest pieces of wood from the floor. A splinter stuck me. "Got tweezers?" I frowned at the needle of wood protruding from my skin.

"Nah," he said. "But I've got your murder weapon."

I forgot the splinter. "What?"

He grinned. His stained teeth were appalling. "And you're never going to guess who found it."

"Who?"

"A dog named Biscuit. Its owner threw a stick, and the dog brought back a Smith & Wesson .45. So the owner, Mr. Dunlop, called us. Found it in Baumer's Pond, which is really just a big puddle a few minutes from the golf course." His smiled dimmed. "Any chance the techs can get prints off it?"

"It's been in the water and in some dog's mouth? Plus the dog owner's hands?"

"Still, we got it," he said.

"Has the lab been notified?"

"Yup."

I put up my non-splintered hand, and Finnegan smacked his palm against it. We had the gun.

"Way to go, Biscuit," I said.

Finnegan examined his hand. "I think you got glitter on me."

# SATURDAY, SEPTEMBER 20TH
## 1000 HOURS

Suds was quiet. The bar was closed. Next door, the Laundromat was occupied by the few people whose washing machines or driers had died recently.

"Hey, Nate," I said. "You have a pet?"

"Yup. An Irish setter named Lewis." He didn't raise his head. He fiddled with one of the tap lines below the bar. Something was clogged or stopped. I'd tuned out as soon as he'd started talking wrench sizes. "I named him after Meriwether Lewis. Dumb dog gets lost going to the front yard." Something clanked and he cursed. "Why—you in the market for one?" he asked.

"Not exactly." My mind had just been circling animals. The ones my dead girl had tried to save. The cats Tiffany Haines peddled. And let's not forget Mrs. Ashworth's dogs.

"There's a breeder over near Windsor," Nate said. He stood. He held a rag in one hand and a wrench in the other. His hair was tied back with two leather strips today. He wiped his forearm against his brow. "I could ask if they're expecting pups."

"No, thanks," I said. "I'd probably get a mutt." Because last week Tiffany Haines had told me how many pets are abandoned each year. How many mixed-breeds need a loving home. Not that I needed a dog. Hardly.

"Well, if you change your mind, let me know."

"Thanks. Think I'll get my laundry." I'd dropped off an enormous load three days ago after I'd made the mistake of sniffing my sheets. I set some bills on the counter, thanked Nate for the coffee, and walked next door, where it was ten degrees warmer and the air smelled of fabric softener. Lucy stood, her back to me, arranging dress shirts on a rod.

"Morning, Lucy."

She turned, and I saw she wore no makeup. Her face was pale with freckles by her nose. Her brown eyes looked bigger. Her mouth was naturally red. God, she was pretty. Even with her purple hair.

"Don't." She held up a finger to her mouth.

"Don't what?"

"Don't say whatever you were about to say about my face. I've had enough this morning."

"Okay." But she looked so much better without that white mask she always wore. "I'm here for my laundry."

She walked to the corner, where two bulging bags stood. Both mine.

"Some of this stuff really needed cleaning." Lucy set the bags down near me.

"Hey, I don't talk about your makeup; you leave my cleaning habits alone."

"Fine. But maybe you should bring the towels in sooner next time. They practically marched into the machines."

"Yeah? Well, you look awfully pretty today."

She slapped her hands over her ears.

I mouthed words at her until curiosity got the better of her and she uncovered her ears. "What?"

"What grade are you in?" It occurred to me that Lucy might know some things.

"Eleventh. Why?"

"You know Chris Warren?"

Her hands tensed around a garment bag. "Yeah. He's a year below me."

"Any thoughts on him?"

She glanced at the patrons. Two read magazines while they waited for their machine cycles to end. The third folded towels on a square table. "Why you asking?"

"I think he might be involved in something."

"Something bad?"

"Yes."

"That would be him. Everyone thinks he's a great kid, but underneath it all he's a psycho." Her voice was low, the words fast.

"Psycho? How?"

"He manipulates people, even teachers. Everything he does is about him, but no one sees it. He volunteered at this charity rockathon. You stay up all night, on rocking chairs, to raise money for cancer research. He raised the most. But he took a cut. I heard him tell people there was an administrative fee for their donation. Which was total bullshit. He pocketed the money."

"Did he get caught?"

She bit her lower lip. "He claimed it was a misunderstanding. Gave the money back. But he probably got it from his parents. They're loaded. His dad owns some software company."

Embezzling from a charity was bad behavior, but not blueprint-of-a-killer stuff. "Anything else?"

She picked up a pen, tapped it on the counter. "I caught him blowing up frogs with fireworks once. Plus, he ruined Jennifer Gilmore's reputation. He asked her out. She said no. Next thing you know, everyone at school is calling her a slut and claiming she slept with half the football team. Which isn't true. Chris started the rumors. When he doesn't get what he wants, he gets nasty."

"Interesting."

"What's awful is that most people think he's like, amazing. I mean, on paper he looks good." She tapped the pen faster. "Does well in school, plays sports, has friends. But behind it all, he's just not right." She tapped the counter harder. Noticed what she was doing. Stopped.

"He bother you?" I asked. She seemed too upset for this not to be personal.

Her nod was small, a quick bob of the head. "We went on a date, two years ago. He asked me out for weeks and weeks, and finally I said okay. His parents drove us to the movies. *Billy Madison*, with Adam

Sandler." Her voice was wooden. Her face flushed. "He, uh, took my hand and tried to push it into—"

In a low voice I said, "His pants?"

Her head jerked, as if pulled by a string. "Yeah. I tried to pull my hand back. But he wouldn't let go. It hurt. He kept . . . and so I squeezed him, hard, and then yanked my hand back. He zipped up and then he left."

"Left?"

"Called his parents. Told them I had left him and gone home. He stranded me there. I had to call a cab because my parents had gone out that night. The next day at school, everyone is looking at me. Whispering." She blinked fast, several times. "My wrist was all bruised."

"What did he tell them?" Another slut story?

"He told them I was a Satanist. That I'd tried to get him to sacrifice a puppy with me. And those idiots believed him. Wanted to believe him. It's much more fun to gossip about someone than actually investigate. After four months of being called 'Satan Girl' and finding pictures of dead animals in my locker, I decided to give them what they wanted. Went fully Goth. The makeup. The clothes. And then they backed off. Started acting afraid."

"And today?" I asked, gesturing to her bare face.

She huffed. "I have to visit my grandmother after work. My mother won't let me wear makeup when I see her." She pushed her hair forward, the better to hide her beauty.

"Thanks for telling me," I said.

She watched me from behind her hair. "You going to nail him?" she asked.

"I hope to."

"Good." She smiled. Her teeth were as white as her absent face powder.

An hour later, I took my suspicions with me to work.

"Anybody know this kid?" I push-pinned a photocopy of Christopher Warren's yearbook photo onto the crime board.

Billy's brow wrinkled. "Chris Warren. I coached him at soccer camp a few years back."

"Anyone else?"

Wright rubbed the corners of his eyes. "Isn't that one of the kids you busted at the golf course?"

"Yup."

Finnegan wiped pizza grease from his chin. "You think he's involved?"

"He wears distinctive sneakers. I think they're a match for those at the crime scene."

"What do the techs say?" Wright asked.

"Their print expert is out now."

Finnegan chewed another slice of pepperoni-and-pineapple. His combos were disgusting. No one would share. He always ended up with extra slices. Those of us who ordered normal pizzas never had leftovers. They got poached.

Billy said, "Chris is a good kid. He's on the honor roll. He raised like two grand last year for cancer research at this school fundraiser they had. I don't think—"

"He fits the profile." I chafed my hands. "So far, we know he was at the golf course, looking to remove evidence. He also claimed to have seen a flashlight no one else saw."

"That's not evidence of a crime," Finnegan said. He set his pizza down. "What about the three other kids you caught? You think they were in on it, too?"

No. I couldn't picture Tiffany Haines shooting someone. "I think he was playing me," I said. It sounded lame, even to my ears.

"What about the gun?" Wright asked. "He have access?"

"Not that I know of."

Wright scratched his neck. "What's his motive?" His question and tone were curious, not hostile. Since we'd partnered on searching Gary Clark's house, we'd settled into an easier back-and-forth.

I couldn't tell them about the sex act on the golf course. Not yet. Warren was a minor, and I didn't have enough on him. "Let's just keep our eyes and ears open, okay? Now, what's all this about?" I tapped the picture of Revere on the board. His face was a constellation of dart holes. One dart remained stuck in his left earlobe.

"Detective Benedict fucking Arnold?" Finnegan said. "No idea."

"Look, his station called him back. It wasn't his call to leave. Okay? Besides, we can solve it without him," I said. "Any word on the gun?"

Finnegan said, "They're 'cautiously optimistic' they can lift the serial number. But they wouldn't say how long it would take."

"Okay. Keep pushing. We should have the sneaker confirmation soon. And let's keep this under wraps." I tapped Chris's picture. Thought about it. Removed it from the board. Better to be safe.

"Mum's the word," Finnegan said. Wright nodded.

"Billy?" I said.

He met my stare. "I won't say anything."

Their words should've reassured me. They didn't. I didn't think they'd talk. But not because they didn't want to. Because they thought I was nuts, pursuing some honor-roll teen for the murder. It didn't bode well. If I couldn't convince my fellow cops, how could I hope to convince a district attorney?

# TUESDAY, SEPTEMBER 23RD
## 1600 HOURS

"**S**o this is where you saw the flashlight?" I asked Chris. We were in the wooded area beside the eighth-hole green of the Nipmuc Golf Course. Fallen leaves crunched underfoot. He looked up and down the stretch. "Around here," he said. Twenty feet from us, in a circle of sunlight, a golfer practiced his swing. The course was in use, but we were away from the action unless someone really shanked it.

"And how many times did you see the light flash on and off?" I had my notepad out. I kept my voice curious. And while I watched him I thought, "You're a killer." The forensic lab had come through on the sneaker treads. A Nike Air Jordan XII sneaker made the 11.5 print. But because the crime-scene print was a partial and not a good one, an exact match to the killer's shoe might not be possible. So I'd called Chris and asked for his help.

He scratched his chin. "Six times, maybe seven. Like I said, it flicked on and off. Like someone was looking for something."

"We've been up and down this strip and haven't found anything."

"Maybe he found it," he said. "Whatever he was looking for." He bit his lip. Furrowed his brow. He was trying a little too hard with his concerned-citizen act.

"Maybe. Damn." I swatted my notepad against my leg. "This case. I don't like to admit it, but we're stuck."

"I heard you found the gun," he said. Did that worry him?

"Yeah. But the serial number's been erased. Not much good without it."

"Oh, really?" His lips moved upward. A smile he quickly squelched. But not before I saw it.

"Yeah." I walked to a damp spot where the ground was softer. Peered at the mud. "If only I knew what he was looking for. The guy whose light you saw."

Chris approached. "Maybe a bullet casing?"

"Nah, we got those."

He moved into a patch of sunlight. His ginger hair glowed. Rick's hair. But he wasn't like Rick. Rick was weak. He'd fallen to temptation. This kid was cold through and through.

I looked at the golfers. They chatted about club selection and the weather. "Beautiful day," I heard for the fourth time. When they saw me, in the trees at the periphery of their putting, they pretended they didn't. I was a reminder of what had happened here. Heaven forbid they recall that a young woman had bled out on the grass where they enjoyed playing a silly game.

"Hey, what's this?" Chris said.

His voice brought me back. Made me focus. I moved deeper into the woods. He held something in his right hand. "Where'd you find that?" I asked.

He pointed to a small patch of leaves and twigs. "In here." He held it out.

Pop Rocks. Strawberry. The packet damp and dirtied with leaf debris. I pulled a baggie from my rear pocket, and he dropped it inside.

"You think it's evidence?" he asked.

She'd held this packet. As she walked home. It was in her warm hand as she headed home, thoughts of her comfy bed in mind. She'd held on to it until after she exited Gary Clark's car. Not before she'd reached the cabin, as we'd supposed.

"Maybe." I fought to keep my voice neutral.

"Huh. Maybe that was what the guy was looking for?"

"A candy packet? I doubt it." We hadn't made public the details of her visit to Cumberland Farms. He'd no way to know I realized this was evidence. Evidence the little fucker had given me. With his own hands. So of course his fingerprints would be on it. He was smarter than most.

I sighed and scratched my hairline. Thought about hitching up my pants, but thought that might be a touch too folksy. "Well, thanks for your help, Chris. I appreciate it. You need a ride home?"

"No, thanks. I think I'll walk up to the club. My dad's usually here by now."

I watched him go. Counted to one hundred. And then I radioed to my car, where Mike Shannon waited. "It's ready."

A few minutes later, he appeared. He wore booties and carried a box. "That it?" He nodded at the sneaker prints Christopher Warren had left behind. In the muddy spot I'd lured him to.

Mike photographed the prints from several angles. "This will cast up nicely," he said. "And see that mark across the right print? That line?" He snapped another picture. "Something's cut the tread on his sneaker. Was your crime-scene print a right or left?"

"Right shoe," I said.

"This will do very well indeed." He put his camera down and unpacked a wooden frame that he set around the print. Next, he mixed up dental stone. He poured the mixture onto the print. "Now we wait."

"How long?"

He checked his watch. "Temperature's good. Weather's dry. Half hour, maybe forty minutes to be safe."

"Let's be safe," I said.

"So, your killer's a kid? How'd he know the vic?"

"I'm not sure he did."

He looked over the mold again. "Why'd he kill her, then?"

I shrugged. "Maybe because he could." I looked at the evidence baggie and the Pop Rocks packet within. This was the last thing she'd held, before she fell to the grass.

"Can you take a left print, too?" I asked.

He crab-walked toward a second print. "You don't ask for much, do you?"

"I'll owe you," I said.

He glanced up from the print and grinned. "That you will."

# FRIDAY, SEPTEMBER 26TH
## 1430 HOURS

'd uncovered another secret of small-town life. Don't shop for groceries on the weekend. Everyone and their granny shops at that time. And despite the fact that the grocery, or "market," as locals say, is the size of Giants Stadium, on a weekend you can't navigate its two-lane aisles because people park their carts to stare at the nutritional labels on boxes of Twinkies. As if they need to read the label. There shouldn't even be a label on Twinkies. Just a warning sticker like they have on cigarettes and alcohol.

The best time to shop is weekday evenings. Place is a ghost town. But I'd missed those due to work, so I settled for a weekday afternoon. When my only competition was the elderly and some stay-at-home moms and their kids. No problem.

There was a problem. In the form of an unattended toddler whose cart was parked sideways next to a salsa display. Effectively cutting off the entire aisle. The kid sat in the cart's seat, tugging at his truck T-shirt. Revealing a flash of whale-white belly when he pulled it up. When he noticed me, he stopped tugging and stared. He had a stare most corner boys would envy.

I looked for his mother, but there wasn't anyone in the aisle. I felt strange about moving him out of the way. The kid didn't know me from Adam. I was just a big, strange man in civvies. I could back up and go to the next aisle, but the milk I wanted was right at the end of this one. And I'd already walked a half mile just to get my six items. I grabbed the cart's handle and steered it so that it was facing lengthwise, opening up a walking path.

"Gavin?" a woman cried from behind me.

The child's chubby face split into a gummy smile. He kicked his legs and squealed.

"Gavin!"

I stepped away from the cart. The mother, dressed in sweats, ran to her child and patted his downy blond hair. "You okay, sweetie?" She turned to fix me with a look.

"You left him parked in the middle of the aisle," I said. She didn't get to glare at me. This was her fault.

"Baby, did that man touch you?"

Gavin clapped his hands and said, "Touch! Touch!"

Oh, God. She turned around and said, "I'm calling the manager." Her ponytail bobbed with each word.

I would never shop during the day again. "I moved your cart. It was blocking the whole aisle."

She pointed her finger at me. "I don't know what kind of world we live in, where a mother can't leave her child for two seconds without a stranger trying to —"

I was about to tell her exactly what sort of world we lived in. Throw some cold data on her fiery speech. About how many kids are abducted each year, and how little time they're out of sight when they're snatched. But before I could, I heard, "Chief Lynch."

Mrs. North stood a foot away.

"Mrs. North," I said.

"Chief?" the mother said, her hand on Gavin's chubby ankles.

"Police chief," I said.

"Oh."

"You want to call the manager?" I asked. "Have a conversation about parental negligence?"

Gavin watched us with his wonderful, unblinking stare.

"No." She wrapped her hands around the cart, so tightly her knuckles whitened. "No, we'll just be on our way."

"Bye!" Gavin yelled, opening and closing one hand as his mother half jogged away.

Mrs. North watched them. When they were out of sight, she said, "At that age, Cecilia was such a charmer. I'd take her shopping, and she'd make eyes at everyone, especially men. I'd look back, and there'd be a trail of men who'd been lured into waving at my baby."

Her cart had fewer items than my basket. Paper towels, pancake mix, butter, and corn on the cob. Grief has a way of tumbling the mind. It makes sustained concentration impossible.

"We haven't heard anything," she said. "About the case."

"We're pursuing leads." I couldn't say more. Didn't dare. Hope is a terrible gift. The return policy is heartbreak.

She looked at bags of pretzels. Touched a few but chose none. "I just don't get it. Cecilia was sweet. Not perfect, of course. When she was a teenager, there were days I wanted to give her away. She had a temper, and stubborn!" She picked up a bag of honey-mustard pretzels. "But she was a good girl. Sometimes I'd find things she left around the house as surprises. Flowers or drawings she'd done." She hugged the pretzels. "I just don't understand why anyone would kill her."

A man with tortilla chips edged past us, whispering, "Sorry." Either he'd caught her words or he'd figured out that this wasn't a moment for interruption.

Mrs. North looked at me. "Some days I find myself looking at people and thinking, 'Did you do it? Did you shoot my baby?'" She released her hold on the pretzels. Set them in the cart as if they were eggs. "The other day, I found myself thinking that of the minister. The minister!" She tilted her head and asked, "Am I going crazy? Will I always think this way?"

I set my basket on the floor. "You're not crazy. You've experienced a terrible loss and you're trying to make sense of it. But it's just—" I stopped.

"Just what?" she said.

"It will never make sense. If we catch who did this and bring him to trial, if you find out every detail of what happened, it still won't make sense. I'm sorry."

She blinked. A tear fell. She wiped her cheek. "Thank you, for telling the truth. So many people keep saying, 'It will get better' and 'God has a plan,' and I want to scream at them. I want to ask, what kind of awful plan does God have that involves murdering my daughter?"

"Some people give God too much credit." I took her hand and squeezed it. "Or too much blame." She squeezed back.

# MONDAY, SEPTEMBER 29TH
## 1020 HOURS

Beside the crime board, Wright sat at his desk, muttering as he stacked papers. At his elbow was a *Sesame Street* video. "What's that?" I asked.

He glanced at the video. "Present for my daughter. Her birthday's this Thursday. She loves Elmo." He tapped the video. A red, furry creature with arms wide open stared at me with eyes as big as tennis balls. He grunted. "Could be worse. She could like that stupid purple dinosaur."

I wasn't up-to-date on children's television, so I said nothing.

Wright pointed to his papers and said, "There's nothing in there. Not one damn thing. A woman is killed on a golf course. A golf course! And we can't find the guy." He wasn't sold on Chris Warren as our suspect. None of them were. He emptied Finnegan's overflowing ashtray. "Damn case. I sneaked a few smokes last night. Figured they might relax me." He said, "The wife smelled it on me. Made me shower before bed." He rolled his eyes.

So I wasn't the only stress-smoker here.

"We need the serial number off that damn gun. I'm going to the lab," I said.

"Want company?"

"Sure." I hadn't planned on a partner, but maybe he'd come in handy.

In the car, he asked, "You ever have an unsolved murder before?"

"You kidding? I was a New York City homicide detective for twelve years."

"How many cold cases?" He tapped out a rhythm on the dashboard with his long fingers. His nail beds were shiny. Did he buff them? Rick had done that.

"Forty or so, I think."

"You think?"

"The eighties were rough. Lots of drugs. Gangs looking to establish territory. More guns. Some of it was accidental. Those could be bitches to solve."

"You still think about them?"

"No. Most of the vics were likely to end up on the wrong end of a knife or a gun the way they lived. Their murders didn't come as surprises, not even to their mothers. There was only one. An old guy who ran a bodega. Nice man. Knew the kids in the neighborhood. Gave them candy on their birthdays, that sort of thing."

"Holdup?" he asked.

"No. That would've made sense. He was tied to his kitchen cabinet and beaten to death."

"Beaten?"

"With a brick. It lay a few feet from the body."

"You never found the killer?"

"No. But we found things in his bedroom under a floorboard. Some money, pictures, papers."

"And?" he said.

"He'd been some sort of fighter in Spain during their civil war. He'd kept records, had killed a lot of men. Not just men. Women, children."

"You think someone from Spain offed him?"

I scanned the horizon. Traffic was moving. The sky was the color of a robin's egg. "Don't know. The brick had no prints. A few people had spotted a repair van that day, but it turned out to be legit."

"And it doesn't haunt you?" He seemed surprised.

"No." Those late-night theories I'd had about the old man's death? Those were just exercises in curiosity.

"Well, this one's getting to me." He stopped tapping on the dashboard. Pulled out a cigarette. I tensed. He noticed. He swapped the cigarette for a piece of gum.

"You buff your nails?" I asked.

He looked straight ahead. "Why?" Was he turning pink under his cocoa skin? Had I made Wright blush?

"They look like my old partner's. He told me a man's hands were a reflection of his inner self." Which explained why Rick had let his nails go to shit after he'd developed a taste for drugs.

"Your partner?" He glanced at his fingernails. He said, "My mother used to say dirty nails were a sign of sloth." He tapped the dashboard. "Just about everything relates back to sin with her. She's big on the Bible." I thought of what Finnegan had told me about Wright's mother. Her getting hit when he was a kid. Him developing a hatred for men who hit women. We carry so much with us on this job. It's a miracle they give us guns.

I said, "Everything relates to literature with my mother. Specifically nineteenth-century English literature written by women."

He grinned. "Must have made for great bedtimes stories."

"What young boy doesn't love *Pride and Prejudice?*"

He laughed and said, "At least the Bible has lions and fighting."

My radio crackled. "Chief Lynch?"

I answered, holding the radio in my right hand and steering with my left.

"We got a call from the lab."

I cursed. We were ten minutes away.

"They got the serial number. It's a match for Browning's stolen gun."

My hand squeezed the radio. "You're sure?" My fingers tingled.

"They are."

"We're coming to the station. Have Donny Browning picked up."

"10-4."

"Son of a bitch," Wright said. "You think he did it?"

"No." Donny wasn't smart enough to have killed her. And he'd been on shift all night.

"So what then?" he said.

"I think he took the gun and never told his dad. He's afraid of his old man." I pressed my foot down and started up the siren. "So let's find out when Donny last saw the gun."

They were still looking for Donny when we returned to the station. They'd checked his house, his job, and a couple of his friends' places. No joy. I stared at the board, at a photo of Cecilia's corpse. We had the gun. We were almost there.

Inside my office, I called Elmore Fenworth. Maybe he knew something about Donny's whereabouts. But Elmore's phone rang and rang. So my feet led me to my second largest source of local information. She looked up from the mail, a lethal letter opener in hand.

"Good morning, Mrs. Dunsmore. I need your help."

Her frown wavered. "What can I do for you, Chief?"

"I'm hoping you can help me find Donny Browning."

"Now, Chief, I warned you about that family."

"His gun killed Cecilia North. Mr. Browning's gun."

She smiled. It wasn't a nice smile. It was the kind evil witches make before handing you a poisoned apple. "Well, well," she said. "The devil will be paid his due." She reached for her phone. "Give me a few minutes."

She located Donny Browning in twenty-five minutes. She didn't say how. He'd bought a ticket to see *The Game*, a movie starring Michael Douglas, at the theater in Manchester. He was one of about twelve people in the theater at this hour.

I sent two patrolmen to fetch him. "Disregard the speed limit as much as you can," I told them. They smiled, happy to oblige.

Wright had been checking area hospitals. He saw my smile and hung up the phone midsentence. "You found him?"

"Mrs. Dunsmore," I said.

He grimaced. "She's goddamn spooky sometimes."

"Sometimes?"

"Maybe Mr. Browning did it," he said. "Our vic had a thing for older men."

"I don't know." As far as we knew, she'd only dated one older man. Gary Clark.

"So, what, their gun was stolen and used to kill her? And that's it? Or you think Donny had a hand in it somehow?"

We both glanced at the clock. Another four minutes gone. To kill time, we drank coffee. Thought out loud. We were abuzz with caffeine by the time the patrolmen brought Donny in. He looked bad. We let him stew, alone, in the interview room for a few minutes. Then we went in. I cleared my throat. Wright adjusted his narrow tie. Donny removed his cap. "I'm ready," he said. We hadn't even sat down yet.

"Ready for what?" asked Wright. His tone was curious, with a strong hint of impatience.

"To tell the truth."

"We're all ears," I said.

"Do you have to tell my father?" He picked at a hangnail.

"He'll probably find out, sooner or later," I said.

Donny thought on that. Too long. So I nudged him. "You stole your father's gun."

He didn't shake his head or meet my eyes.

Wright looked at me. I jerked my head toward Donny. Wright circled him, slowly. Donny didn't like that one bit. "Let's hear it," Wright said, his voice low.

Donny said, "I took his gun, four years ago." We waited. He rushed to fill the silence. "I just wanted to check it out. But he always kept it locked up. So one time he went to New York for this case, and he was going to be gone a few nights. So I borrowed it. Just to shoot cans and stuff." He'd stolen the gun to shoot cans. Some stories are so mundane, they have to be true. No one would invent them.

"And?" I prompted.

"He got back early. The trial got settled, and he came home. I don't know why he checked the safe that day. I hadn't had time to return the gun. He discovered it was gone and flipped out." He cringed.

"Did he ask you if you took it?" Wright said.

He frowned. "Of course. If anything went wrong, he asked me about it, even when stuff wasn't my fault. It was always, 'What's Donny done now?'"

"So you lied," I said.

"He would've gone ballistic if I'd told the truth. He'd have tossed me out of the house, no question. So I said I hadn't touched it. I actually stood up to him. For once."

"And then your father blamed the cleaning staff," Wright said.

"I felt bad about that." He stared at his sneakers. "But I knew they'd be okay. They hadn't stolen it, so they weren't going to get into trouble."

Wright exhaled, hard. He looked ready to make a speech. But I didn't care about the past or the cleaning ladies. Not now. "What happened to the gun?" I asked.

Donny scratched his head as if it were covered in bug bites. "When I moved to my apartment, I took it with me. I worried my father would find it." He was still worried about his father. What he wasn't worried about was that he'd just claimed ownership of a murder weapon.

"Donny, did you shoot Cecilia North?" Wright asked.

"What? No!" He quivered like a wet dog. "I didn't have the gun when she died."

"Who did?" he asked.

"I rented it." Donny munched on his bloody hangnail.

"You what?" Wright's voice bounced off the bricks.

Donny looked at me. As if I'd protect him. I would, for now. I approached him and said, "Rented? What do you mean?"

"I got this idea. You can rent movies and even video games. So I thought, why not rent the gun?"

Wright palmed his face and struggled not to answer.

"So you rented the gun. How?" I asked.

"I let some friends know they could borrow it. If they bought me stuff. They told some friends. Word spread." He smiled. "Homies as far away from Hartford asked to rent it."

"Homies?" Wright said, his voice one hundred percent disdain. Donny wilted under his gaze.

"Who'd you rent it to last?" I asked.

"A kid from here. But he lost the gun." He blew a short blast of air at his scruffy hair. "Now he owes me." I looked at Wright, who had one shoulder leaned against the bricks. His eyes were wide. Donny thought the kid was going to pay him? He was in for a world of surprises.

"Who lost the gun?" I asked.

"I'd rather not say."

I crossed the room in two seconds and shoved my face so close I saw a whitehead ready to erupt on Donny's nostril. "Who?" Our foreheads almost touched.

"Kevin Wilkes! He rented it for target practice." I stepped back and he slumped in his chair. "Kevin's a good kid. Hell, he's a Boy Scout." I remembered Kevin. He was short. Not the standing man. But he could've been the second man, the one kneeling.

Donny said, "If you found the gun, I wasn't worried, cuz I'd filed the serial number off, but then I watched a cop show. They raised a filed number. I knew I was in trouble."

"But you still didn't come forward," Wright said.

He shook his head. "I knew my dad would lose it if he found out."

I gestured to Wright, and he followed me out of the room. "Kevin Wilkes was one of the golf-course kids. Call Finnegan. Get him in. But first, what's the restriction on interviewing minors here?"

"If he's under sixteen, a parent must be present."

"Kevin is fifteen. They all were, except Chris. He's sixteen."

He said, "In Connecticut, sixteen ages you out of juvie. You commit a murder at sixteen? You do adult time."

"In an adult prison?" I'd thought New York was tough on kids. Seemed like Idyll wasn't any friendlier.

"Yup."

I said, "Call Mr. Browning. Tell him we're charging his son with illegally selling a gun to a minor, defacing the serial number, and obstruction."

"But he's terrified of his dad."

I cracked my knuckles. "Well, I guess it's not Donny's lucky day now, is it?"

Wright chuckled. "I guess it isn't."

# 1525 HOURS

Kevin Wilkes's mother answered the door, holding a clarinet. Wright introduced himself. I didn't. She'd met me once, and I doubted she'd forgotten the event. I asked if her husband was at home. Best to deal with both parents at once.

"Jim? He's in Southbury. He teaches piano." She held up her instrument. "We give lessons." Her words came fast. There were two cops on her door. She had every right to be nervous.

"We need to talk to Kevin. Is he at home?" I asked.

"He's at soccer practice. What's this about? What's he done now?" She looked at our faces, trying to guess. "We just took him off grounding, for trespassing on the golf course." Right. That was going to look very minor very soon.

"Mrs. Wilkes?" a small voice called.

She looked over her shoulder. "Just a minute, Matthew." She told us, "I'm teaching now."

"We're going to need you to bring your son to the station," I said. A small blond kid walked toward us, his clarinet two-thirds his size. Either he was a child prodigy or he was small for his age.

"Matthew, I'll be with you in a moment. Practice 'Happy Birthday.'" The kid blinked at her command but did as he was told. He went back inside. Tinny squeaks emerged from his instrument. No prodigy, then.

"You should call Matthew's parents," Wright said. "Have him picked up."

"Wait!" Mrs. Wilkes pointed. Wright nudged me with his elbow. At the curb, getting out of the backseat of a BMW, was Kevin Wilkes. "Here he is."

"Everything okay?" the woman driving called. Two other teens sat in the car, rubbernecking.

Mrs. Wilkes put on her best brave face. "Fine. Thanks." She waved at them like her hand had springs in it until they drove away.

Kevin cradled a soccer ball to his chest. His shin guards were bright red. His face matched.

"Kevin, the police want to speak to you," Mrs. Wilkes said.

He looked away from his mother. "I don't have it," he said. He directed his comment to me.

"Have what?" his mother asked.

"The gun," he said, his voice barely audible. "I don't have it."

"I know," I said. "We do."

"Gun?" Mrs. Wilkes's voice brought Matthew back to the door. "What gun?" she asked. She grabbed her son's jersey sleeve. He winced, but didn't move.

"You have a gun?" Matthew said, eyeing Kevin. "Cool. Can I see it?"

"Matthew! Go practice!" she shouted.

He took a step backward, tripped, and fell. His small, pointed face got white. "It's okay," I said. I helped him up. "Want to see my gun?" He nodded. "Let's everyone step inside."

Mrs. Wilkes led us inside to the living room. There was a piano and another clarinet and two guitars. Also records. Lots and lots of vinyl near a stereo that resembled one I'd had back in the seventies. The furniture looked like an afterthought. Nothing matched, and it was arranged not for comfort but to allow space for the music. I sat on the rose-print sofa and patted the cushion beside me. Matthew hopped up onto it. His legs dangled a foot above the floor. Wright, Kevin, and Mrs. Wilkes stood near the piano.

I jerked my head at Wright. He picked up my cue and said, "Kevin, we'll need you to come to the station with your mom."

"What? No! I didn't do anything. I gave the gun to Luke."

"Luke Johnson?" Wright asked. He pulled out a notepad.

I unholstered my weapon. "This is my gun," I told Matthew. "Its safety is on, which means it can't be fired. You never take the safety off a gun unless you plan to use it." The boy's small hand reached out. I withdrew my firearm. "No touching," I said.

"Luke Johnson," Wright said. "Why did you give him the gun?"

"Yes, why?" his mother shouted. "And where did you get a gun?"

Kevin looked from his mother to Wright. And decided to answer the person not yelling at him. "We were supposed to go target shooting," he told Wright.

"Target shooting?" Mrs. Wilkes's cry made Matthew turn. But the lure of my gun soon recalled his attention.

"This gun is always locked in a safe when I'm not carrying it. Do you know why?" I asked Matthew.

"We were supposed to go shooting together, but I felt sick, so Luke and Chris went," Kevin said.

"So bad guys can't get it?" Matthew said.

"Chris Warren?" Wright asked. He looked at me. Gave me a slight nod. Score one for the chief.

Matthew tugged my shirt. "What?" I said.

"Do you lock your gun to keep it away from bad guys?" he asked.

"Yes. And to prevent accidents."

Kevin said, "Yeah. Chris slept over that night. He snuck out and met Luke. I'd given Luke the gun because I knew my folks would flip if they found it."

Mrs. Wilkes held up her hand. "Whoa. I think maybe, maybe I should call my husband. We might need a lawyer. I don't think—" She glanced at Kevin and chewed her lower lip.

Wright flipped his notepad closed. "Of course. You can call your husband. Consult a lawyer. That's absolutely your right. But honestly, ma'am, it's just going to slow things down. Kevin will have to make a statement. He can do it now, with you beside him, at the station. Or you can call a lawyer and buy a day or two. When news of this will have spread through town." He paused. Let that sink in. "It's up to you."

Nicely played, Wright.

She looked at her son and then glanced outside. "Okay. I want to call my husband, though. Let him know where we're going and tell him to meet us there."

"Sure thing," Wright said. "I just have one more question." He waited for her to protest. She crossed her arms but remained silent. "So Luke had the gun, and Chris went to meet him. Which night was this?" he asked Kevin.

"August ninth." His voice was low.

I holstered my gun. "We're going to need that statement. Mrs. Wilkes, could you please call Matthew's parents?" I asked.

"I want to go to the police station," Matthew said.

"The ninth?" she repeated. Her face got pale. "But wasn't that . . . ? Oh my God. The dead girl." She covered her mouth and crouched. As if she might be sick.

"Can I see the other cops' guns too?" Matthew asked.

"Mrs. Wilkes?" Wright asked. He held his hand out. She made a small sound and waved him away. After a few moments, she stood and steadied herself against the piano. Looked at us and said, "I'll call Matthew's mother now. Have him picked up."

"Darn!" said Matthew.

The Warren house reminded me of Elmore Fenworth's. It had the same well-groomed, historic look. But Elmore's house didn't have a pool or a three-door garage. Chris answered the door, a half-eaten cupcake in hand. Chocolate with white frosting. There were rainbow sprinkles on top. He leaned against a marble-topped table in the foyer. "Hi, Chief Lynch. Can I help you?" He was so natural, so friendly. Award-worthy.

"I need you to come to the police station." I waved an arm toward my car.

"Why? Is this about the candy wrapper I found near the golf course?"

"No," I said. "Would you come with me, please?"

He lifted the cupcake to his mouth. Took a large bite and chewed. I waited. He swallowed. I said, "Now."

"You can't take me without my parents being present."

"I can." And I suspected he knew that.

He squinted at my car, which needed a wash. "I think I'd rather stay home." He looked over his shoulder. "I'm in the middle of watching *The Usual Suspects*."

"Come on." I reached forward but didn't touch him. Who knew how hard I'd grip? He might bruise easy.

"It's a real cliff-hanger." He finished the cupcake.

"Verbal Kint is Keyser Söze," I said.

He dropped the cupcake liner onto the floor. "That's plain rude," he said, "spoiling the ending." He closed the door behind him. Stayed on the front step. "My parents will be worried when they come home and I'm not here." He smiled. "They do funny things when they worry. Call people they know. Like the mayor."

From what I'd learned, his parents were rarely home. Too busy working or socializing to spend time with their son. "You can call them from the station," I said. As for his threats, they meant less than nothing. The mayor wouldn't back a killer. No matter who his parents were or how much money they donated to town causes.

He sat in the back. I didn't cuff him. He was a minor. Even if Connecticut saw fit to try him as an adult, for now I had to treat him like a baby.

"You haven't told me what this is about," he said.

I closed the door. Started the car. Checked the rearview. He stared out the window, at his family's lovely house. He didn't look worried.

"I'm arresting you on suspicion of murder. Would you like me to read you your rights?"

A smile spread across his face, and he turned slowly, his eyes meeting mine in the mirror. "Oh, why not?" he said. "I bet you've been practicing."

He was protected from my fist by a panel of Plexiglas. And by years of training. *Don't fight, Thomas. Violence creates problems. It doesn't solve them.* But how I longed to connect my right hand's knuckles with the bridge of his nose. To hear the crunch, to feel the bone collapse beneath my anger.

But I couldn't. So I recited *Miranda* at him while I drove us to the station. Every time I glanced in the rearview mirror, that self-satisfied smile was on his face.

# 1735 HOURS

The station smelled of burnt coffee. Everyone talked, smoked, and paced. Finnegan was out, getting us warrants. Wright helped Kevin Wilkes review his statement while his parents huddled near him. Christopher Warren sat alone in the interview room, awaiting his family's lawyer. We couldn't find Luke Johnson. Or his mother.

Finnegan stomped into the pen, smelling of wood smoke, and said, "We've got warrants for both boys' homes. However, the judge was less than delighted by our pick of suspects."

"No one likes kids as killers," I said. "Disturbs the natural order." I massaged my hands. They were sore. I'd been clenching them so as not to punch Chris Warren.

"I still can't believe you got it right," he said, "on nothing more than a look at his sneakers and a hunch." He was impressed, at last.

Wright led Mr. and Mrs. Wilkes to the hall. Each parent kept one hand on Kevin's shoulders. "Is there anything else?" Mrs. Wilkes asked, equal amounts hope and fear in her voice.

"No, not now. Thank you," Wright said. He walked them outside to their car. They were on the good guys' team now, and we needed to coddle them. In the coming months, we might need Kevin to testify against his friends in court. Of course, if he resisted, we'd threaten him with an accessory-to-murder charge. Being on the good guys' team isn't all fun.

When Wright returned, I put him in charge of both search teams. "Take all their boots and sneakers," I said.

"Will do." He set off quickly, then stopped and returned to me. "You made a good call," he said. "Sorry I doubted you." He met my eyes, steady, and I knew he meant more than doubting my pick of suspects. I also knew apologies didn't come easy to Wright.

"Thanks." I tipped an imaginary hat. "Now go get me some evidence."

He saluted and hurried out the door.

"What about me?" Finnegan asked.

"You're on interviews."

"Poor Revere," he said. "He's missing it all." He didn't sound sorry.

Thirty minutes later, Christopher Warren's attorney arrived. She was a tall woman who looked like she took her coffee black and her clients wealthy. Her first words were, "I'm Melissa Simon, Christopher Warren's attorney. Where is he? And why aren't his parents with him?"

"Hello," I said. "I'm Thomas Lynch, Chief of Police. Your client is in an interview room. His parents aren't home. He's sixteen years of age, so they don't need to be here."

"When did he turn sixteen?" she asked.

"Three months ago. Given the rates you charge, I'm surprised you didn't know."

She didn't respond. Just tightened her grip on her briefcase.

Forty-five minutes later, Luke Johnson and his mother arrived, both pale and slump-shouldered. His mother held Luke's hand and leaned toward his ear. Finnegan showed them into the second inter-view room, the room we used as an informal gym. We'd moved the weights and bench into the equipment space and set up a spare table and some folding chairs.

"I'll take Luke," I said to Finnegan.

He said, "You don't want Chris? I figured, since you had such a hard-on for him—"

"I want to give him someone new. See how he behaves. Be careful. He's clever."

He scratched his chest. "Guess he'll be too smart for the likes of me, then." He leaned harder on his accent. With any luck, Chris would buy Finnegan's dumb act.

Mrs. Johnson and Luke refused a lawyer when I suggested one. "You understand what *pro bono* means?" I said.

She harrumphed and adjusted the purse on her lap. "You get what you pay for," she said. "Luke's dad had pro bono lawyers. Look what that got us."

"From what I heard, it kept him out of jail after he knifed a guy." I watched Luke. His knee jiggled under the table. Up and down, cocaine-user fast.

"We paid for *that* lawyer." Under her breath she said, "Still paying for it."

"So, you going to ask me questions or what?" Luke said. He had a hard time keeping still. Why not counter that with relaxation? I took a deep breath. And regretted it. Good lord, the funk in here was terrific. We needed another interview room. A proper one not used by men as their gym.

"So, where were you two earlier?" I asked.

"Apartment hunting," Mrs. Johnson said. "The bank's going to foreclose. So you can imagine how delighted I was to find two cop cars in my yard after I'd spent three hours looking at crappy apartments."

"Idyll doesn't have crappy apartments," I said.

"We weren't looking here. Can't afford it. We were in Hartford." She pulled out a cigarette and lit it. I didn't complain. It might improve the room's scent.

"So who shot Cecilia North?" I asked Luke.

His knee stopped jiggling. "Didn't do it," he said.

"So it was Chris?" That would be music to my ears.

"Chris?" Mrs. Johnson said. "Warren? The little rich boy?" She coughed. "You pull him in here, too?"

"Sure did. He's in the other room. He has a lawyer."

"Of course he does." She looked around. "Ash tray?"

I fetched it from the windowsill. The window was set high in the wall, above everyone's head but mine. "Here." I set it on the table. It clanked. Luke flinched.

"Didn't do it," he said, unprompted.

"We know you had the gun. We have footprints from the crime scene. We're going to bring all your shoes inside, and then the techs will match them. You'll be found guilty of murder. On the bright side, you won't have to move to a crappy apartment in Hartford."

He got sullen. Pouty lips. Crossed arms.

"So when's moving day?" I asked Mrs. Johnson.

She looked away from Luke's muddied sneakers and said, "Next month. We have to be out by the fifteenth."

Luke's scowl deepened.

"You have any idea what your sentence will be like?" I asked him.

He straightened and kicked one foot out. "A year or two in juvie." He smirked.

Ah-ha. He hadn't denied the crime. And he banked on a soft sentence.

"Connecticut's been known to try minors as adults. Would you like me to list some examples?"

"Maybe we should get a lawyer." Mrs. Johnson stubbed out her cigarette with short jabs.

"Sure," Luke said. "But a real one." He emphasized the last two words.

"But, honey—" Her voice cracked. She faced foreclosure, was paying for her long-gone husband's lawyer, and her son needed expensive counsel.

"Don't worry," he said. "We can afford it."

"How?" she asked.

Yes, how?

"Call him," he said. "The guy who got dad off." His voice was steady.

"I want to call a lawyer," she said to me.

I took her outside to the phone.

Twenty minutes into the wait for their lawyer, Mrs. Johnson asked that the room's door be left open. She complained that the smell was overwhelming. "We can't have the door open," I said. Too much risk she or Luke would overhear something. I dispatched Billy to find me a solution. He returned with a plug-in air freshener. Now the room smelled like body odor and vanilla.

Finnegan emerged from the interview room, a broad smile on his face. When the door closed, his smile dropped. "Chris is a bright little shit. How's yours?"

I told him Luke had denied killing our victim and demanded a lawyer.

"Any word from Wright?" he asked.

"Not yet. The Warrens' house is big. Gonna take a while to search, and I imagine they're gonna put up a fuss."

My prediction was proven true in less than ten minutes. At 8:30 p.m., Mr. and Mrs. Warren came to the station. Mrs. Warren wore pearls she twisted back and forth. Mr. Warren had one of those *Star Trek* earpiece devices so he could make telephone calls without using his hands. They demanded to know where their son was and why they were the victims of a vicious prank. Why we were treating them like criminals, rooting through their valuables?

"It's no prank," I said. "Your son's been arrested. He's with his lawyer."

"We want to see him."

I had no objection. Finnegan and I were regrouping. I didn't want to talk to either boy again until the house searches were complete. While the Warrens reunited, we made a list of what we'd learned thus far.

1. Chris insisted that he'd left Luke with the gun at the golf course. He'd thought better of firing a weapon and had returned to Kevin Wilkes's house.
2. Luke wasn't talking and wanted a lawyer.

It wasn't much. But we knew our suspects' defense plans. Both involved denial.

Wright returned at 10:00 p.m. "Guess what I found?" he said. "Timberland boots. Size eight and a half. At Luke's house, in the pantry, under a box of trash bags. And a pair of eleven and a half Air Jordan sneakers found in the Warrens' entryway. Chris didn't even bother to hide them."

Finnegan brought Wright up to speed. He said that Chris claimed he'd been at the golf course, but that he'd left before Luke shot Cecilia.

"Chris says Luke admitted he shot our vic?" Wright asked.

"No," Finnegan said, "But he's implied it. He's smart. Full of 'maybes' and 'it's possibles.'"

"You turn up anything else?" I asked Wright.

"We've got Chris's laptop," he said. "Might be something there."

"He has his own laptop?" I pointed to the old Selectric IIs we used.

"The kid has everything, far as I can tell. Oh, and he had these stashed in a drawer." He pointed to a group of baggies. Each held a package of Pop Rocks.

"Most of them are untouched," I said. "Don't test those. She'd eaten some of the candy, remember? Crystals on her hand."

"Right," he said.

"Why did he buy them?" Finnegan asked. "Is he just trying to make the techs' lives hell?"

"Trophy?" Wright asked.

"Don't know," I said. "Don't care." Not true. I suspected Chris bought the Pop Rocks as a reminder of what he'd done. What he'd gotten away with. Until now. But I wasn't going to get hung up on it. Because thinking about it made me want to march into the interview room and rough up both boys in front of their mothers. "Where's Luke's lawyer?" I asked. "I can't have another run at him until he shows."

Luke's lawyer, Mr. Benjamin Walsh, showed up at 10:45 p.m. On the attorney scale, he was somewhere in the middle. His clothing? No suit from London, but no Men's Wearhouse two-for-one special either. He wore wire-frame glasses that made him look older. I pegged him at thirty-five. He was shown into the room where the battle between air freshener and body odor continued.

We drank coffee and pinned what we knew on the board. Finnegan told the Warrens to stop alibiing their son. We'd already confirmed they were at a fundraising event until 1:30 a.m. two towns away the night of the murder. And Chris hadn't slept at their house that night. He was at Kevin Wilkes's house. They finally stopped after their attorney told them they weren't helping him.

At 11:55 p.m., Mrs. Warren left the interview room. She looked bad. She asked one of the men if she could bring her son a blanket from home. He told her no, gently. Instead of arguing, she hiccupped softly, pressed her knuckles to her mouth, and hurried outside.

At two minutes past midnight, Mr. Walsh, Luke's lawyer, requested that I come in to hear a short statement by his client. Brows rose around the pen. "This might be it, boys," I said.

Billy said, "Go get him, Chief." His hair was cowlicked and his uniform rumpled. All in all, he looked like the rest of us, but better rested. Wright extinguished his cigarette. "Good luck," he said. Finnegan said he was going to put Revere on speed dial so that when we broke the case, he could call him right away. And gloat.

"You'll have to call his home number," Billy said.

Finnegan tapped his phone. "No problem," he said.

I brought two water cups into the room. Decided to let them fight over who got the beverages. The lawyer declined. Mrs. Johnson took quick, shallow sips from hers. Luke drained his in one go. "Want more?" I asked.

His knee was still. His hands clasped together, on top of the table. "No, thank you." This was a transformation. Was the lawyer responsible? Mr. Walsh sat a foot from his client.

"I have something to say," Luke said. His mother gripped her cup, and water rose over the rim, splashing her. She didn't notice. He said, "I shot her. I killed her. Chris wasn't there." His voice was monotone, with no inflection at all.

It was a confession. At last. There was just one problem. It was a lie. His tone, his posture. He hadn't done it alone. Years of experience, intuition, and my funny vertebrae all argued that he was stringing me along.

"Was anyone else with you?" I asked.

"No."

"You're sure?"

His eyes flicked to meet mine. He swallowed. Looked at his lawyer, who nodded a fraction. "Yes. I was alone."

"You weren't. I have evidence that you weren't." Not that Mrs. Ashworth had seen the boys shoot Cecilia. But he didn't know that. There were other things he didn't know I knew. Like what he'd been doing before the shooting.

"Chris was with me, at first," he said. "We were going to shoot the gun at targets we'd brought. But Chris got worried the Wilkeses would notice he'd left their house. So he went back to Kevin's. I was the only one there when she showed up."

I played along. Asked him questions. Where had he been, what had he been doing? Where had she approached from? Did she see him?

He'd been standing, reloading the gun. She came from the eighth hole. Yes, she saw him. She yelled at him. He got scared and shot her.

"Four times," I said.

His fingers unclasped. He tapped them on the table, as if playing piano. "Yes, four times."

"Why?"

Mrs. Johnson took a shuddering breath and wiped a fuzzy tissue under her eyes. The lawyer remained mute. I revised my opinion. This guy was worse than pro bono. Luke looked down. Saw what his hands were up to and clasped them together. "I don't know. I panicked, I guess."

"You guess? You guess?" My voice rose with each word. "You murder a young woman, toss the gun, and pretend it never happened. And when you tell me all about your amazing crime, all you can do is guess as to why you did it? No. Sorry, Luke. Try again."

"I was afraid she'd tell on me." His hands came apart. That had a ring of truth to it.

"Why?"

"Because she saw me . . . with the gun. And I was afraid she'd call the cops."

His mother grabbed another tissue from her bag. It fell apart in her hands.

"You two are going to let him do this?" I said, to Mr. Walsh and Mrs. Johnson. "Confess to a murder?"

"What do you want from us!" she yelled. "He's telling you what you want!"

I planted my hands on the table. "No, he isn't. What I want is the truth." I slammed a hand against the table. It rocked to one side.

The lawyer spoke up. "Chief Lynch, you may choose to disbelieve my client, but he'd like to make a formal statement."

I stepped back. "Fine. I'll send someone in to take it."

"You won't do it?" Mr. Walsh asked. He leaned forward in his chair.

"I have better things to do than listen to lies. Since he's fifteen, he'll need to be transferred to a juvenile facility. But it's nearly one a.m. They probably won't take him until morning." I walked to the door.

"My client is fourteen," he said.

"What?" I spun around.

Luke looked down.

"You told me you were fifteen. The night I picked you up for trespassing." He was in the same grade as Tiffany and Kevin. Jesus, had he skipped a grade? Talk about buying into someone's dumb act. I'd bought front-row tickets.

He raised his head and met my stare. "I'm gonna be fifteen in a few weeks."

"When?"

"November seventeenth."

"November seventeenth is almost two months away."

He ducked his head.

"You lied," I said. "Why am I surprised?" I left without another word.

In the pen, Wright looked up, his expression hopeful. "He confessed," I said. Billy let out a war whoop and put his hand up, expecting me to slap his palm. I didn't.

"He's lying. Story has more holes than a wheel of Swiss. Oh, and it turns out he's fourteen."

"Shit," Wright said. "Fourteen is a tough sell."

"Will you take his statement? His lawyer is insisting. Then see that he gets a cell as far from Chris Warren as possible. We'll have to call Juvenile. See when they'll take them."

"You're keeping Chris?" Billy said. I didn't like the way he said his name. As if he deserved better treatment.

"We have evidence he was involved. I'm not letting him go. God knows where he'd fly off to if given the chance. His parents have money and resources."

Finnegan arrived with three large pizzas. "Mine has macaroni and cheese," he said. Wright groaned. Once again, Finnegan had found a way to keep a whole pie to himself.

"Luke confessed," I said.

Finnegan's droopy face tightened with a smile. "All right!"

"He's lying." I scratched my scalp. Sniffed my shirt. I smelled like the weights room.

"You sure?" He wanted to believe we'd done it. Hell, I wanted to have done it. But we hadn't. I hadn't.

"I'm going to nip home. Change clothes. I'll see you in an hour." I said.

"You don't want pizza?" He held up the pies.

"No. Finnegan, have another go at Chris. If you get nowhere, put him in a cell. You have my home number in case anything breaks?" They nodded. "See you soon."

"Why does he think Luke's lying?" Finnegan asked. I slowed my steps to hear the answer.

Wright said, "He claims his story was inconsistent."

Finnegan said, "Chris is a shit, but I think the chief wants it to be him. He spent time with Luke this summer. Maybe he got too close."

Wright said, "He worked homicide twelve years. He can probably spot a liar faster than Billy can miss a layup."

So maybe I'd earned a little respect. Too bad it didn't mean shit unless I could get one of those boys to tell the truth about what happened the night Cecilia North was killed.

# TUESDAY, SEPTEMBER 30TH
## 0220 HOURS

removed my uniform and hung the pants and shirt on a bathroom hook. Maybe the steam from the shower would render them wearable. I had to return to the station soon. My mind went around like a revolving door. Why would Luke confess? It was possible he shot and killed her. But not alone. Chris was there. Or was he? His behavior. His footprints. His belt buckle. The Pop Rocks. No, he was guilty.

I showered. Got dressed. Drank some orange juice. Listened to the hum of the fridge.

A rap on my kitchen door made me jump. Who the hell was outside this time of night? Expecting Billy or Finnegan, it took me a second to recognize the handsome man standing in the dim glow of my porch light. Damien Saunders.

I opened the door. Two moths danced near his head.

"Hi," he said. "May I come in?"

I said nothing, but held the door wide. I was glad I hadn't turned more lights on. No need for him to see my peeling floor and avocado fridge in all their glory.

"In the neighborhood?" I said, gesturing toward a chair.

He looked around. I wished he wouldn't. He sat.

"Sort of. There was a three-car accident out by Tolland."

I nodded.

"I realized you lived quite near, and so I thought I'd stop by." After midnight. On the off chance I was accepting social calls. Huh. "Look, I saw your light on when I drove by, and I just wanted to apologize."

"For?" I asked.

"For blowing up at you that night, and just . . . bringing my shit to your table. You didn't deserve it." His eyes were tired, but blazing blue. Beautiful.

"Don't sweat it," I said. "I shouldn't have blindsided you with my request, which reminds me." I got up and went to the safe. Retrieved Elmore Fenworth's list. Rummaged through my kitchen drawers until I found matches. "You're not looking for a date, are you?" I asked, waving the papers.

"Pardon?" he said.

I showed him the list. Waited until his expression changed. Knew he'd seen his name. Knew what he was thinking. "Is that—?"

"The name of every able-bodied gay man in the immediate area. You were included because of your profession."

I struck a match. Listened to the scrape and sizzle. And then held the wavering flame to the bottom of the list. Waited until it really caught and the names burned. Before it singed me, I dropped the papers. The remains floated down to the sink, char settling in a Rorschach pattern. Then I ran the tap until all that remained was black goo in my sink trap. I felt lighter.

"Who made that?" He sounded scared. Even though he was out. He must've realized many of the men on that list, like me, were not.

So I told him about Elmore Fenworth and the list, and he asked why I went looking for that information to begin with, so I had to explain about Mrs. Ashworth.

"She had no idea what she almost witnessed," I said.

"So you've been looking for two gay men all this time." He picked up a pen and rotated its bottom, withdrawing the ink tube. How very like Revere. "And you never told your team."

"I didn't want to give them an excuse to re-create the Stonewall riots," I said.

"They're that bad?" Here was the sympathy I'd been denied. By isolating myself.

"They're no worse than your average cops."

He didn't say anything.

"We've got two suspects at the station now. Kids. It's odd, because I wouldn't have pegged either of them as on our team."

"Maybe they were experimenting? Just fooling around?"

I opened the cabinet under the sink. Pulled out rubbing alcohol and some cotton swabs. I put a dishtowel on the scarred table and set my badge on it.

"What are you doing?" he asked.

"Rubbing alcohol gets the gunk out." I unpinned my badge and dipped a swab in the alcohol.

"You clean your badge?" I saw him fighting a smile. The smile was winning.

"At home. If I did this at the station I'd be nicknamed 'the cleaner' for life. It helps me think."

"Cleaning helps you think?"

"Sometimes. Sometimes I do crunches instead."

He waved toward the floor. "Don't let me stop you."

My smile was short-lived. I rubbed at the badge's upper right corner. The swab turned gray. I set it down. Picked up a fresh one.

"You know, my hiding things from my men. It hurt the case. If I hadn't been hiding that I'm gay, I would've gotten to this point sooner. If I hadn't been trying to protect gay male witnesses, I might've moved on that info faster."

"You're not exactly a villain," he said.

"And not a hero either."

"You take things hard, don't you?"

I wanted to make light of what he said. Turn it into a dirty joke. But he was being kind. And maybe I wasn't undeserving. "Sounds like something my father would say."

"Do your parents know?"

I nodded. "They probably knew before I did."

"Are they . . . supportive?"

I looked up from my half-cleaned badge. "Being gay is probably my best feature. They're liberal, Catholics in name only. Academics. To them, my being gay gives them something to bitch about during tenure-track meetings. How their poor son is mistreated by the world."

He leaned forward in his chair. "You're full of surprises."

I didn't ask if they were nice ones. Didn't want to risk it.

"Hey, since I'm here, can I see your Eileen Gray table?" he asked.

I winced. He'd see more of the house.

"Try not to look at anything else, okay?" I said.

"Why?"

"You'll see." I led him to the living room and flipped the switches.

He didn't keep his eyes on the table only. His mistake. "Spend a lot of time in that chair?" he said, looking at my recliner.

"Perhaps."

"I think I can see your body imprint." He walked toward it and I tugged on his shirtsleeve, pulling him back.

"No touching the antiques," I said.

He laughed.

"So is the table real?"

He took a walk around it and peered at its underside. "Yes. Congratulations."

"Thanks. Let's celebrate with a drink."

We returned to the kitchen. I gave him a beer. I didn't have any spirits in the house. Then I sat down and continued cleaning my badge. "I just wish I knew why he was lying."

"Who?"

So I told him about Luke, about everything. "Luke confessed, but I don't believe him. He wasn't telling the truth."

"Why would he lie?" He picked up a catalog from my pile of unsorted mail. Set it down. "To protect someone?"

"That would be Chris in this scenario. Why?"

He shrugged. "Love? Money?"

"He doesn't have any. Shit." I set the badge down. "That's it! Money."

"Really? He killed her for money?"

"No." I capped the alcohol bottle. Stood and tossed the swabs in the trash. "He's taking the fall for money. He got himself a lawyer tonight. He told his mother he could afford it. Just after she got through telling me their house is being foreclosed on. I also found out he's fourteen. Chris is sixteen."

"This isn't getting much clearer," he said.

"I think Chris convinced Luke to take the rap. He told him he'd pay him and his lawyer fees if Luke claimed to be the lone shooter. Chris is sixteen. He can be tried as an adult. But Luke's two years younger. He'll probably do time in juvie. That's a much easier stint. I bet Chris knows that."

"So Luke goes to juvie and Chris walks?"

"I won't let that happen." I gave my badge a final wipe and put the cleaning supplies away.

"How can you stop it?" he asked.

"By having a little talk with Luke."

"Doesn't he have to have a parent present?"

"Yes. But I'm the police chief, remember?" I pinned my shining badge to my shirt.

"Need to get to the station?" he said. He sounded disappointed. I tried not to let it go to my head. Or other regions of my body.

"Yeah."

"Good luck," he said.

We walked outside. He studied my face. "You look really . . . happy," he said, as if naming a foreign emotion.

"I am. I cracked the case."

"You love being a cop, don't you?"

"Yes." I did. Always. Even when it was hard.

"Good," he said. "It's good to find something you love."

I thought he was going to say something more, but he just walked to his car and waved at me before he got in and drove away.

# TUESDAY, SEPTEMBER 30TH
## 0445 HOURS

Luke Johnson slept on his cot. A thin, gray blanket was pulled to his neck. In the dimly lit six-by-eight cell, he looked troubled. His face puckered as he dreamed. I whistled, low and short. He moaned and turned to face the wall. We had a drunk next door, sleeping it off. But two cells down was Chris Warren. I couldn't risk waking him. I whispered, "Luke!"

He sat up. "What?" he said. "Who?"

"Here."

He looked my way. His eyes shuttered. His face drooped. "Oh. You."

"Come on." I opened the cell. He looked at it. "This is a limited-time offer."

He shuffled over, touched the bars, and dropped his hand. "Quiet," I said. He followed me past the drunk. In the next cell, Chris snored, his blanket on the floor. Luke followed me to the end of the hall and through another door, into the central station. The night-shifters answered calls and played card games. Finnegan, on his way to the cof-feepot, saw us. He raised a brow but said nothing as I led Luke to my office.

I closed the door. "Sit." I pointed to a chair. "Here." I handed him a mug of cocoa I'd prepared. He was about to get the good-cop treatment.

He rubbed his eyes. Sipped the cocoa. Seemed to like it. Took a larger swallow. "You're not supposed to talk to me without my lawyer or mom present."

"True. Did you know that before you killed Cecilia North?"

He scowled and set the mug down. "Who cares if I did or didn't?" His knee jiggled.

"Not me." I sat. Rocked back and set my hands across my middle. "Because I know you didn't kill her."

"Oh yeah?" He reached for the mug again.

"Yeah. And I know why you're claiming you did. And I'm here to tell you something, son. Whatever money Chris Warren promised you, you're not getting it."

The mug shook in his hand. His eyes darted away from mine.

"In a couple months, your mother is going to call you from some shitty apartment in a crime-ridden neighborhood in Hartford, and when you ask how she's doing, she's going to tell you the truth. That she's working three shifts to pay your lawyer's bills. Because guess what, boyo? Chris Warren and his rich parents aren't going to give you a dime. It would look awfully suspicious if they did."

"You don't know anything." He rocked forward on his chair.

"I don't know *everything*," I said. "For instance, I don't know why you agreed to suck Chris's dick." The mug fell to the floor. Cocoa soaked the carpet. The brown stain spread outward. "Frankly, he doesn't seem like your type."

Luke knelt to pick up the mug.

"Don't worry. The janitors will get it."

He set the mug on the desk, his face paper white. "How did you— You can't tell anyone!"

"Why not?" I asked.

"Because! Because they'll think I'm a faggot and then—" He broke off. Tears ran. Snot flowed from his nostrils like water from a tap. "How did you know? Did Chris tell you? He promised!" He ran his hand under his nose. I handed him a tissue. "Chris said he'd never, and that it wasn't a big deal. Guys on the track team did it. Like an initiation."

I rather doubted that. "Why did Chris shoot her?" I asked.

He wiped his nose. Snuffled. "I can't believe he told. He said he'd never tell."

"Chris is not a boy to be trusted."

He balled the tissue. His wet face hardened. "That fuck."

"You know, he's been setting you up for some time. He was talking smack about you at Idyll Days. Saying you got your criminal instincts from your father."

Luke raised his head to look at me. "That prick."

I looked at the ceiling and said, "Why did he shoot her?"

He looked away from me, toward my plant. "I don't know. She startled us. She yelled at us and jogged by. Chris started talking to himself. Something about how she shouldn't be there. He had the gun. He pulled it up and shot. And she fell. But she was still moving, so he shot her again." He swallowed convulsively.

"And twice more?" I pictured Chris with the gun. Most likely shooting a corpse. But maybe not. She'd bled to death. That took time.

He wiped at his eyes. "Yeah. Two more times. He kept saying, 'Stupid bitch' as he shot her. He was so angry. And then he got real quiet. He's like that. He has a temper. And then it passes." He looked at his hands. I remembered Chris at Idyll Days. Hitting the cat's cage and then apologizing seconds later.

"What happened then?" I asked.

He closed his eyes, but whatever he saw made them snap open again. "He grabbed something that she'd dropped. Some food thing. And he took a thing from her hair. I told him to stop touching her, but he wouldn't listen. And then he said I had to get rid of the gun. He told me to dump it in Hought's Pond. It's deep, if you go out far enough."

"But you didn't," I said.

He rubbed his arms. "The pond is miles away. I was scared. It was dark. I kept hearing noises. And I thought the cops would come any minute. The neighbors would call in the shots, and I'd be arrested. But no one came, so I just walked until I reached Baumer's Pond, and I dropped the gun in. Chris had gone. He'd told me to keep my mouth shut and he'd take care of every-thing." His knee went up and down, like a carousel horse.

"Why'd you go back to the golf course a few days later? That wasn't smart."

"Chris kept insisting. He told Tiffany and Kevin we were going to hold a séance. But I think he just wanted to go back; he was so happy he'd gotten away with it. I didn't want to go."

"Why did you?"

"He threatened to tell, about the sex stuff. He said I'd do as he said unless I wanted to be known as a cocksucker the rest of my life."

Because that was the world's worst punishment. Being thought a faggot. I said, "Why didn't you walk away that night when he suggested the sex?"

His eyes got dark. He reached for the mug. Dropped his hand when he recalled it was empty. He radiated fear. A harsh, animal smell seeped out of his pores. "He had a gun in his hand. That whole time, on the golf course. When he was telling me it was no big deal." He drew a shuddering breath. "He had the gun aimed at me. And I thought, if I don't do what he says, he'll shoot me."

So that's why Luke had given in to Chris's sexual demands. Because he'd had a gun pointed at him. And if he'd believed then that Chris would shoot him, why would he disbelieve any other threat Chris made?

I set my hands flat on my desk. "Luke, you can't say you killed her. You have to make a new statement."

"I can't! He's going to give my mom money so she doesn't lose the house. And I'll be out in a couple of years. I'm only fourteen."

"Luke, listen to me. I'm not going to charge you with a murder you didn't commit. I'm going to nail Chris Warren, and you're going to help."

"But he'll tell," he said. "About, you know."

"Yes, and he had a gun to your head. Now stop thinking like the two of you will be back at school together. You won't. Ever. He's going to prison. Adult prison. And if he ever gets out, he'll be a very old man. Understand?"

His eyes. He doubted me. He was still afraid of Chris Warren. Fear can enslave a person. It was time to set him free.

"Listen, son. Chris had a gun, once. He used it to scare you. And he has a temper. But he's locked up in a cell now. I have a gun, always.

And I have a temper. I don't shoot young women." I stood up, at my full six foot four inches. "I shoot perps. So which of us do you think is the bigger threat?"

His knee stopped moving. His eyes went to my holster. His eyes tracked upward to my unsmiling face. "You," he said.

"Bingo. Now let's get your lawyer back in here."

## 0800 HOURS

I stood outside Chris Warren's cell, watching his chest rise and fall. Sunlight striped the foot of his cot. I knocked my Maglite against the cell bars and called out, "Good morning!" Next door, the drunk muttered, "Keep it down." Chris sat up. I watched his face figure it out. Squinted eyes, open mouth, turned head to take it all in. He was still in a cell. No nightmare then.

"Sleep well?" I asked.

He grunted and looked at me. His face was puffy. His ginger hair stuck up in back. "Never better," he said. His voice had gravel in it.

"Glad to hear it. I've got good news and bad news. Which would you like to hear first?" I leaned against the opposite brick wall.

He stared at me, face full of distrust. And a little curiosity. "The bad."

"Luke recanted his confession. Says you shot Cecilia North."

He rubbed his neck. "Right. I'm sure."

"I can't quite figure you out," I said. "Sexual sadists don't always go on to murder. But I guess maybe you're just a complicated guy."

He looked startled. One hand clutched the sheet. But he said nothing.

"Piece of advice for the future. Don't keep trophies and don't trust anyone to keep your secrets. People are a constant disappointment."

His jaw clenched. "He wouldn't talk to you."

"Sure he would. I'm the guy who can see that he doesn't serve more than six months in the nicest of the juvie facilities." An exaggeration, but a useful one. "You're the guy who wants to send him away for years. And honestly, I don't think he's forgiven you for the blow job at gunpoint."

His mask fell. He no longer looked like Rick at all. His face was so hard, it was statuesque. "Luke!" he yelled. "Luke!"

"Quiet down," the drunk in the next cell said. "People are sleeping."

"He's not here," I said. I'd had Luke transferred to the juvenile facility a half hour ago.

"Guess I'll see him later." A small smile appeared.

"Nope," I said, approaching his cell. Getting so close I could smell his cologne and sweat. Fear sweat. Good. "You won't be seeing him ever again. At least, not until your trial." I'd moved heaven and earth this morning to get the boys housed at separate facilities. I suspected I'd be paying this favor off for some time, but I didn't care. "Do you want me to pass on a message to him?"

He stood and walked toward me. Made himself as tall as he could. Good trick. He'd need that inside. He'd need a whole lot more, too. He was going to be competing against kids who'd grown up in slums, who'd been incarcerated multiple times. He'd be beaten badly within a week.

"What's the good news?" he asked.

"Ah, right. The good news. Today is Tuesday. Taco Tuesday. Best day of the week, where you're going." I whistled a happy tune.

Chris smacked his palms against the bars. "You think you're so fucking smart!" He hit them again. A dull clang echoed. "I'll get out of this. I will!" He smacked his hand again. The palm was red. He'd bruise himself if he didn't stop.

"Knock it off."

"Yeah!" called the drunk. "Shut up."

Chris dropped his hand and scowled at me. "This isn't over," he said. But his face told a different story. He knew he might not make it out. That this might be just a preview of coming attractions.

I walked away, whistling.

We'd regrouped in the pen and were staring at the board. Pictures of footprints hung alongside pictures of the corpse. Papers competed for space. A time line. The first page of the ballistics report. Photos of Luke and Chris. It was all there. The whole case.

"You found her hair pin?" I asked Wright. "In Chris's room?"

"Tucked under his socks. Thought it was odd, so I bagged it."

"He took it from the body after he killed her," I said.

Finnegan tsk-tsked. "Don't these kids watch TV? Never keep trophies."

Billy sat in the chair that had supported Revere's flat ass. He nibbled his fingernails. "So Chris shot her and then he took a keepsake?" He squinted at Chris's photo. "I taught that kid soccer. I don't understand why he did it."

"She scared him. I'm not sure he meant to kill her with the first shot. But the other three?" I tapped the picture of Cecilia, face down on the grass. "He meant to kill her then."

"I'm just glad the sixteen-year-old shot her," Wright said.

"What about the Johnson kid?" Finnegan asked. "Only fourteen."

I planned to have words with the DA. "I'll try to plea him down. He didn't shoot her."

"Yeah, he only aided and abetted," Wright said. "He admits he tossed the gun?"

"Yeah. His good friend Chris told him to."

We stared at the board some more. Until I roused myself. "I'll call the DA. Tell him about Luke's new statement. Finnegan, you rattle the techs and see if those imprints of Chris's sneakers are ready."

"Still can't believe you tricked him into leaving fresh prints at the course," Wright said. Was that admiration I heard?

"Why didn't he toss his sneakers?" Finnegan asked. "They nailed him. Without them, we'd still be staring at our navels."

Billy whistled low. "You know how much those things cost? New Air Jordans are almost one hundred fifty dollars. I'm guessing even Chris's parents might get mad if he lost those shoes."

"Huh," Wright said. "Well, thank you very much, Michael Jordan."

Only in movies do cops go home triumphant after they've solved a big case. Real cops sit at their desks, piled high with debris, and hunt and peck their way through reports. I had all the other business of being police chief I'd put on the back burner. Mrs. Dunsmore reminded me that I had a meeting with the selectmen next week to discuss the budget, and I needed to create that bicycle patrol I'd insisted Yankowitz would be on. But every hour or so, another man would stick his head in the door and say, "Good catch, Chief." And that kept me going until I had to leave, and well past quitting time.

# WEDNESDAY, OCTOBER 1ST
## 1000 HOURS

**W**hen I woke the next day, everything felt different. More and less real, by turns. I looked around me and made a decision. After I'd had coffee, I drove to a stadium-sized Home Depot and filled a cart with supplies: a tarp, paint, rollers, putty knives, big sponges, and a million things I didn't know the names for and wasn't sure I needed but that the orange-aproned men who worked there insisted would "save me time and money in the long run." Those men, with their easy confidence and scarred hands, were all about the long run.

I started on the room with the sailing-ships wallpaper. It didn't come off easy. I destroyed two putty knives prying the paper from the wall, cursing the idiot who'd applied the glue. But I had empty hours and the kind of loneliness that welcomes sore shoulders, tired arms, and a neck that cracks like a popcorn kernel after relentless manual labor. After a week of long evenings, I had a room with clean, white walls. When I'd removed the last of the adhesive, I thought about what it meant to hold on, too long.

I unpacked the boxes in the sewing room and found some photos from the old days. John and me on vacation with our parents, the year they took us to the Grand Canyon. A few pics from my old precinct, clearly taken with work cameras. Rick and me mugging in front of an FBI poster, thumbs to our chest, indicating what? We'd caught the guy? We hadn't. Or that we were the most wanted? The joke was forgotten to time. My smile was wide. I'd forgotten that face—that it belonged to me. And Rick. God. He looked like a baby, with his freckles and squinted eyes.

I put the photo of Rick and me on the living-room mantel. Then I opened the gun safe. Metal winked at me. The key ring. I picked it up and sat in my recliner. The cool metal coil grew warm in my palm. I exhaled hard, the noise like a steam train.

"Hey, Rick." I looked at the metal ring as I spoke. The way some people talk to headstones. "I um . . ." I cleared my throat.

"I just wanted to say I'm sorry. I'm sorry I didn't get you help. I should've forced you into rehab. Should've applied the cuffs and dragged your scrawny ass there. Stood guard til you got clean. I really wish I had." Would it have worked? Impossible to say, to know. "It's been tough without you." I closed my fingers over the key ring. "Really tough. You were the best partner I ever had. The best friend too." The ring no longer felt cool, but the same temperature as my hand. I didn't notice it unless I squeezed hard enough to feel the coils. I sat in the silence, holding the key ring, not squeezing it. Just letting it be. Just letting us be.

# FRIDAY, OCTOBER 10TH
## 2000 HOURS

I stared out the windshield at Suds. The bar was lit up and lively. Half the station celebrated inside. Earlier today, a judge had remanded Christopher Warren to Hartford Correctional Center. He'd stay there until he stood trial for second-degree murder. Cause for a party, or so the men had decided. "Come to Suds tonight, Chief! Drinks are on us." How could I say no? I turned off the car. The engine ticked as it cooled.

The noise inside Suds was at post–victory game levels. Mostly caused by my men, who'd gathered in a crush near the tables at the back. The locals stayed near the bar, watching the action. Finnegan came over and clapped my shoulder. "About time you got here. Billy's competing against Wright in a free-throw contest."

"Using what?" I lifted my chin. Over the sea of uniforms, I saw someone had attached a laundry basket missing its bottom to the wall. Billy stood behind a row of chairs, a squishy ball in his hands.

"This is going to get ugly," I said.

Finnegan laughed. "Get?" He drank from his glass.

"Hi, Chief," Nate called from behind the bar. I walked over to say hello. "Haven't seen much of you," he said. His dark eyes searched mine.

"Been doing work on my house."

"Ah, a handyman. Drink?"

"I wouldn't go that far. I've only just learned how to use pliers." I held out my nicked and scraped hand. "And how not to use them."

He slid my drink toward me. "You need help, let me know. I grew up helping my dad build houses."

"Thanks."

He nodded at the cops. "Never seen them so happy. Wish you'd warned me they were coming."

"Causing trouble?" I asked.

"Nah. Just busier than expected. I had to call Donna in to help out. It's her night off." I scanned the room, fast. "She's in the kitchen," he said. "Want me to tell her you're here?" He flashed me a big grin.

I walked away. "How's it going?" I asked Yankowitz when I reached the action.

His eyes widened, and he made room for me. "Um, Wright's winning, eight to six."

"Come on, Hoops!" Hopkins cried as Billy handled the ball.

"You got money on this?" I asked Hopkins. Billy's forehead was shiny. His lips wet. How many drinks had he consumed? And would they diminish or improve his aim?

"Yeah, I bet ten bucks he'd lose," Hopkins said. "That money is safe as houses."

Billy lifted the soft foam ball and tossed it at the makeshift hoop. It bounced off the wall and sank through the laundry basket. "How you like me now?" he shouted.

"If he makes this one, it's sudden death," Yankowitz said.

"Worried?" I asked Wright. He stood nearby. He'd removed his jacket and loosened his tie. His button-down shirt was untucked.

"Nah," he said. "He'll choke." He drank from his bottle and wiped his mouth with the back of his hand. "He's never not choked."

Billy tossed the ball. It sank through the middle of the white plastic basket. A cheer went up from those who'd taken the long odds and bet on him. Finnegan took the ball from Billy and explained that a coin toss would decide who shot first. After that, the first man to miss a shot lost the competition.

Billy called the coin. He chose heads. It came up tails. Wright told him to shoot first. Billy sank it. Wright bit his lip. "Lucky shot," he muttered. He accepted the ball from Finnegan and got ready. There were calls of, "Don't muff it!" and "Come on!"

The door opened. A cold breeze made its way inside. I looked back. A tall figure stood, ramrod straight with a buzz cut. Revere. I scooted past the trash-talking cops and said, "You made it."

He surveyed the scene and walked to the bar. "What are you drinking?" he asked.

"Laphroaig."

He rapped his knuckles on the bar. "Your sainted Irish ancestors know you're drinking Scotch whiskey, you wretched heathen?"

"They weren't purists when it came to alcohol," I said.

Revere ordered a Hooker Irish Red. While Nate worked the tap, Revere said, "So. Christopher Warren. What set you onto him?"

"He lied on the golf course. Said he saw a flashlight no one else saw. And every time I ran into him, he brought it up. Once he registered as fishy, I noticed his sneakers. From there, it was just a matter of forensics."

He accepted his beer from Nate and set bills on the counter. "Drink's on me," he said. He raised his glass and said, "Sláinte." I repeated it.

A roar went up from the crowd. We looked over. "Ha!" Wright yelled. "Take that, youngster." He threw his hands into the air.

"Looks like Wright beat Billy," I said.

"No surprise there," Revere said.

"So, how are things at the Eastern?" I asked.

"Same old, same old. There's rumblings that the acting head might not get the permanent appointment." He rubbed his nose. "Politics. It's all bullshit."

Finnegan and Wright came over. "There he is!" Wright said. "Our favorite turncoat."

"Now, now, gentlemen," I said. "Detective Revere is an invited guest."

"Invited to celebrate our solving a murder that stumped the staties!" Finnegan said.

"Hello, Wright. Hello, Wrong. So gracious in victory," Revere said. "I'd expect nothing less. Or more." Wright and Wrong. Not bad, for nicknames. Right up there with Wright and White.

Billy wandered over, a little off-keel.

Revere said, "Well, Chief, I got to hand it to you. You guys did all right."

Billy interjected, "You're a good detective, Chief." He pointed. His finger made circles as he rocked on his feet. He probably thought he stood perfectly still.

"You okay, Hoops?" Finnegan asked, one hand out, ready to prop if needed.

Billy waved his hand as if shooing a fly. "Fine. Fine. This guy." He stabbed his finger at me. "This guy solved the murder. And now that little shit who killed Cecilia can spend years in prison getting fucked in the ass." Revere winced. "Serves the little homo right."

"Billy," I said, "I've told you. Chris Warren's not gay. He's a sexual sadist. He had girlfriends. And by all accounts, he abused them too." Now that Chris was behind bars, lots of people felt free to share their feelings about him. And they weren't that he was so quiet and polite that they never saw it coming.

"Pervert," Billy said. He swayed. Finnegan stepped closer. "Never convince me he's not gay."

"Billy, it's done," I said. "Enough with the gay slurs. Why don't you go ask Nate for some water?"

He belched softly. Covered his mouth. "'Scuse me." Then he frowned and said, "When did you become such a faggot friend, Chief?" He giggled.

He was drunk. He'd had too many beers. He wouldn't remember half of what he said when he awoke tomorrow with sore eyes and a heavy skull. It would be so easy to say nothing. To let it go. But I'd been letting go of these things for years. And look what damage it had done. I'd resolved to stop running. Maybe now it was time to stop hiding.

"Hey, Billy." I tugged on his shirtsleeve.

"Yeah?" He smiled, his teeth large and bright. A happy drunk now, all his animosity forgotten.

"I'm gay," I said.

"What?" He reeled backward.

I pulled at his shirt. "I'm gay. A butt pirate. A faggot. Queer. Ass bandit. That's me." I jerked my thumb toward my chest. A trail of sweat ran down my back, caught on the storm-predicting vertebrae.

He tugged away from my grasp. Looked to the others for help. Finnegan and Wright stood, wide-eyed and silent. Revere watched, a smile at his lips. He knew. Or had known. From his friends in New York? Maybe. Or maybe he was just a good detective.

Billy shook his head. Licked his lips and said, "Nah, you're playing with me." He wagged his finger. "Can't be true."

"Why not?" I asked.

"'Cause." He hiccupped. "Because."

"Because I don't fit the profile?" I shook my head. "You're such a rookie." A tremor started in my hands. I flexed my fingers. I'd done it.

"How about that water?" Wright asked, jerking his thumb toward the bar.

"I don't—" Billy said, but he followed Wright.

Finnegan said, "Excuse me," and headed for the cops.

My eyes followed Finnegan. He leaned into Hopkins and whispered something. Hopkins looked at me, then away. I looked around Suds. The cops, clinking bottles together. Billy and Wright, heads close, talking. Donna at the bar, listening to them, her eyes the size of coasters.

"Maybe I should go," I said. I could start rehabbing my bathroom. I'd been reading those old Time Life series books on home improvement. Maybe I could see about replacing those pink and black tiles.

The door opened. And in walked Dr. Saunders, his hair disheveled by wind. He spotted me and waved.

"Oh, I think you should stay," Revere said. He clapped his meaty hand on my shoulder. It felt like an anchor. "Definitely stay."

# ACKNOWLEDGMENTS

This book owes much to many.

My Novel Incubator group midwifed the heck out of this book. My amazing instructors, Lisa Borders and Michelle Hoover, helped me revise and market this work, and I am so grateful for their efforts. My fellow students: Lisa Birk, Carol Gray, Michael Nolan, Patty Park, Hesse Phillips, Elizabeth Chiles Shelburne, Ashley Stone, Mandy Syers, and Gerald B. Whelan—thank you for inspiring and encouraging me. I can't wait to hold your books in my hands!

To Grub Street, for challenging me with every class, workshop, and event I've attended. I'm lucky to be part of such a wonderful writing community.

To everyone at MIT who has made my day job a pleasure and who has encouraged my "other" job, especially those in Computing Culture, High-Low Tech, Lifelong Kindergarten, and the Finance group at the Media Lab.

To my agent, Ann Collette, for loving Thomas Lynch as much as I do, and for gambling on both of us.

To my editor, Dan Mayer, for giving me the hard truth (you should get rid of the ghost) and for providing so many smart, insightful suggestions.

To my friends who are a delight and are always understanding when I go off the map to write: Karen Brennan, Maggie deLong, Jeff Hawson, and Tracey Schmidt.

To Sayamindu Dasgupta for taking a very good picture of me.

To my family, especially my parents, who always encouraged me to write. And to Grandma Gayle, who once sassed back with, "Well, my granddaughter wrote a book!"

And to Todd, for living with me and my characters every single day.

# ABOUT THE AUTHOR

Stephanie Gayle is the author of *My Summer of Southern Discomfort*. She's twice been nominated for a Pushcart Prize for her short fiction, which has appeared in *Kenyon Review Online*, *Potomac Review*, and *Minnetonka Review*, and elsewhere. She co-created the popular Boston reading series Craft on Draft. When not writing, she is often playing board games. Her Settlers of Catan skills are exquisite.